C000147956

DEATHDAY

Colin Philpott

Fisher King Publishing

Deathday

Copyright © Colin Philpott 2023

Paperback ISBN 978-1-914560-54-5
Ebook ISBN 978-1-914560-55-2

All rights reserved.

No part of this publication may be reproduced or distributed
in any form or by any means, or stored in a database
or electronic retrieval system without the prior written
permission of Fisher King Publishing Ltd. Thank you for
respecting the author of this work.

The right of Colin Philpott to be identified as Author of
this work has been asserted by him in accordance with the
Copyright, Designs and Patents Act, 1988.

This is a work of fiction. Names, characters, businesses,
places, events and incidents are either the products of the
author's imagination or used in a fictitious manner. Any
resemblance to actual persons, living or dead, or actual
events is purely coincidental.

Published by Fisher King Publishing

fisherkingpublishing.co.uk

To the many older people, including family
members and friends, whose stories have
influenced this book.

Acknowledgements

My thanks to Rick Armstrong and the team at Fisher King and to the following people who have offered invaluable help and advice at various stages during the writing of this book – Kit Monkman, Dave Kennedy, Di Burton, Rod Taylor. My particular thanks also to Alys West for her invaluable advice and my very special thanks to Hilary Philpott for her advice, support and encouragement.

November 2045

PART ONE

PART ONE

CHAPTER ONE

Bromley, Greater London
Sunday 5 November 2045

Maybe history would judge a journey like this to be remarkable, even though, in November 2045, it didn't seem so. Holly's thoughts wandered as the driverless car led them towards their destination with the warm afternoon sun glinting through the windscreen. Even she, a strong supporter of what was now normal, had to concede that she would have been surprised, even shocked, had she known two decades earlier that she would be doing this. But she had no doubt it was for the best.

She could see that Jake was agitated as they rode along the A21 out of Bromley. They were about an hour late after a series of traffic jams, mainly at roadworks which were the result of a major government programme to renovate routes allowed to fall into serious disrepair over the previous decade or more. The satnav seemed to be taking them a long way around to reach Mary's house. She suspected, though, that it wasn't really the hold-ups that were bothering him.

"We said we'd be there by one," said Jake grumpily to his partner, "I can't stand being late for anything."

"Just chill out," replied Holly. "I don't suppose many people will get there on time."

Holly knew that Jake was devoted to her and, for that reason, was worried he was doing this to please her rather than out of genuine belief. She often thought him too reasonable, too keen to please and to keep the peace. Sometimes she wondered how he had cut it in the rough and tumble of London's financial sector which, though much reduced in size from its millennial heyday, still provided him with the opportunity to earn good money. So did Holly, fifteen years his junior, in her job with a London PR company. Despite this, they were always worrying, and arguing, about money. Theirs was a second partnership and Jake had serious financial commitments from his first which had ended acrimoniously.

"I'm sure that's the road," said Jake as the driverless drove past a turning on the left.

It carried on and it indicated a left turn one kilometre ahead.

"Relax," said Holly. "This is a better way."

"Where's the card we bought?" replied Jake. "We need to write it before we get there."

Holly rooted in her bag and found the 'Happy Deathday' card.

"Oh, I don't know what to write in one of these."

"'Have a nice death?' 'Hope you've enjoyed your life?' 'Thank you for bowing out at ninety and leaving us your money'?" suggested Jake.

"Don't be ridiculous!" interjected Holly, "we can just say something simple like 'Thank you for your love and friendship' or something like that."

"That sounds sentimental," said Jake.

As they continued to agonise over the wording, their attention was brought back to the road as the driverless turned left.

"This is it," said Jake. "Oh me of little faith!"

As the vehicle turned into the street, it slowed as it approached the security gate. Jake put his arm out and held it against the auto-guard. After about thirty seconds, the barrier lifted and they were able to continue along the street.

"I can remember when you had to be seriously rich to have one of those," observed Jake as the driverless cruised.

"One of what?" asked Holly.

"Security gates at the end of your street."

"It's just common sense. Don't you remember all those break-ins in the twenties?"

Holly knew that gated communities were no longer the preserve of the wealthy. They had become commonplace even on fairly ordinary housing estates with a perimeter fence or wall and a security guard at the single-entry point. So, here in middle income Bromley, it was quite normal for relatively small houses to be part of communities protected in this way. She'd seen many new housing developments built like this and countless existing estates remodelled to incorporate fences, gates and security points.

A few minutes later, the driverless slowed and announced that they were at their destination. Even though they were late, Jake and Holly sat for a moment composing themselves for an occasion about which even Holly had to admit she wasn't confident. She knew pre-death day parties were all the rage now but she hadn't been to one before so she was still nervous about exactly how she would feel. A few moments of silence followed.

"Right, let's go in," said Holly as she got out of the car, already regretting her decision to wear a long winter coat.

She left it on, though, partly because she thought it might get colder later in the garden and because it was a comfort to her. It was a coat she'd recently bought - soft, black leather, quite expensive but it made her feel good. And that had a lot to do with the memories associated with similar coats she'd worn in the past when they were part of the unofficial uniform of supporters of the 90 Law. Holly realised that it gave her confidence. Jake, dressed in a short-sleeved shirt and chinos, now quite normal for November, gathered up the flowers they had bought en route and the card upon which they had finally settled on this message deemed suitable by both of them, 'Thank you for so many great memories and our love and best wishes for the journey ahead.'

Mary's house wasn't grand but was solidly and comfortably middle-class. Built in the 1980s, it was a product of the boom in house-building under the Conservative government of the then United Kingdom led by Margaret Thatcher. It was in a style which had gone out of fashion in the late twentieth-century but which had more recently acquired a certain retro appeal. Holly paused again on the driveway as she summoned her courage one more time. As they approached the front door, it was opened before they needed to press the entry panel and Mary stood in front of them.

"Hello Holly, so nice to see you," she said in a commanding way reminiscent of her younger, healthier days.

Holly hugged her grandmother. Immediately, she could feel the genuine warmth that existed between them, a warmth that stretched back to Holly's childhood but which had been deepened more recently by the shared experience of living through the decline and death of Holly's mother, Susan. Holly had to fight back tears as she was brought up sharply by the thought of her grandmother no longer there, of her grandmother lying in her coffin, of her grandmother having the injection.

"And so nice to see you too," added Mary as she disentangled herself from Holly and offered her arm to Jake.

Jake embraced her warmly, ignoring the fact that he knew that Mary couldn't remember his name. In the past, on more than one occasion, she had called him a variety of names, often those of former partners of Holly.

Holly stepped in to help, "Jake and I had a terrible journey. Lots of hold-ups. All these roadworks that should have been done years ago."

As Mary turned in the doorway to lead the couple inside the house, Holly was struck by the still elegant profile of her grandmother but saddened, as she was every time she saw her, by her mental decline. The sadness she'd felt moments before was supplanted by an emotion with which Holly felt more comfortable. Mercy was how it was labelled in the early days of the League. Although Holly now baulked at the terminology, she still agreed with the sentiment. Far better, she convinced herself, that Mary should be freed from the degradations and indignities of dementia.

As a child, Holly had admired rather than adored her grandmother who, it seemed to her at the time, was always immersed in her work as a GP in the inner suburbs of South London. Holly was sure that Mary loved her family and had wanted to spend time with them. But she also knew that Mary had used her job as a platform to campaign for social change, to fight the austerity of the 2010's. She was always on her way to one or other meeting to fight this or that injustice.

Holly's private thoughts lasted only a few moments as she and Jake were soon immersed in the warm greetings of the wider family. During their journey there, Holly had tried to give Jake a quick reminder of who all the more remote relatives were but Holly was soon engrossed in animated conversations with cousins, aunts and uncles, almost all on her late mother's side. As the adults caught up, a clutch of children buzzed around. She knew Jake would be having a pang of regret when he saw them all, a regret that his own children weren't there. He rarely saw them and they would certainly not want to be at a gathering involving their father's new partner. When his previous partnership disintegrated, the children took their mother's side.

It was early afternoon and the twenty or so members of what Holly in her professional PR capacity would categorise as a typical English middle-class family, drifted out into the garden to enjoy the fading autumn sunshine. A few parents were still administering sun cream to their children's faces but it was getting cooler. Holly, now glad of her coat for warmth as well as comfort, had noticed that Jake was doing what he usually did on family occasions, avoiding direct contact with her father, David, Mary's only son. She believed Jake when he said he had tried his best to get on with him, but theirs was a difficult relationship.

Even Holly privately shared Jake's irritation at her father's behaviour on occasions like this. He was assuming the position of master of ceremonies and was clearly enjoying his starring role in his mother's party. He was supervising the younger generation who were acting as helpers with the barbecue and the drinks. At the same time, he was flitting from guest to guest catching up on their news with a few, often barbed, questions.

"Still enjoying the fruits of your ill-gotten gains in the City then, Jake?" he said as he advanced on his daughter's partner, wearing his trademark lounge suit with open necked shirt.

"Yes, we're doing OK, thanks, David." Jake replied trying to take the wind out of the older man's sails. "How's the drone hire world, then?"

"We manage, we manage," was David's self-deprecating reply.

Holly observed this exchange and was unsurprised. It was pretty much what happened every time the two men met. Her father, despite his denials, was motivated by money and status. His latest venture was to be one of the first to set-up a drone hire company when the licensing rules were loosened in the twenties. He had soundly rejected his mother's left-wing views, her campaigning stance and her permanent state of political battling. As a young man, he had been swept up in the political turmoil of the twenties, joining the League of Youth and persuading Holly to do the same as a teenager.

"Ah, Holly, wearing your League coat, I see. Anyway, it

suits you. You look very elegant."

"It's new actually Dad," Holly replied, slightly offended that her father thought she might still be wearing something she owned more than a decade ago.

"Pricey, I imagine. Well, I reckon you must be pretty astute at the dark arts of public relations."

Holly smiled weakly but otherwise ignored her father's comments. She was already upset that her father hadn't said hello to her until this point in the party. He moved and put his arms around her and she did likewise. Before her mother's death, he had rarely done this but their shared grief had brought them closer together. Holly's sympathy for her father's loss, never mind her own, had reinforced her love for him. Since her mother's death, she had rediscovered much of the zeal she previously had for the intergenerational struggles and for the politics that had led to the 90 Law. But she knew that the relationship with her father was a complicated one and she struggled at times to disentangle the political from the personal.

"It looks like the upstarts in the Party are going to have another go at repeal," announced David. "They just don't get it, do they? I just hope that slippery Prime Minister of ours stands up to them."

"I can't see things changing, Dad," responded Holly, not out of great conviction but more in an attempt to shut down this line of discussion before Jake rose to the bait. But she was too late.

"I think you'd be surprised, David, how many people want to see some change."

But David's response was never heard as he was summoned away by the arrival of more relatives, leaving Jake muttering to himself and Holly increasingly tiring of the business of keeping things sweet between her partner and father. For a while she and Jake stood away from the crowd, with their drinks as people mingled, chatted, ate and drank in this suburban garden. It was as though, Holly thought, this was a birthday party or just a family gathering without a specific purpose.

All this while, the person in whose honour the party was being held, moved around the garden, sometimes on her own and sometimes guided by her ubiquitous son. Sometimes, Holly noticed, Mary seemed to be completely mentally sound but at other times she forgot names and faces and confused her guests with random conversation with little or no connection to reality. And one thing remained unsaid in all these conversations; the impending death by legally mandated termination of the party's host and star.

Just before 3.30 p.m., as the sun disappeared behind clouds, David suggested that everyone go inside. In the lounge placed on a table was a three-tiered cake, in the style of a wedding cake, iced and decorated with great precision. On an adjacent table, cards and presents brought by the guests had been gathered together unopened. David ushered his mother in front of the table, tapped a glass with a spoon to call everyone to order and addressed the assembled company.

"Thank you all for coming today. It's great to see so many family members together in one place and we particularly appreciate the presence of those of you who've travelled some distance, hopefully by drone, to be here."

A modest ripple of laughter greeted the drone reference as David continued, "We all know why we are here today. In a few weeks' time Mum will be bidding us farewell as she reaches her ninetieth birthday. Of course, when the time comes, this will be a moment of sadness but today is a time for celebration, celebration of a life lived well and to the full. It has been a life full of fun and excitement and a life which has brought so much happiness and joy to so many people. We will all have our own particular memories of Mum but I would just like to say, in front of all of you, that she has been the most wonderful mother you could ever have, when I was a child but also as I have got older. She was always there to support me and to advise me (quite a bit of advice, in fact, and it hasn't stopped) and she has also been a fantastic grandmother to my children."

Holly, standing at the back of the assembled crowd, had deliberately placed herself out of the direct eyeline of her father. She rarely enjoyed her father's speeches which she considered overblown and often only bearing passing resemblance to the truth. She had little doubt he loved his mother but she knew that his words today completely glossed over the vastly different outlooks on life between the two of them. However, it was his reference to 'children' which, even though she had half expected it, brought her up short. Her father hardly ever made reference to Emily, killed in a road accident when she was five, the sister Holly could only recall through photographs. The rest of her father's speech went past in a blur and she only refocussed on what he was saying as he drew to a close.

"We are now able, through medical advances and the wise decision we took as a country to draw life to a close at ninety, to live our lives with dignity until our final days. We have been freed from the worries and traumas that once plagued old age. So, we will of course be sad to see her go but we will be thankful for her life and glad that she will leave us in a fitting, humane manner."

As David paused, several people started a tentative round of applause which gathered strength as others felt compelled to join in. Without any invitation, Mary then cleared her throat,

"Thank you, David, and thank you all for coming today.

I'm not going to say very much and, as you know, I am quite forgetful sometimes but I have been very lucky to have such a loving family around me. Of course, I will miss you all but I am looking forward to slipping away quietly on my ninetieth birthday. As you will all remember, umm, umm..."

Abruptly, Mary's uncharacteristically lucid speech came to a juddering halt. Holly knew immediately what it was she had forgotten. The name of her husband, Colin, who had undergone voluntary euthanasia a few years before. She wanted to call out his name but the moment passed as Mary resumed,

"Oh dear, I'm sorry, I just have trouble with names and places, every now and then. My husband went the same way of his own accord a few years ago. I am sure it is for the best. All I will say to all of you is that, when I'm gone, the fight must go on, the fight for a fairer society but that will be for others. Thank you all."

As Mary finished speaking, polite applause was accompanied by quiet sobbing from several family members. Holly was pleasantly surprised when her father went to put his arm round his mother. Then a succession of family came up and embraced Mary, some crying, some just tearful, others just saying a few words.

After a few minutes, the previous equilibrium was restored. David then called the room to order.

"Now it is time to cut the cake, or at least part of it. You will see that the cake has three tiers, Well, with the deathday cake, we will cut one tier today, the second, we will keep for Mum's deathday and the third will be for us to have after she has gone. Mum, would you like to do the honours?"

Mary picked up the knife and guided by her son's hand, made a ceremonial cut. As the hubbub of conversation resumed and the cake was cut and offered round, Jake stood quietly with Holly at the back of the room.

"This feels unreal," he said, "how has this become normal?"

"It's for the best, Jake. It's best for all of us and best for Gran that she doesn't go on like this for years."

CHAPTER TWO

Otterburn, Northumberland
Friday 10 November 2045

Wilfred was humming a tune but there was nothing unusual about that because he was nearly always humming a tune. It was part of who he was and he knew that people had come to expect it, including his son, now walking a few paces ahead of him. Today, his musical whisperings were being carried away on the squally wind that cut into them both as they walked away from where the taxi had left them. The autumnal afternoon lights of Otterburn were fading into the distance but it was still a long trek to the border and they wanted to get as close as possible before they lost the light completely.

It had been difficult finding a taxi but Wilfred hadn't been surprised. He knew they were few and far between these days even in the big cities but, in somewhere like Morpeth, it was like looking for a needle in a haystack. Most people used driverless pick-ups but Northumberland didn't seem to have any. So they had to resort to an old-style driver taxi and, eventually, they'd found one heading back towards the train station and they hailed it in the street.

Wilfred was sure that the driver was a bit suspicious. A man clearly in his final days with someone who looked very much like his son wanting a cab on a chilly Autumn evening and then asking to be dropped off in Otterburn. The driver hadn't voiced any concern. In fact he hardly said anything at all. But Eversley had given him a sizeable tip to minimise the risk.

Earlier, Wilfred had taken the unscheduled termination of the train at Morpeth in his stride. His son, on the other hand, had become very agitated, swearing and complaining to station staff before he remembered that he shouldn't be drawing attention to himself. The original plan had been to go to Berwick where they had been promised help by a 90+ supporter to get across the border. However, it was just their luck that the power lines went down and all the trains had to stop for the evening. The Government had taken a lot of flak about this recently, power failures that afflicted trains, people drones and car-charging points. Wilfred reflected that, in the middle of the twenty-first century, travel around England often seemed like it had regressed to the nineteenth, never mind, the twentieth century.

Wilfred agreed with his son that Otterburn was the last safe place they could ask the taxi to leave them. Any closer to the border would have looked highly suspicious but it meant they would have to walk about twenty kilometres to reach Scotland.

"This is the path. I remember it, Dad," said Eversley as they walked on a narrow, badly maintained lane past the last cottage in the village.

The footpath ran up the side of the garden but, fortunately, there didn't seem to be anyone at home as they turned off the road onto the muddy path.

"I trust you implicitly, my son, you're a good man," replied Wilfred with a touch of irony.

"You should," whispered Eversley back," I had to run along here in all weathers when I did my training. It's not somewhere I will ever forget."

They fell into quietness and headed purposefully along the path. For Wilfred, despite replacement body parts, the aches and pains of old age had not really been eliminated. He knew others often thought he could walk reasonably well but, more often than not, it was a struggle even on the flat. He had trimmed his beard before they'd set off on this trip but it was still quite bushy and therefore offered useful protection against the cold. His trusty overcoat, which he tended to wear almost whatever the weather, was also a bonus.

Every time he met his son, Wilfred was still mildly amused by the fact that he had a quite broad Mancunian accent. He knew it was hardly surprising since that was where Eversley had been brought up and had spent most of his life. Wilfred, though, was proud of the fact that he had preserved what he described as an African-Caribbean Cockney accent, a badge of the heritage of the Windrush generation. Now, though, their linguistic differences somehow symbolised the gap between them.

But it was what he said rather than how he said it that marked Eversley out from his father. Already several times on the train journey, ill-advisedly in Wilfred's opinion, Eversley had voiced his anger at the termination laws they were now seeking to evade.

"Look how fit you are, Dad," he'd said more than once, "what sense does it make in your case?"

And Wilfred had been treated to Eversley's forthright views on how England, the England he had fought for, could possibly have taken the decision it had. England, ah yes, England. The England which had waged those 'wars against terror' back in the noughties. The England Eversley had voted for in the Brexit referendum in 2016. But Wilfred knew that, for his son, all that was irrelevant now and that his only concern as he walked two paces ahead of his father was saving him.

Wilfred noticed that Eversley kept turning and looking back towards the receding outline of Otterburn as they trudged on. There was no sign of life. There was no reason to think that anyone had seen them head out on a country footpath late in the afternoon on a November day. Had they done so, any onlooker would probably have thought it odd. But whether anyone would have acted on their suspicions was another matter, particularly in a rural backwater like this.

Wilfred's thoughts drifted back to his music. Earlier in the day when his son arrived at his smart but cluttered Victorian house in Chorlton, Wilfred had been at the piano wrestling with the troublesome third movement of his latest composition. Eversley had shown no interest in his father's creative dilemmas and Wilfred was now annoyed that, as he walked, he couldn't recall the idea he'd had to resolve the issue. Eversley had been fretting about whether they had enough food and sufficient clothes for the journey. There was a change of clothing for them both and food to keep them going for a day. But Eversley kept telling him how he didn't want them to have to sleep out overnight because it might be near freezing. Wilfred knew that Eversley thought he was really much frailer than he looked.

As they walked on, Wilfred struggled to get his thoughts to focus on his music. Instead, he found himself recalling each room of the house they had left hours before, making sure he could picture the bathroom, the kitchen, the attic room, the cellar. He wondered whether he would ever go back there. Somehow the idea that he'd escape to Scotland and live happily ever after still seemed unreal. But so did the idea of the escape attempt failing and his termination happening in a few weeks' time.

Wilfred knew that Eversley would judge it to be too dangerous to try to make contact with 90+ this far from the border. Had the train worked, that would have been fine but they couldn't expect people to take undue risks. Although the authorities waxed and waned with their enforcement of the law, it wasn't fair to put others in danger. For now they were on their own. Although Wilfred had taken some time to be convinced of the merits of this expedition, he was now invested in it. And he started to feel the anxiety that was radiating from his son. As the sky darkened, each step seemed to be louder than the last. The noise of their boots on rotting leaves was both a blessing and a curse, nearer to escape but maybe closer to discovery.

They walked on without conversation, partly for safety to reduce the risk of being noticed but also because they were both deep in thought. For Wilfred, it might have been customary to regard your children with paternalistic favour even when you had fundamental differences with them. But he was different. He had been a creative type all his life, a free-thinker, a liberal and his son hadn't followed in his footsteps in terms of lifestyle or occupation. Nothing wrong with that per se but what he couldn't reconcile was the difference in attitude, particularly the political views his son held. For him, the heritage of the Windrush generation, the generation of his parents, was a fundamental part of Wilfred's identity. Even though he had been born seven years after his dad had arrived at Tilbury Docks, he had grown up almost feeling that he had been on board. It frustrated him that his own son didn't share this heritage although he understood why.

Wilfred suspected that the irony of this expedition was not lost on his son. As a boy, Eversley had loved and admired his father and Wilfred knew that there were many shared memories which made them both feel nostalgically warm. Throughout Eversley's adult life, though, the distance between them had gradually widened. Not because of any specific issue or incident but more the slow realisation that they were very different and had very different world views. Blood ties may matter, thought Wilfred, but ideas and beliefs do count for something even, maybe particularly, with your closest relatives. Now, though, here they were on a lonely footpath right at the limits of their country trying to escape its clutches because of a shared desire for Wilfred's continued existence.

By 5.30, it was fully dark as they continued across what was now more open country. The rain had held off but it was increasingly chilly. Away to the left, Wilfred could hear the distant low hum of the A68 and its drone corridor. There were very few drones and not that many driverless on the road. But they were interspersed with old-style lorries which, contrary to the predictions of twenty years before, were still operated by people.

Wilfred surmised that Eversley would be thinking about calling his 90+ contact now but he also knew that they needed to cover a few more kilometres yet before they could commit to a definite rendezvous point. The older man was dubious about the security of I-COMs. There were stories every week in the news about information leaks. But he knew that his son, an early adopter of these devices, believed the technology had made secure communication implants impenetrable even by governments. So, when the moment came, Eversley would think up his contact and find out whether they could help them get to Scotland and to safety.

The silence was interrupted suddenly by Eversley, causing Wilfred momentary alarm.

"Let's stop in that wooded area over there and have something to eat," Eversley suggested to his father who nodded his agreement.

They had been walking for two hours and had covered only about a quarter of the distance they had to do, and Wilfred welcomed the chance for a rest. Without a word, they sat down against a tree which afforded a bit of shelter from the wind, tucked into their sandwiches, each lost again in their thoughts about this unlikely journey. It was a journey they could not have envisaged as being necessary twenty years ago. Nor was it a journey that seemed at all likely even a few weeks ago.

Wilfred had been unaware that Eversley had thought about

it several years back but had only dared mention it to his father a couple of months previously. At first Wilfred had dismissed the idea as ridiculous and Eversley had pretty much dropped it. However, something had clearly kept gnawing away at Eversley – a belief, Wilfred thought, that the law that required his father's life to end was fundamentally unjust.

For Wilfred, he had agreed to make the journey for a mixture of motives. Partly, it was the residual self-preservation instinct that remained in everyone despite the cultural shift of the last ten years. It was also a strong desire to see some new surroundings which might inspire him to finish his latest composition. But mainly, he thought, he was doing it for his son and for the relationship between them. However, whatever the reasons, here he was, sat under a tree on a cold autumn evening in Northumberland, about to break the law.

They finished their sandwiches, took some tea from a flask and stood up. Wilfred observed the military precision with which Eversley packed away the provisions and stuffed the silver foil in which the sandwiches had been wrapped into his bag.

The course of the footpath they were following took them closer to the A68 but still far enough away not to be noticed from it. Wilfred was rather vague about the geography but he couldn't help calculate the distance still to be covered to get close enough to an unguarded part of the border for a meeting with someone who could help them. There were at least three hours more of walking in his estimation, so it would be between nine and ten at night before they could rendezvous. Today it was the left knee in particular that was hurting and, as they trudged along and the temperature dropped, Wilfred found himself wondering whether he could make it.

But being here also made him think about the awkward times years ago when Eversley had signed up for the Army. The bleakness and the fear he was now experiencing transported him to the dark days of the past. Eversley had joined the Army just after the Millennium when he was in his early twenties. It was partly pragmatism. He didn't know what else to do. But Wilfred knew it was partly a rebellion, a rebellion against his liberal father. It was also a rebellion against what he saw as the increasingly degenerate society that was often dubbed 'Cool Britannia'. But when he was training on the Otterburn Ranges, Eversley hadn't expected that he would be going to war so soon. Tony Blair's decision to support America's invasion of Iraq had changed everything. Before he knew it, the practice exercises in these Northumberland moorlands had become the precursor to something very real and very scary.

It was as if they had been thinking the same things, thought Wilfred, as unexpectedly Eversley stopped, turned towards his father and spoke into the darkness.

"It's nice in a weird sort of way being back here, you know. A black man stood out then in the Army. Some of them called me all sorts but, actually, most of them were fine with it. Thinking about it now, it was the easy bit compared with what came afterwards."

Wilfred felt that his son was expecting a response.

"We were worried about you at the time. Your mother was certain you'd be killed and I just didn't like the idea of a son of mine in the Army. But it was your life to lead."

Eversley slipped back into silence but Wilfred now appreciated that, for his son, being back here now made him feel secure in a strange sort of way. Wilfred wasn't letting on to Eversley that now he was starting to feel the pain in his hip as well as his knees that usually happened after he'd walked more than a few kilometres. He wouldn't mind another rest but knew that they had to keep moving to get closer to the border. So he struggled on a few metres behind his son whose pace he couldn't match. His thoughts wandered back to his music but the discomfort in his body prevented concentration. He walked as if in a trance with Eversley's combat trousers and camouflage jacket ahead as his guide.

A few minutes later, Wilfred's trance was broken as Eversley turned towards him.

"Don't say anything for a few minutes, Dad. I'm going to make contact."

Wilfred got closer to his son and listened, although he knew he wouldn't hear anything. He realised that the chimera of security, created by the strangely familiar feel of the army training area, had emboldened Eversley to try to make contact with the people who would help them with the last leg of their journey. As it was happening, though, Wilfred was completely unaware of what was being said. He still struggled to understand the technology and, if truth be known, he was still a bit wary of it. Wilfred only knew of the success of his son's communication when Eversley turned to look at his father.

"It's all sorted," he said, "about an hour from now, hopefully."

Wilfred nodded but said nothing. Eversley, keen to reassure his father, continued.

"We're aiming for a farm near Byrness. It's just straight on ahead on this path. I know you don't trust I-COMs but it's all fine. It's all encrypted so we don't need to worry. But just to be on the safe side there was no point actually speaking to him. Take no unnecessary risks. That's the mantra."

Wilfred remained unconvinced. Eversley continued,

"You'd have loved the passwords we used, Dad. 'Regis to Rashford - we're two passes away from a goal!' And his reply?' Dalglish intercepts and Souness tackles'. I bet you can even remember Cyrille Regis can't you?"

"And Dalglish and Souness – much better players than any around today," darted back Wilfred, smiling because he fondly remembered how much he'd loved football in his younger days.

Wilfred temporarily forgot his worries about I-COMs as the two men reminisced briefly about football. He knew most devices could be thought-activated using memorised passwords with the visual information projected onto the false lenses that most people had fitted in their eyes. So it was possible to communicate without making a sound or even any movement visible to anyone else. But for him, it was still science fiction.

Wilfred had already heard Eversley's explanation of how the escape attempt would be organised. Communication with the 90+ group was very much on a 'need to know' basis. Over the past couple of weeks, some of the communication had involved real voice conversations. For Wilfred, the jury was still out on whether Eversley had indeed made genuine contact with the resistance group which had been spearheading opposition to the age termination laws for several years. The group had made a reputation for itself for helping would-be escapers to flee abroad or to secrete themselves in remainder colonies. No one knew for certain but it was widely believed the epicentre of their operation was in the Hunstanton colony on the Norfolk coast. For now, Wilfred would just have to trust his son.

They both went back to the separate worlds within their own heads. The return to silence was short-lived. Feeling buoyed by the confirmation of the rendezvous, no doubt, Eversley succumbed to the urge to call his partner with an old-fashioned voice call. For a few minutes, Wilfred overheard parts of a whispered conversation between his son and daughter-in-law. He wasn't really listening but he heard enough to be reminded of the apparently blissfully happy relationship Eversley enjoyed with his wife, Emma.

"How are the girls?" he heard Eversley say, causing Wilfred a pang of sadness because he rarely saw his granddaughters, both now in their early twenties.

There hadn't been any particular issue with them but his partial separation from them was simply a product of the difficulties he had with his son. Once the call ended, they both continued in silence, as the evening turned fully to night and the noise from the A68 quietened.

The next interruption came from Wilfred who had now been able to turn his mind back to his music. He was humming a tune. He felt it was safe to do this now. Earlier, before conformation of the rendezvous, he might have thought differently.

"What's that tune, Dad? I don't recognise it," asked Eversley.

"Well, you wouldn't because I've not finished it yet," replied Wilfred, letting out a short chuckle.

"I don't know how you can keep music you're still writing in your head like that."

"Neither do I really, but it helps."

Wilfred had been working on this piece for saxophone and orchestra for many months and, as their conversation lapsed, he carried on humming, repeating the same phrase over and over again. What really occupied his mind though, wasn't the technicalities of his composition but the connection he had just felt with his son. He hoped there would be more of this in the days ahead.

This sense of security was only momentary. Wilfred stopped his humming mid-stanza. He could feel the adrenaline running through him. About a kilometre ahead against the silhouette of a farm building he'd not previously noticed, two people, both men he thought, were walking towards them, almost certainly on the same path, shining torches. His first instinct was to freeze but it was Eversley who took command.

"Dad, just carry on walking. We've been on an afternoon walk and we're heading back to our B&B in Byrness if they ask."

They walked on with the silhouettes of the two men getting closer and larger. Wilfred realised his heart was pounding. He had concluded that the game was up, even before it had properly started and walked slightly faster and closer to his son. He thought it was too soon for the 90+ rendezvous but, on the other hand, the police wouldn't bother to come looking for people on a remote path. They caught people trying to cross into Scotland closer to the border. But he couldn't think of any other plausible reason for anyone to be on this path deep into the evening on a November night. In the past, it might have been a couple of men heading to the pub but people hardly ever did that now.

His mind was racing whilst he tried to maintain an exterior calm. The two figures were now much closer, maybe fifty metres away, still shining their torches at the ground ahead and walking at a normal pace in silence. Wilfred was worried that Eversley might activate his I-COM by mistake. This happened sometimes with thought-activated devices.

As the four men converged, the two strangers stopped and one said in a broad Scottish Borders accent, "Wilfred and Eversley? Souness runs half the length of the pitch, evades three English defenders and scores from twenty-five metres."

Wilfred had no idea what any of this meant. Everything happened so fast but he found himself trying to assess whether to place his trust in this man. But he also felt a strange calm with the noise of their steps silenced and the fear of the night extinguished by the men's torches.

Moments later, though, Eversley took away any responsibility Wilfred felt about making a decision as his son simply replied, "Howe." Yet another footballing code word in honour of the great manager who had briefly revived the glory days of Newcastle United twenty years previously.

"Follow us," the stranger said. And they did.

CHAPTER THREE

City of Westminster, Greater London.
Friday 10 November 2045

Every time he made the journey to Buckingham Palace, Edward Watson's attention was drawn to the New Union Jack fluttering above. He had been strongly against the decision to remove the cross of St. Andrew from the flag just as he had been against changing the official name of the country from the United Kingdom. As far as he was concerned, Scottish independence was illegal and the UK should retain a claim to the territory of Scotland under international law. In the end, a messy compromise had left the Union flag altered but the name of the country unchanged. As the Prime Ministerial car swept silently through the gates bringing him for his weekly audience with the King, Edward smiled to himself as he remembered how he'd coined the phrase 'Union Jock' to describe the new Scottish flag.

Previously, these audiences had always been on a Tuesday but now it was a moveable feast usually arranged to accommodate the Prime Minister's diary. This was a recognition perhaps of the much-changed roles and relationships of the monarchy and the government in the tumultuous two decades since Brexit and the Great Pandemic. When he first became Prime Minister, Edward enjoyed these weekly meetings but, perhaps in retrospect, mainly because he was then still in disbelief that this working-class boy from the sticks was mixing in such exalted circles. Now, however, he had an unpleasant feeling in the pit of his stomach as the car slowed to a halt under the Palace arches and he knew that the weekly interrogation was now only moments away.

"Good evening, Prime Minister," said the King's Chief Assistant greeting Edward as he stepped out of the car.

Even though he was a Conservative through and through, the Prime Minister welcomed the dramatic changes made in the size and style of the Royal Family over the past fifteen years. Gone were the equerries and cast list of flunkies dressed in outdated uniforms befitting the nineteenth rather than the twenty-first century. The Royal Household was much reduced in size and those that were left wore ordinary suits and didn't bow and scrape. These changes were the result of the financial crisis of the mid-twenties which had prompted a backlash against the perceived excesses and wealth of the Royals.

The size and style of the Royal Household may have changed but the grandeur of the one remaining Royal Palace persisted. As Edward was led along the ornate corridor, he glanced at the portraits adorning the high walls. He neither knew nor cared who these people were, virtually all of them men. The young King had once given him an impromptu tour of the inner sanctum of the palace and told him the stories behind some of these proud faces from the past. Now it was all a blur.

Edward still had to remind himself that he was perfectly entitled as the elected Prime Minister to walk these corridors of power. However, even after almost a decade in office, he still had the nagging doubt that he was something of an upstart. He was very much the kid from the 'wrong side of the tracks', brought up in an unfashionable part of North London. He had won a place at Cambridge through a special scheme designed to help young people from disadvantaged backgrounds. As the economic recession worsened in the years after the Great Pandemic, he was outraged by the way his generation seemed to take the blame and the pain for what had happened. The League of Youth seemed a natural home for him and from then his journey into politics seemed to continue at breakneck speed. Now, though, he was older and tired and the new generation coming up behind him were making his lifelong insecurities resurface.

"Just wait a minute here, Sir, and I'll check that his Majesty is ready," commanded the Chief Assistant, as they arrived at the door of the Royal study.

The knot in the prime ministerial stomach tightened and, to distract himself, Edward studied some of the portraits close up. The names and the faces meant little to him but he did register the dates underneath the pictures.

'Sir James Cranborne 1762-1811'

Here were people who had lived 200 or 300 years previously and, to qualify to be on the walls of Buckingham Palace, they had clearly been part of the affluent, wealthy strata of society. Despite this, their lifespans were alarmingly short by the standards of the mid-twenty-first century. Most had died in their forties, fifties or sixties, ages of death which would today be regarded as exceptionally premature. He reflected that his generation were the lucky ones to be in a position to argue about whether life should end at ninety. As his mind wandered, he heard the words of some of his fiercest political opponents in the House of Commons only a couple of days earlier. They had lambasted him as a murderer, one even accusing him of genocide for allowing the State to kill perfectly healthy people when they reached their ninetieth birthday.

Edward turned and walked across to the wall of the Royal inner sanctum. A series of portraits encapsulated the tragic set of circumstances which had afflicted the succession over the previous twenty years. Firstly, the still fondly remembered Elizabeth the Second. Then, the rather less popular Charles who, suffering from dementia, had finally been persuaded to give up the throne to the much more popular William whose reign turned out to be tragically short.

Edward was jolted back to reality as the door of the King's study opened. The Chief Assistant beckoned him in and, in a flash, he was inside face to face with a man not much more than half his age who had been propelled onto the throne a couple of years previously in the most tragic of circumstances.

"Good evening, Prime Minister," said the King whom Edward thought bore an uncanny family likeness to both his father and grandfather. "How are you this evening?"

"Good evening, Your Majesty," replied Watson, "I'm fine, thank you. It's rather busy at present but I think we're still winning on most fronts."

As he uttered the words, he knew how false they sounded. He was failing to convince himself never mind persuade the Monarch that all was well with the government of his Kingdom.

King George the Seventh seemed old for his thirty-two years, a combination, no doubt, of being prepared for the role he now occupied and the accelerated learning curve thrust upon him after the untimely death of his father in a helicopter crash.

Edward had read about the relationship between Prime Minister and Head of State the last time a British Monarch had assumed the throne at so young an age. That had been back in the 1950s when the young Princess Elizabeth became Queen at the age of twenty-six when her father, the last King titled George, had died. Back then, by all accounts, an ailing Winston Churchill, in his second term as Prime Minister, had patronised the young Queen and used his status as Britain's iconic wartime leader to try to undermine her.

Conscious of this warning from history, Edward had tried to forge a constructive partnership with the youthful King from the start of their working relationship. However, his hope that George would bow to the judgement of an experienced politician such as himself was short-lived. The King had grown in confidence much more quickly than he had expected.

"Can I bring you up to speed on the Russia issue, Your Majesty?" asked the Prime Minister, in an attempt to start the weekly encounter on less potentially controversial territory. "I believe we are getting closer to a conclusion to this matter."

Russia and Britain had been involved in a long-running dispute for over twenty years about allegations of murders committed by the agents of both countries on each other's soil. It had all begun in 2018 with the poisoning of Alexander Shripol and his daughter in Salisbury by two Russian agents. Edward started detailing the latest developments in Anglo-Russian relations but he could sense the King's impatience.

"Glad to hear it," retorted the King, clearly only mildly interested. "Now tell me where we are with the euthanasia reforms. You have a debate about it at your conference soon, I gather."

"We do, Your Majesty," replied the Prime Minister, the knot in his stomach suddenly making itself known again. "I'm confident that…."

"I have some concerns about the Government's position," interjected the King cutting across Edward before the Prime Minister could muster the first phrases of the argument he had rehearsed for this very moment.

"I was in Leicester last week and met a group of people there who really impressed me. It was a Late Eights group. You'll be aware who they are. There were probably twenty or so there, men and women, and they were involved in a campaign to reduce drone noise in the city centre. They were all in great shape physically, so much so in fact that I struggled to believe that some of them could possibly be that old. More importantly, they were all, pretty much without exception, articulate and entirely in command of their faculties. They had all their marbles, as I believe people used to say years ago. I ended up spending far longer than I should have done talking to them and the rest of the day was all behind schedule. My reason for mentioning this to you, Prime Minister, is that I am increasingly worried about what sort of society we are if we are happy to euthanize people like these just because they are ninety years old. These are people who are making a worthwhile contribution, people who are still clearly enjoying life and people who have nothing wrong with them."

The Prime Minister was momentarily and uncharacteristically unsure how to respond, taken aback by the forthrightness of the Royal rebuke. He knew from their previous meetings over the last few months that the Monarch, privately at least, questioned the idea of euthanasia at ninety. Speculation had been rife in the media that he was almost certainly supportive of the idea of raising the termination age. However, the King had been very careful not to say anything until now which could be seen to breach constitutional propriety. Clearly, he had decided that today was to be the day when he crossed a line.

"I'm sorry to be so direct, Prime Minister, and you may feel I'm overstepping the mark but I'm sure you would agree it is the Monarch's right, indeed responsibility, to advise the Government."

These last few words gave Edward breathing space to frame a response.

"You don't need to apologise, Your Majesty, and I welcome your advice because this is a very difficult issue. As you know, there are some in my own party who express similar concerns to those you've just articulated. These are genuinely held views, I'm sure, but I do think there is a danger here of losing sight of why we introduced euthanasia at ninety a decade ago.

"It's only a few short years ago, Your Majesty, that our country was crammed with care homes full of demented people in their nineties. In many cases, the homes were in a very poor state, dirty, dilapidated and sometimes dangerous. Staff were poorly paid, the food was awful and abuse was widespread. And the costs of running all this, even though the service provided was scandalously bad, were out of control. And we shouldn't forget that the massive costs of saving the lives of mainly older people in the Great Pandemic have burdened all of us since.

"However, people slowly came to realise that quality of life was what really mattered. Living a long life is a nice idea but if the last years of that life are spent in pain, unhappiness and often without mental capacity, then what sort of a life is that? Many of our people had already come to this conclusion themselves and took the option of ending their own lives. Of course, at first, that meant either going abroad or breaking the law. Fortunately, my party, with great support from many others including the churches, was able to convince people that the law should change to allow euthanasia in certain circumstances. As you will recall, that was a change in the law of which many people took advantage. In fact the numbers of people using voluntary euthanasia rose exponentially in the first few years of the new law. And, incidentally, they continue to keep increasing even after the 90 Law came in ten years ago. So even though life ends at ninety, people still choose to end it earlier if it has become intolerable."

The King listened patiently but couldn't help but interject when the Prime Minister made the mistake of pausing.

"I appreciate the history lesson, Prime Minister, but none of that addresses the issue of compulsion at a set age irrespective of a person's health. That's what I am concerned about. If you had told leaders of your party like Margaret Thatcher or Boris

Johnson, I believe you are a great admirer of both, if you had told either of them that within a few decades, the country they led would kill its own citizens for no reason other than the fact that they had reached the age of ninety, they wouldn't have believed it possible."

There was an uncomfortable silence for a few moments punctuated only by the rain which was now rattling against the palace windows and the low hum of driverless and drones in the distance. Edward decided that he should wait for a cue from the King before continuing. The Monarch walked over to the window. Outside, there was still a small crowd of tourists gathered by the Palace gates. Edward noticed that the evening gloom was lifted by the bright colours of their coats, many of them vintage designs reminiscent of the 1960s which had enjoyed a revival in the last few years. This was a reaction, it was said, to the dour austerity of the post-Brexit twenties and early thirties.

But the tourists were not the only visitors to the gates of the Palace. Away to the left, as Edward could see over the Royal shoulder, there was a group of people being kept at a distance from the gates by the police. Many were holding banners and he could just hear, through the double-glazed windows of the palace, the distinctive chants of the League of Youth. In recent weeks, they had taken to demonstrating outside the Royal front door to remind the King of their strong support for the status quo.

"Don't kill the young to save the old."

"90 is more than enough."

"Young Lives Matter."

After reading the slogans, Edward waited for the King to turn back into the room.

"Your Majesty," tried Edward tentatively, unsure whether attack or defence was the better option at this time. He chose the former.

"Sorry if my words felt like a history lesson but we should perhaps not lose sight of the fact that my party was elected on a manifesto that included the 90 Law and that we won a very comfortable majority in that election. Parliament then debated the issue extensively before passing the Law so the 90 Law was, I think it is fair to say, passed with due process and with full public support."

"Look, Edward," retorted the King breaking another convention by addressing the Prime Minister by name, "I understand your position and I know that many people in the country agree with you. But I also know that many don't, including it should be said, many in your own Party. I've been very impressed by your Business Secretary, Evie Smith, who seems to have become the standard bearer for those questioning the status-quo. I thought she was very impressive when I heard her the other day. I'm sure she represents what a lot of people are thinking now and she's young, she's energetic and she is the future. But you must do what you think right. We are after all a democracy. But please bear in mind what I've said."

"Of course, Your Majesty," replied Edward, "I always value your advice and I will think on what you've said this afternoon."

Although he disagreed with the Royal viewpoint, he confessed to himself a secret admiration for the passion with which the King expressed his views, a passion which reminded him of the King's late grandmother, Diana. But it was the mention of Evie Smith that made him recoil inwardly. Smith had been Edward's protégé, young and energetic, as the King had said, but also black and northern and a great asset to the Conservative Party. He had taken her under his wing and promoted her but now he knew she was gaining in confidence and support and was becoming a serious rival.

"Now, Prime Minister, you wanted to bring me up to speed on Russia?" said the King in a business-like manner.

"Yes, indeed," replied Edward as the two of them launched back into the less controversial business of government.

For a further ten or fifteen minutes, they ranged over the usual fare of these audiences – drone accidents, train failures, food prices, rows over the security of I-COMs and various other matters. The King behaved as though the earlier exchange had never happened and displayed a genuine interest and asked some pertinent questions. Edward, however, felt slightly detached as if he were just going through the motions of being Prime Minister.

As he was driven away from the Palace, a blur of bright coats flashed past the rainy window of his car, their owners no doubt keen to see who had been to see the King. His driver had turned on the radio for the news so the shouts of the League of Youth were drowned out. Edward sat back as the Palace faded into the distance and for a few moments he shut his eyes in a vain attempt to forget about the challenges ahead.

CHAPTER FOUR

Bromley, Greater London
Friday 10 November 2045

Holly let herself in to Mary's lounge through the patio doors still sweating and short of breath. She had been running regularly for years, had completed several marathons and other 'ultra' challenges but today a modest 5K run felt like torture. Fitness was very important to her and she made herself use almost any spare moment to take some exercise. But, as she slumped onto her grandmother's sofa, she wondered why it had felt so tough today. Perhaps it was the anxiety she felt about the day ahead.

"Hello dear. How lovely to see you! What a nice surprise."

Holly was unsurprised but still saddened by Mary's confused greeting.

"Gran, I've just been on a run. I've only been gone about thirty minutes. Would you like a cup of tea? I need one."

"Oh, yes please, dear."

Holly headed into the kitchen, ignoring a call coming in on her I-COM from Jake. She knew why he was calling. They'd had an argument before she'd left home earlier. Jake had told her that, in his view, the pre-death day rituals were a fiasco and that he didn't want to be part of them. Holly had told him that he could do what he wanted but that she was going to do everything she could to make her grandmother's last days as pleasant as possible. When she returned to Mary with the tea, she felt the urge to kiss or even to embrace her but, like many other people who'd lived through the Great Pandemic as a child, the norms of social distancing still occasionally restrained her behaviour.

"I'm going to have a quick shower, Gran, if that's OK?"

Holly was back in the room in less than ten minutes and ready for the arrival of her father who was going to take them by drone on this latest pre-deathday trip. He had offered to pick Holly up from her home in Croydon but she couldn't stand the embarrassment of him landing his drone in her street so she'd offered to meet him at Mary's house. Holly had never much liked drones but her father's fascination and then his business interest in them had persuaded her to at least tolerate them. So now, on a warm Friday morning in November, she found herself waiting at her grandmother's home for David to land on the back lawn.

David was normally very punctual so, when he was ten minutes late, Holly had a flicker of concern. What if he had crashed the dammed thing? He had done so several times before, particularly back in the twenties when drones were first used to carry people rather than just goods. On one occasion, he had crash landed in Orpington High Street only narrowly missing two young children. However, he seemed to have become less cavalier as he had got older and the technology had improved.

Then Holly was pleasantly surprised by Mary's next observation.

"Where's David? He's not usually late. He should have been here by now."

Holly knew that, more often than not, her grandmother would not have realised that her son was late. Other times she might not have remembered at all that he was coming to pick her up. The impact of her dementia was variable and unpredictable. Today, though, Holly was pleased in a funny sort of way that Mary was feeling agitated that David was late. However, just as she was about to act on her concerns, Holly heard the distinctive sound of her father's drone circling above.

"He's here, Gran. Can you hear it?"

"Pardon, dear. What did you say?"

As so often, Holly thought, it was one step forward and then one step back with her grandmother's dementia, as she helped her to her feet. Mary stood up a little unsteadily. But with pretty much a full new set of joints acquired over the years, she was, like many of her age, remarkably upright and agile despite her eighty-nine years.

"Good morning, Mother," beamed David as the drone lowered itself to a smooth stop and he climbed out exuding his usual bonhomie. "How are we today?"

Drones had become a regular part of the background soundtrack of suburban life in relatively comfortable middle-class outer London but they were mainly for deliveries of all sorts. Privately-owned drones were rare and Holly thought it was unnecessarily ostentatious for her father to own more than one even though he was the owner of a drone hire company. As it hovered above the garden and automatically manoeuvred itself down onto the lawn, she was pleased to see a wide smile light up Mary's face.

"Hello, David, I'm alright, thank you," she replied. "Isn't it quiet? And it's so compact. It's nice having a little trip in this, isn't it?" addressing the question to Holly who concealed her true feelings about the prospect of a drone trip.

"Now you'll have to remind me where we are going today. I've completely forgotten what we said."

"We are going to Peckham, Mum, to see some of the places where you grew up, remember. And we're going to see where you used to work, at Herne Hill. By the way, sorry I'm a bit late. I had to take Boris for a walk and he kept running off."

Holly nipped back into the lounge and swept up the items her grandmother would otherwise have forgotten – her coat and scarf in case it cooled off later, her SLR camera and the ancient smartphone which she had retained as an emergency means of communication. Like many older people, she had rejected the idea of an I-COM.

From inside the house, she could hear her father climbing out of the drone and could imagine the slightly awkward embrace he would be giving his mother. She could hear their conversation.

"And isn't it nice, Mum, that Holly wants to come with us."

"Holly?" enquired Mary.

"Your granddaughter. My daughter. She's inside getting your things," replied David just a bit impatiently.

"Oh yes, of course. I like Holly. She's one of the good ones."

"What do you mean by that?" responded David, sounding mildly annoyed.

"She understands. She understands," replied Mary enigmatically.

"Understands what?" asked David.

"Understands me," offered Mary.

Holly paused at the door before going out, not wanting to interrupt this revealing conversation. But, Holly concluded, her father had clearly decided that further probing would be unproductive.

He helped his mother into the drone, buckled her in and got back in himself. They sat in silence as he programmed the nav. Holly joined them. She had decided against the leather coat today, worried that it would get crumpled and creased in the confined space of the drone. Instead she wore a padded jacket which, she hoped, would keep off the chill she nearly always felt on a drone flight.

"There we go. We're all set for your old stamping ground. Herne Hill, here we come," announced David with an unnecessarily theatrical flourish.

Less than a minute later, with the drone cleared for take-off, they lifted slowly into the air and rose almost vertically to their cruising height as the streets of suburban outer London opened up below them. Even though she wanted the flight to be over as quickly as possible, Holly did enjoy looking down on the familiar landscape below. It was a clear day with very little cloud and from the air you could see the millennial additions to the area's housing, late twentieth century accretions to the older Victorian, Edwardian and pre-Second World War stock. Very few new houses had been put up in the last twenty years but, unseen from the air, many shops, offices and factories had been converted to homes, including the flat she shared with Jake in Croydon. She tried to make out her street from the air.

"That's my street, down there, Gran."

Mary appeared not to hear and, after two repetitions, Holly gave up.

"I thought we could land in Brockwell Park first. I've had a word with Daniel and they're expecting us at the office sometime this morning," interjected David.

David had told Holly some time previously that he was planning a number of these farewell trips for his mother. Like many things in her life, Holly was ambivalent about the idea. She knew that, even before the 90 Law, people had sometimes done a similar thing after they received a diagnosis of terminal illness. Often, though, people were overtaken by events and they never got the time to complete a tour of their favourite people and places. Nowadays, it was in theory easier given that people had a definite date for their death. However, like many people, Holly still found it awkward to discuss these sorts of arrangements.

At this moment, huddled in a drone high above London with her two closest blood relatives, Holly's overwhelming emotion was sadness. In her lucid moments, Mary was fully aware of David's plans for her and in agreement with them. On other occasions, she seemed confused and oblivious but went along with them in a fog of partial understanding. Today she was somewhere in between, happy to let others determine the shape of her last few weeks but hazy about the exact details of what was happening to her. Holly was torn between thinking it was best for her grandmother to be released from the indignity of her condition and railing against the unfairness of it all.

Partly to jolt herself out of her dilemma, Holly engaged her father.

"How's work been the last few days, then, Dad?"

"Fine, fine, all good," was David's unconvincing reply.

If anybody deserved the epithet 'Panglossian', it was her father. Holly was rarely able to penetrate his emotional defences and he was even more secretive about his work. Holly strongly suspected that he was lying. He'd occasionally given the odd hint that all wasn't well with his business. Or she'd overheard a conversation. Once or twice she'd read something on the news-sites where his company's struggles had been documented.

They said little on the first part of the journey. Holly felt momentarily unnerved by the automatic sharp slowing of the drone as they approached the M25 corridor. It was one of the busiest drone routes in the country and, even though they were counter-intuitively now heading out of London, they needed to join the corridor in order to access a route into inner London further round. They slowed, curved round to the right and joined the clockwise flow of drone traffic, mainly pilotless cargo machines but interspersed with taxis and a few private drones. They continued on the corridor for a few minutes safely spaced from drones in front and behind. Then they accelerated automatically and veered right and across the anti-clockwise channel to continue northwards towards inner London.

Even though she had flown along it and over it many times, Holly was still fascinated by the sight of the M25 below them. She could just remember how crowded it was thirty years ago, how it had been widened, made into a so-called smart motorway but still had seemed to be badly congested more often than not. It was still in use although only the original clockwise lanes, now split into two lanes in each direction. The old anti-clockwise carriageway had been abandoned. Parts had been built over and giant weeds were growing in the unrepaired cracks in the concrete, all but obscuring the faded remains of the white lines and cats' eyes. Individual car ownership was almost a thing of the past. Freight transport was much reduced as people's desire to buy and own things had waned, partly out of economic necessity and partly because of changing values.

As the drone climbed back to its cruising height and then onwards in the direction of central London, David spoke.

"Have you had a good week then, Holly?"

"Yeah, OK," she replied, "It's been busy at work and we've been decorating the flat until late each evening so I'm a bit tired to be honest."

"No pain, no gain," was her father's entirely predictable response which dented Holly's enthusiasm from detailing why she had been busy at work or how she and Jake were getting on with the decorating.

Instead she drifted back inside her own head. This nostalgia trip was the product of her inner conflict over what was happening to her grandmother. Mary had been a great influence on Holly as a child, imbuing her with her social radicalism. But so also had her father whose brash capitalism had in part rubbed off on his daughter even though she never admitted it when she was younger. She had many arguments with her father over the years, particularly when he had poured scorn on her original career plan to find a job in the charity or campaigning world. However, father and daughter had unsurprisingly become closer since the death of Holly's mother. By joining them on the journey, she was in a way trying to please both her father and grandmother.

"Are you looking forward to today, Gran?" asked Holly.

"Yes dear," replied Mary slightly feebly. They chatted intermittently and the journey passed quickly. The tell-tale signs that they were nearing the middle of London soon came into view. Looking away to the east, Holly could see the vast expanse of water which now occupied the area which had previously been Greenwich Park. They had to circle northwards passing over the boarded up streets of Borough Market, London Bridge and New Cross. It all reminded her of the breaching of the Thames Flood Barrier eight years before - one of the iconic events of all their lifetimes.

Eventually, the drone manoeuvred itself above the parking lot in Brockwell Park. It was unusually busy and there didn't appear to be enough space for them to land. Just as David was about to engage manual override and look for an unofficial space somewhere else in the park, a chill ran through Holly. Twenty or so metres away from them, just above the ground, was the unmistakable shape of a vehicle which embodied the 90 Law and the power of the state to enforce it. Holly, even though she was a supporter, shivered, held her breath and felt a dryness in her mouth.

"There's a narabanc, Dad. What's happening?"

"Oh, I'd better obey the parking rules, I suppose, and hover here and hope for a space."

Holly knew it was highly improbable that the occupiers of the police drone would be in the slightest bit interested in a drone traffic violation. Even though her father didn't acknowledge it, she knew it was a particular type of police drone, highly sinister in the popular imagination, which belonged to the National Age Regulation Authority, the agency which enforced the age regulation laws. But David seemed chastened into lawful behaviour by their arrival. So he continued to hover, waiting for a space to open up below.

The scream cut through Holly like a knife. The urban landscape of most English cities was much quieter than it had been twenty years before so almost any unexpected noise was now amplified against the ambient silence. It was all over almost before it had begun. Three agents bundled a man into the drone despite the protestations of a screaming woman, presumably from her age his daughter. He put up little resistance and, within what seemed like less than a minute, the drone was airborne leaving the woman sobbing at the roadside and being comforted by bystanders.

Holly was still so shocked by what she had seen and wanted to shout out but she was inhibited by the almost certain knowledge that her grandmother had not appreciated the significance of what they had just seen. But she wasn't going to let it go.

"What's happening, Dad? We should land and see if they are alright," she said in a raised whisper to her father.

"We can't," he replied, "we'll be late for Daniel and anyway, there's nothing we can do. It would be so much better if people complied with the law. It's better for everyone if people obey the rules and enjoy their last days and weeks, as we are with Gran."

David had seen the NARA in action before but it was the first time Holly had witnessed it for herself. Mary belatedly realised that something unusual had happened.

"What's all that noise?" she asked her son as she turned her head in the direction of the sobbing and shouting.

"It's just the police arresting someone, Mum," offered David as soothingly as possible as he steered the drone hurriedly across the park away from the noise.

Inside, Holly was mounting a spirited argument against her father's line of reasoning but again thought better of it. She sat in thoughtful silence as her father cruised above Brockwell Park looking for somewhere to land. She had seen many older people suffering greatly in their last years and she could see the sense in the compulsory ending of life at ninety. But she was still shocked to see the raw horror of the policy she had voted for being implemented.

After a few minutes of fruitless searching, David gave up looking for a safe but illegal landing spot and headed back to the official parking area and found a space. The upset appeared to be over and the screaming woman had disappeared. David helped his mother from the drone and all three walked swiftly down the street, crossing the road towards Mary's old workplace. Holly was grateful for her coat as it seemed to be a few degrees cooler here than in Bromley. In a moment they were at the door of the office and were buzzed in by Daniel who greeted his former colleague effusively.

Mary hugged Daniel warmly as David and Holly exchanged greetings with Daniel's colleagues. Stepping back in time seemed to bring a new energy to Mary.

"Well, this seems just like yesterday," she said to the assembled company and smiled broadly in a way that she rarely did these days, "I should have come back before now. It's been too long."

"This all looks very different. Where are you hiding the patients?" joked Mary. These new ways of working had all started after she had retired as a doctor more than thirty years before.

"We don't see that many patients here. It's mostly online.

But there are a few here today for minor operations and for some consultations which just can't be done remotely. Let me show you round."

During the brief tour that followed, Holly could see that it was rekindling many memories for Mary. Even though the building felt more like a call centre than a medical surgery, there was enough left of the old layout to jog recollections. When she spotted a poster on the wall with information about debt counselling, Mary was particularly animated.

"They told me I couldn't do that. The other partners and some interfering NHS managers said it was not the job of a doctor to get involved. But I just did it anyway. We linked with the, now what were they called, oh dear, I can't remember their name. Whatever, it worked well. So many of the patients we saw had all sorts of practical problems with money and housing and other issues, that affected their health."

"Citizens Advice Bureaux," offered Daniel, "you were a pioneer, Mary and a fighter for the communities round here. People haven't forgotten that."

"Yes, Citizens Advice – that was it," chorused Mary as she launched into another memory.

Daniel led Mary by the arm and Holly was pleased to see her grandmother in animated conversation with him as she relived her career and tried to comprehend the changes to the job she had done such a long time ago. Her father stood awkwardly next to her looking as though he didn't know what to do with himself.

"It's so nice to see Gran enjoying herself, isn't it, Dad?" observed Holly quietly.

"Yes, of course," her father replied, "but I do wish she'd just let go of all that left-wing stuff. I had my fill of it when I was growing up. She was never at home. She was always at meetings, campaigning and agitating. I don't know how she had time to see any patients. Sometimes I thought she cared more for the poor of this area than she did for her own family."

"You know that's nonsense, Dad, don't you? She loved her family and she still does even if she can't show it very much."

Holly was quite taken back by her father's forthright tone. He rarely let his emotions show, although she had heard his political analysis many times before. She could recite his speech – how his generation, whose prospects had been wrecked in the twenties after the Great Pandemic, had learned to stand on their own two feet. How he was the epitome of the 'self-made man'. His mother, love her though he did, represented the do-gooder, nanny-state which, thankfully in his view, England had left behind.

Now, though, wasn't the moment to rehearse all this so Holly made small talk with Mary's other former colleagues leaving her father standing on his own and covering his embarrassment by reading the noticeboards. Holly's thoughts were elsewhere. The events of an hour ago in the park were running around in her mind. She knew that she was starting to feel troubled by the plan that her father had designed and was now implementing for Mary's final days on earth.

CHAPTER FIVE

Near Byrness Village, Northumberland.
Saturday 11 November 2045

Even though it was now after midnight, the large open fire in the farm kitchen was still giving off considerable heat. The smell of the slightly burnt toast they had just consumed was lingering in the room. The comfort of the second mug of piping hot tea now in his hands enveloped him. All in all, Wilfred felt much more secure here than he had alone on the country path earlier even though he knew that the riskiest part of their escape still lay ahead of them. The various pains in his legs hadn't gone away even though he had now been sitting down for a while.

The farmers had introduced themselves as Susan and Richard. Richard sat quietly by the fire, poking it occasionally. Wood burning fires had been outlawed in the early twenties but in remoter areas, it was a law honoured in the breach more than the observance. Susan bustled about nervously, repeatedly offering more food and drink to her visitors who were now ranged around a set of battered leather chairs.

Hardly anything had been said so far between Wilfred and Eversley and the two minders who had greeted them in code a couple of hours before on the track. The minder with the Scottish accent had put his finger to his lips indicating that it was best to say nothing as they set off as a foursome along the path. The would-be escapers had duly obliged as they had walked in single file, first the Scottish minder, then father and son following him with the other minder, who had yet to say anything, bringing up the rear. They had arrived at the farm after a further hour's walking but it was only after sitting for a while and enjoying their refreshments that the conversation started.

Wilfred, still in his trademark overcoat despite the heat in the room, feared that Eversley's impulsive character would surface. He was right.

"OK. Thanks for the refreshments. Very nice of you. Can we get moving now? I'm feeling edgy," announced Eversley.

"OK, not so fast. Everything's fine. Now we have all had something to eat and drink, it is time to explain what is going to happen next," said the man with the Scottish accent.

"Forgive me for not introducing myself earlier but we have to be careful. I'm Joe and this is Chris," pointing to the other man who nodded with a weak smile in response.

"There is one formality we must do before we go any further," announced Joe. "I just need to see your identity cards please just to make sure we're taking the right people to freedom, so to speak."

Curiously, in a world that had become largely paperless, it was still compulsory for everyone in England to have a printed identity card. They had been introduced by the English Conservative Government after the Great Pandemic allegedly to help enforce the social distancing rules for future outbreaks of deadly diseases. Despite a vigorous campaign of opposition, the new measure had won Parliamentary approval.

Wilfred and Eversley reached into their pockets, produced their cards and handed them to Joe who gave them a cursory examination and then returned them.

"As you know, Scotland is very welcoming to people in your situation but we do need to have a record of who is crossing over and I do need to get you to read this and sign something please. It's just a formality but it means that you understand the risks involved, that you are making the journey at your own risk. It's also to emphasise that, when you make it to Scotland, you will be able to stay there but that you won't formally acquire Scottish citizenship. It just protects us all."

Wilfred was aware that escapees across the Scottish border had sometimes been the subject of hostility. Usually this had been only verbal, no doubt encouraged by the rantings of some on the radical right of Scottish politics who believed the English had made their bed and needed to lie in it. There had been a few cases of English refugees being attacked physically or subjected to harassment but this seemed a low risk to him given the alternative if he stayed in England.

Joe handed over a sheet of A4 paper to each of them. Wilfred skimmed through it quickly rather like he might when presented with the small print of a contract to buy something. He knew his son would study every word and would no doubt ask questions. As Eversley read through the document intensely, Wilfred instead studied the two men sat opposite him and on whom his escape apparently now depended. Neither gave anything much away in their facial expressions. And they had said so little that it was difficult to discern much about them or their trustworthiness.

Wilfred prided himself on his ability to locate someone by their voice even though accents had gradually become more homogenous over the past forty or fifty years. Joe's was, he reckoned, a sort of posh Glasgow. It certainly wasn't the working-class Glaswegian that many people south of the Border still found difficult to understand. Joe was probably about fifty, he thought, and from a professional background but it was difficult to know as the range of 90+ volunteers was said to be very wide. As to Chris, he looked maybe late thirties or early forties but he radiated an air of apparent indifference to the proceedings. He alternated between staring blankly ahead and then observing the features of the room as though taking in and committing all the details to memory was important to him.

The most nervous-looking person in the room appeared to be Richard who was sitting on the edge of his seat. Wilfred understood that members of 90+ took considerable risks in helping people escape to Scotland and sometimes elsewhere. Richard was shifting in his seat and giving the strong impression he wished that his guests would leave as soon as possible.

Much had been written about the 90+ group and there were plenty of rumours about it but it was difficult to separate the myths from the reality. Undoubtedly, as Wilfred knew, many of the group were motivated simply by their strong opposition to the euthanasia law. For others, it was a manifestation of their general anger at the rightward drift of English politics over the past quarter of a century. There was an element of Scottish nationalism that had got tied up with it as well. But, amid the idealists, there was also, Wilfred believed, a sinister side of smugglers and people traffickers who exploited the desire of people who wanted to escape the euthanasia law.

"OK, this seems fine to sign but just one question," said Eversley interrupting his father's silent musings. "What happens if something goes wrong? Are we on our own?"

"There is of course a chance that something could go wrong but we do everything we can to minimise risks," replied Joe with a reassuring tone. "Just leave it to us and do exactly as we say."

Eversley signed the document, handed it back to Joe and motioned to his father to do the same.

"There is just one more thing before we set off," added Joe. "I need to ask you for a contribution to the costs of this. We ourselves will not make any money out of this but there are of course costs involved. The hospitality of our friends here at the farm this evening, for example. We will need fuel and food and one or two other bits and pieces."

"How much?" interjected Eversley abruptly.

They had anticipated that this might happen and knew they would have to hand over some money even though he doubted it was really about covering costs.

"500 English," replied Joe leaving both Wilfred and Eversley looking visibly surprised.

"I knew we'd have to pay something but I wasn't expecting that much," replied Eversley.

"Wow, that's the equivalent of £2,000 in old money," said Wilfred joining the conversation for the first time, "Just pay it, Eversley. We need these people's help."

The English pound had been revalued in the mid-twenties after the economic collapse and even fifteen years on, many older people still thought in terms of the previous currency. Wilfred knew that his son would have loved to argue about the money but, thankfully, his anxiety to get on with the journey overrode his sense of exploitation. Eversley counted out 500 English silently and handed it to Joe.

"Thank you," said Joe with the air of a man who was used to getting his way. "OK, we are now all set to get going. Let me explain what will happen now. We have to vary the places where we cross the border. As you know it's not patrolled all along its length but the Border Force play a guessing game with us. They use mobile patrols so that we can never know which parts of the border will be safe and which difficult. We've decided where we are aiming tonight and it's about another fifteen kilometres from here. We reckon it's a bit too far for you to walk given the distance you've already covered. And we could do with getting across the border in the next hour or so because the Border Force guys often start up about five in the morning so this is a bit of a window of opportunity, as they say, in the wee small hours."

Eversley shot up out of his chair a little too quickly revealing his mounting anxiety at a time when he was trying to put on an outward show of composure.

"Steady on, not so fast," interjected Joe. "We've still got a few minutes because, as I was saying, we've still fifteen kilometres to cover so we are going to go by car to within about a mile of the border and then walk the last bit. The car will be here in about five minutes."

"A car? That sounds incredibly risky, particularly in the middle of the night?" blurted out Eversley, now abandoning any pretence of remaining calm and collected. "Nobody ever mentioned the idea of being driven so close to the border. I'm not happy with this."

"Calm down, Eversley," responded Joe addressing him by name for the first time. "You have to trust us. We've done this quite a few times before and our success rate is very high. If you keep calm, do as we say and keep your wits about you, you'll be fine."

"I don't like the idea of a car. Who the hell would be driving around the wilds of Northumberland at the dead of night for any purpose other than trying to cross the border illegally?" protested Eversley, the volume of his voice rising.

"Keep your voice down, Eversley," said Wilfred, surprising his son by joining the argument.

"We have to trust these people. They're taking a big risk themselves as well, you know. Let's just do what they say and get on with it."

Eversley slumped back down into his seat opening the palms of his hands in a gesture of apology. There was an awkward silence for a few moments punctuated eventually by Susan's attempt to lighten the mood.

"One for the road, gentlemen?" she uttered.

"A cup of tea before you set off, or we might find something a little stronger?"

"What a splendid idea!" said Joe as Susan produced a bottle of Scotch whisky from a cupboard.

"Everyone for a small one?" asked Susan, "or a wee dram, as I think you say in Scotland?"

Susan presumed assent from the muted laughter and nodding heads and poured six glasses, handed them round and, taking control of the situation, invited a toast.

"Here's to a successful crossing, and may you all be in Scotland before we've had time to clear up and get to bed."

All five men duly obliged and followed Susan's lead by raising their glasses and knocking back the small measures. Wilfred, no great lover of whisky, felt it hit the back of his throat and, for a moment at least, was able to allow a sense of adventure to overcome the more rational undertone of anxiety that was gripping him. A moment later, he spontaneously broke into a hum which was instantly recognisable to all present.

"When the sun shines on Loch Lomond,
Where me and my true love spent many days..."

Joe, smiling, was the first to join in. The others pitched in nervously and by the time they reached the best-known lyrics, all six people brought together in a remote cottage late at night were united in song, even the hitherto highly restrained Chris.

"You'll take the high road and I'll take the low road,
And I'll be in Scotland afore ye."

Even though Scottish folk tunes were not Wilfred's natural musical territory, he knew all the words and led the others right through the song which ended in a round of enthusiastic cheering and further toasts and good wishes.

As they replaced their glasses on the table and said their thanks, Joe prolonged the lightened mood by referencing the code used a few hours before on the footpath.

"I'm a very proud Scot, particularly when it comes to

football, but I have to give it to you that Eddie Howe was one fine manager and what he did at Newcastle was quite remarkable. I never imagined they'd ever be a top side again but he pulled it off. A big football fan, are you, Eversley?"

Before Eversley could answer, Joe was visibly distracted as people often were when something came in on their I-COMs.

"Right, we need to go. The car's outside. Get your stuff. Thanks Susan. Thanks Richard. We'll see you again, I'm sure."

"Good luck to you both," offered Richard, speaking to the fugitives directly for the first time and, as he did, he offered his hand.

Susan copied her partner as she wished them good luck as well. Wilfred responded to Susan's gesture, moving his hand, gripping Susan's in a warm handshake as he thanked her for the hospitality. Eversley did the same, although less enthusiastically, with Richard. At that moment, in a swift and skilled movement which they had clearly done before, Joe and Chris swung round, produced handcuffs from their pockets and, in a matter of a few seconds, both Wilfred and Eversley were restrained, their hands cuffed together behind their backs.

It all happened so quickly and came as such a total surprise to them that it took Wilfred a few moments to realise what had happened. As Joe and Chris started guiding them towards the door, Eversley tried to resist.

"What the hell is going on?" he shouted.

"What the hell is this?" he screamed as he started to kick out and attempt to pull away from the two men who, until a few moments before, had appeared to be their saviours.

Joe and Chris instinctively decided to concentrate on Eversley. The former soldier was a strong man but the two of them were able to march him relatively easily to the door, as Wilfred stood impassively without resistance.

"Dad, do something, stop them, what the hell?" bellowed

Eversley as he was forced through the farmhouse door out into the cold night.

Wilfred could see the door of a car being held open by a uniformed policeman outside and a second later his son was bundled inside the back of the car.

"Don't say anything, Eversley. Just keep quiet," Wilfred implored his son, already aware that questioning was bound to follow soon and that they would have to try to cobble together some sort of plausible explanation.

The two men, whom by now Wilfred assumed must be police or even maybe NARA agents, returned to the house, gathered up Eversley's backpack and guided Wilfred without aggression towards the waiting car. Wilfred's last memory of his short visit to the farm was passing close to Susan's drained face and hearing her whispered apology.

"Sorry, I'm very sorry but we have no choice."

The regular police often used driverless but not in the middle of the night near the Scottish border. The uniformed policeman drove with another policeman sat in the front. Joe sat in the second tier of seats of the people carrier with Eversley handcuffed to him with Wilfred and Chris similarly linked in the back row. Eversley appeared to have taken notice of his father's imploring him to keep quiet. But Wilfred's mind was racing, anticipating the questioning that he knew was to come and trying to formulate a believable story for his captors. There were all sorts of rumours about the interrogation methods employed by the NARA. He was confident that some of the more lurid ones were exaggerations but nevertheless he expected it to be rather tougher than a polite conversation.

As the blackness of rural Northumberland sped past the car window, Wilfred knew that they were very unlikely to have the chance to compare notes before they were grilled. He feared that Eversley would adopt a belligerent approach throwing caution to the wind. He worried that his son would say that their journey was a matter of principle against an unjust law. Wilfred, on the other hand, instinctively knew that he would take a more pragmatic line, invent a story and hope for the best.

The three agents of the state accompanying them on their journey through the night said nothing. In a sense, nothing needed to be said. Wilfred knew that they had either been betrayed or, presumably given the footballing reference earlier, that their I-COM communication had been intercepted. It hardly mattered which now.

After about an hour, the darkness of the night sky was slowly replaced by the few lights which a town gave off in the small hours. At first Wilfred had no idea where they were but a sign announcing the boundary of Berwick flashed past the window. The car slowed in the town's main street, turned up a dark side street and stopped in a forlorn looking carpark where he spotted a faded sign bearing the logo of 'Northumbria Police'. Tension gripped his insides and for a moment, Wilfred thought he was going to be sick.

60

CHAPTER SIX

City of Westminster, Greater London.
Sunday 12 November 2045

The wind whipped along Whitehall but it was warm and strangely comforting and reminiscent of summer breezes from Edward's childhood. Like his fellow politicians, he stood in line in front of the Cenotaph in a suit but no coat. Edward noticed how some of the veterans wore overcoats but that was probably more to hide their frailty than for warmth. The young King was in uniform, of course, but the overall sartorial style would have been appropriate for May or June thirty years earlier rather than for November.

The climate may have warmed but the tradition of marking Armistice Day persisted almost unchanged even though it was now more than 125 years since the end of the First World War and a hundred since the Second. If anything, the desire to commemorate military victories of the past and to honour the dead of war had strengthened rather than weakened. Edward knew that, when the present is troubled and the future uncertain, the past feels an even safer haven.

As Big Ben chimed for eleven, the assembled crowd fell silent. The Prime Minister always found it difficult to keep his thoughts on the matter in hand during these public silences. This was particularly true when he knew that, for at least part of the time, onlookers and TV cameras would be scanning his expression. Today, it was more difficult than usual and two minutes seemed like an eternity. He was preoccupied by the task he would face only an hour later as his party was meeting for a special conference to discuss the 90 Law. 'Butterflies in the stomach' was actually a very good description of the physical sensation he had at that moment - a mixture of nervousness and excitement about a difficult task ahead which translated itself from the brain to the stomach. He had discovered years ago that breathing deeply did help in moments like these.

Eventually, the Last Post sounded and Watson was released from his internal torment. Now, however, a new cause for concern emerged. He faced the ordeal of stepping forward onto the steps of the Cenotaph, laying a wreath and then retreating backwards to his position. Every year he dreaded tripping up or seeing his wreath topple over after he leant it against the memorial wall. Neither indignity had ever befallen him but he convinced himself that these fears were entirely rational and one day this would happen. The angst was accentuated by the wait as members of the Royal Family must lay their wreaths first.

As his turn to step forward drew closer, he hoped that the tension he felt inside wasn't visible. He found himself doing what he suspected everyone did in such situations. He focused on the minute details of something very concrete and physical, in this case, the tie in his shoe-laces. It was, he supposed, a form of displacement activity designed by the sub-conscious brain to lessen the importance of the moment whose imminent deadline drew ever closer. And then time seemed to speed up and the moment was upon him.

Afterwards he was unsurprised that everything had passed off without incident and he relaxed. Before he knew where he was, it was over and he was walking with his fellow dignitaries into the Foreign Office building for a cup of tea and some small talk. He paid his respects to the King and other members of the Royal Family and chatted about this and that with the leaders of the Opposition parties who had also laid wreaths. He couldn't help reflecting on the fact that the real opposition was nowhere to be seen on this occasion. But they would be waiting for him, knives sharpened, in just a few minutes and a few hundred metres away as delegates even now were gathering for the special conference. The Prime Minister knew that he would have to leave soon but he put it off until the last possible moment so as to allow himself the luxury of a few more minutes inside the warm embrace of those who were technically his political enemies.

"Prime Minister, your car is ready. We should leave now," said one of his advisors.

He knew he could postpone the inevitable no longer, bade his farewells, went to the car and enjoyed the two brief minutes of calm before the expected storm as the car made its short journey down Whitehall and round to the Queen Elizabeth Conference Centre. As his car drew up outside the Centre and his door was opened, he was thrust straight away into the passions that the 90 Law aroused. He knew there would be protesters but he hadn't anticipated so many nor their level of anger.

"Stop state murder... stop state murder." The chant rose up above the shouting and booing welling up from the crowd. "NARA killers, NARA killers."

He was ushered through to the door, protected by his detectives and a line of police. He didn't feel physically threatened but hearing such direct challenge to his policy from people just centimetres from him brought home the scale of the task he faced.

"This way, Prime Minister, to the green room. We have a few minutes before the conference is due to start," his bodyguard suggested.

Once inside, the noise from the protesters outside was barely still audible but Edward was disturbed by what he had witnessed. In the past few months, as the debate about the

90 Law had intensified once again, he had convinced himself that the calls for change were primarily driven by those who wanted to damage him politically. He refused to believe that there was widespread public opposition to the euthanasia law. Just at the moment when he needed firm resolve, his equilibrium was disrupted.

He took the script of his speech from its folder, as much an act of self-confidence as a genuine last-minute rehearsal. He scanned the familiar phrases about 'dignity in death', 'balancing the rights of the generations' and the 'natural human desire for certainty' and thought briefly about how many times he had uttered these and others. But how much did he believe in them? To what extent were they now empty mantras to which he clung for political survival? Was he now locked on a trajectory which earlier choices had dictated but which he might now want to change?

Before any of these internal rhetorical questions received any sort of answer, the clock ticked faster and he was being led into the hall, into what he now regarded as an overwhelmingly hostile environment. He had to remind himself this was his own party. He was pleasantly surprised that the applause which greeted his arrival appeared to be more than just polite. He was momentarily buoyed by this as he took his seat. But there was hardly time to gather his thoughts before the Party Chair rose to his feet to start proceedings.

"Good afternoon fellow Conservatives and welcome to our special conference called as a result of a party petition. Welcome to all of you here with us in London and also to those of you in our other venues in Manchester, Birmingham, Nottingham, Bristol, Cardiff, Southampton, Gateshead and Plymouth."

The voice retained its distinctiveness even at the age of eighty-one. Nigel Farage had adopted the role of elder statesman of the Right ever since he had been readmitted to the Conservative Party in the wake of Britain's departure from the European Union. Edward Watson and Farage had been political soulmates for a quarter of a century and the Prime Minister still believed that in Farage he had a crucial ally.

"As you all know, we are meeting today to discuss a proposal put forward by the Worsley Constituency Association calling on our Party to introduce legislation to amend the age regulation laws. The key proposal is that the age at which euthanasia takes place be increased from ninety."

Farage still liked being the focus of attention and was clearly enjoying being the ringmaster of what he knew would be a lively and probably acrimonious few hours of political cut and thrust.

"I'm first going to call on Evie Smith as proposer of the motion to open the debate."

Twentieth century style political party conferences had become a thing of the past more than a decade previously. Virtual conferences and meetings, not just in politics but in nearly every walk of life, were now the norm. Edward felt that something had been lost, particularly the opportunity to lobby behind the scenes in the bars and cafés.

He also knew that the physical division of party members into several different locations could also create an 'us and them' mentality and today that would undoubtedly be the case as his chief opponent, now standing to open the attack, was in Manchester. However irrational it was, the emotional symbolism of Manchester v London, North v South did little to diminish difference and would almost certainly exacerbate it.

Farage's image on the various giant screens around the room was replaced by Evie Smith on her feet in the Bridgewater Hall in Manchester and starting her speech. Edward had to remind himself that his visceral dislike of Smith was a relatively recent phenomenon. When she had shot onto the political scene as part of the new intake of English Conservative MPs in the General Election of 2030, Edward had admired her, or at least liked what she represented – northernness, ethnicity, working-class conservatism, plain speaking. He'd identified her as a useful ally and gave her a junior ministerial job within a few months of arriving in Parliament. They'd worked together as genuine political allies both committed to getting the ex-Brexit Party members and the mainstream Tories to work together. On most issues, they saw eye to eye.

In the last few years, however, it was personality rather than policy which had come to the fore in their relationship. Edward instinctively knew that his grip on power was gradually slipping, that he now represented the 'old guard' and Smith the 'young blood'. And it was this which divided them, not any fundamental differences of belief. The euthanasia debate might be the current dividing point but Edward's strong belief was that this was little more than a peg on which the 'enemy within' his own party could hang their opposition to the old elite.

Evie Smith was young enough to be Edward's daughter. She had grown up in Manchester's inner suburbs, lost both parents when she was just ten in the Great Pandemic, but brought up by an aunt and uncle, had won a place at Oxford. It must have been there, mused Edward, that she had acquired her posh accent. Unlike black politicians of earlier generations, she hardly ever made any reference to her ethnicity but spoke often about her humble origins. Her politics harked back to an earlier age and was reminiscent of so-called 'One Nation' Conservatism combining a belief in capitalism with a strong sense of social justice. But Edward had convinced himself that Evie had no genuine belief in the need to change the euthanasia laws. To him it was nothing more than political ambition which ignited her passion on this issue.

As ever, Smith sounded emollient and reasonable as she launched forth.

"Fellow Conservatives. We are gathered together today to discuss one of the most important issues of our time. As ever, I will come straight to the point. Those of us supporting this motion believe that the current age regulation law is wrong. We are of the view that the present age limit of ninety needs raising but it is important for all of you to understand why we've reached that conclusion.

"We are proud to be members of a Party which had the courage ten years ago to recognise that things could not go on as before. The last years of life for many of our fellow citizens had become unbearable. Often they were living in incredibly run down homes with inadequate care and bedevilled by physical and mental deterioration. Our Party recognised the growing public mood for greater control over the end of life. We saw that there was a yearning for greater certainty and we made the bold proposal of a legally mandated fixed maximum lifespan. All the arguments that led to that decision then still apply today. We are not standing here today to advocate a return to the bad old days of unregulated lifespans."

As he listened, Edward had to suppress the urge to raise an eyebrow. Was this what she really believed? Was it just a matter of raising the age? He was doubtful but knew now was not the time to unravel that. Evie Smith continued.

"We still believe that control and certainty are important. We still believe that we must continue to avoid the spectre of dilapidated care homes, overcrowded hospitals and impoverished older people. So fixing a lifespan is still the right thing to do. What's more, we shouldn't forget that the climate crisis demonstrated the need for much tougher population controls. We simply had, and still have, too many people on this planet. So, quite correctly, we limited the number of children people could have to two per couple and that is now hardly even controversial. But the laws governing the end of life are, we believe, now in need of review. Advances in medicine, particularly in physical health, mean that in our view ninety is no longer the right age to conclude life. Widespread public support for fixed lifespans will soon reduce if we continue to euthanize thousands of people each year who are to all intents and purposes perfectly healthy at the age of ninety.

"The motion before you today instructs the Party leadership to bring a bill before Parliament within the next three months raising the limit from ninety to a higher age. We believe this will attract cross-party support in the House and, more importantly, widespread backing across the country.

"One final point before I conclude if I may, Chair, and that is this. Many of you will be thinking – well it's all very well proposing that the age should be raised but to what? How can we be expected to vote for this motion unless we know what the new higher maximum lifespan limit would be? Our proposal with regard to this is that a special citizens' panel be set up straight away to hear expert medical advice and to reach a conclusion on this matter."

"So, to sum up, Party members, I urge you to support this motion and to help ensure that it is we Conservatives who once again lead the way on important social reform in our country."

As she sat down, the cameras in Manchester widened to show the assembled party membership from Smith's northern heartlands. A strong ripple of applause and cheering rang round the Bridgewater Hall. Edward, observing this remotely from 300 kilometres away, couldn't help be distracted, probably another act of subconscious displacement, by the scuffed woodwork of the great northern concert hall, now showing the effects of years of underinvestment in cultural venues.

The applause in Manchester was soon taken up around the country and the screen in London offered up shots of supportive faces and enthusiastic clapping from Gateshead, from Cardiff, from Nottingham and eventually from every location. Edward scanned the faces of his fellow Conservatives scattered around the country in search of some scepticism, some sign of opposition to what had just been proposed. He found little encouragement but enough, he thought, to embolden him in the seconds before he would be called to speak.

"Thank you, Evie. Now I call on the Prime Minister to respond," announced Farage, with his usual pomposity.

"Chair, thank you and also an enormous thank you to Evie for putting the case for the proposal before us today so succinctly and clearly. I wish to start by reinforcing the point that she made and upon which we agree wholeheartedly. The argument for a fixed lifespan is something this Party pioneered in the twenties. It is an argument which still holds good today and it is an argument which still has the support of the vast majority of our fellow citizens. I do not need to rehearse the arguments as to why because Evie has just done that brilliantly. Let me simply say that it's about quality of life and certainty. For centuries humans have struggled to free themselves from the ravages of poverty, poor health and lack of freedom. I would argue that the 90 Law was one of the great social reforms in recent history, an idea copied incidentally in several other parts of the world. It was a reform that achieved several important objectives – better quality of life in one's final years, greater equality of resources between the generations, better control of population and perhaps most importantly, certainty. The whole history of humanity has been one of developing control over things we previously couldn't control – birth control, disease prevention, climate control. Death is no different. I am pleased to hear that Evie agrees that all this still holds true.

"The point of difference between us is the matter of the exact age. Of course there is no easy answer to this. There are two reasons why the Government believes that increasing the age from ninety is mistaken. First of all, there is no conclusive evidence that more people are healthy at ninety than they were when the law was introduced. I have read studies which argue in both directions. It is a case of you can find whatever study you want to support your view. And so much of the case for raising the age is based on individual case studies which are not necessarily representative of the population as a whole. Secondly, raising the age would represent in our view a slippery slope. Once you go beyond ninety, where do you stop? Before long, we would be back just where we were a decade ago with millions of frail elderly people living on towards 100 with no meaningful quality of life. Is that what you really want for yourselves or your loved ones?

"And just one more point. I appreciate that Evie has suggested a citizens' assembly to consider the evidence and propose a decision on what the new maximum lifespan should be. But it does seem to us that, as a matter of principle, asking Parliament to increase the age without knowing what the new limit would be, is procedurally questionable.

"So, this Government believes in compassion. It believes in justice. It believes in improving the quality of life of all our citizens and it believes that this is best achieved by retaining the current 90 Law. Thank you."

As he sat down, applause and even some cheers of approval started up in front of him in London but also elsewhere and he felt buoyed both by this apparent support and by the fact that he felt he had delivered what he wanted to say better than he was expecting.

During the remaining hour or so of the special conference, Edward felt strangely relaxed as he listened to delegates at the Bridgewater, the Rose Bowl, Cardiff Castle and elsewhere making their points. Opinions appeared to be pretty evenly divided if judged by the content of the speeches which represented only a small proportion of those who would vote. Some delegates supported his view even more strongly than he did. Some supported his opponent's views not because they wanted the age raised but because they wanted the whole law scrapped. Edward knew that was the elephant in the room.

He and Smith both made brief closing statements. And then came the vote. These electronic votes always took longer than they were supposed to. Some people's I-COMs failed to connect to the voting app and those whose votes were registered manually by push buttons always seemed to take longer to count. During the fifteen minutes or so, Edward chatted amiably with advisors exuding a calm which he convinced himself was a result of a belief that the vote would go his way.

Farage stood up suddenly, called the conference to attention and announced the result: –

"Those in favour of the motion 532, those against 498. The motion is carried. Thank you for your attendance today and for your contributions. The conference is now closed."

The screens were switched off straight after these words so Edward could not see the reaction from Evie Smith in Manchester. The result wasn't really a surprise but he had convinced himself during the afternoon as the debate went on that he might just edge it. But that had been a fantasy, although it was very close. Immediately his thoughts turned to whether he could now argue that the vote was so close that it wasn't binding on the Government and whether he could use this to delay things. However, he pretty much concluded this wouldn't work. As he left to get in the Prime Ministerial car, his mind turned to his next challenge. He must visit his frail eighty-seven-year-old father, a challenge arguably greater than the political one he now faced. How he longed for a quiet Sunday free from care.

CHAPTER SEVEN

Oval, Lambeth, Greater London.
Sunday 12 November 2045

'To the memory of all the sporting greats who played here', read the inscription on the plaque commemorating the site of what had once been one of the most famous cricket grounds in the world. Holly had never understood cricket but it was in Jake's blood even though the game had changed out of all recognition in his lifetime. Their visit there today was not however born out of Jake's sense of sporting nostalgia. Rather it was part of the programme the family were laying on for Mary as death approached.

When they had woken up earlier at their flat in Croydon, Jake had been slow to get out of bed. Holly knew why.

"This is the last way I want to spend a Sunday," moaned Jake, "A row with my daughter last night, now a day going through this sick charade with your grandmother."

"We've discussed this before and you've agreed to do it, so you're coming with me. Whatever you do, I'm going whether you're in or not. Anyway, you're mad about sporting history, so you'll enjoy it!"

"I would if I could spend a bit of time going round the Oval on my own. I will come but only because I think it's dangerous round there and I don't want you and Mary wandering all over the place on your own."

Holly had already unburdened herself on Jake the previous evening describing the narabanc incident in Brockwell Park in great detail. At first, thought Holly, he had brushed it away, and she decided he wasn't treating it seriously.

"How do you expect the NARA to enforce the law? With

polite requests and email reminders? OK, you happened to witness it, but it's happening all the time. It's the inevitable by-product of a law you believe in and helped bring in. If you don't like the heat, get out of the kitchen."

They argued back and forth about it and, in the end, Holly decided it was best to drop the subject. However, in a strange sort of way, she was rather enjoying being able to talk to Jake about something which gave her the chance to take her out of herself. It was a cause to focus on which was bigger and ultimately far more important than her everyday concerns about her job and her relationship with Jake. Until now, the euthanasia debate had seemed rather remote to her. Now for the first time, there was someone close to her directly affected by it, and an issue which previously had existed for her in the political and the theoretical was made real.

Holly's doubts were growing but she suppressed them. Mary had dementia and going peacefully at ninety was the best thing for her. Holly's job was to make the last weeks of her life as pleasant as possible. She would park her internal conflict for resolution another day. Today she was going to the Oval and she knew that Jake, whatever he said, would come as well. Even though it was a Sunday, her father was away on business. A few days before, he had suggested to Holly that she and Jake might like to take Mary on her next nostalgia trip. And, when she realised it involved cricket, she had jumped at the idea in the hope that this would entice Jake to be involved.

Jake and Holly declined David's offer of a drone but instead hired their own driverless and went across to Bromley to pick her up. When they arrived, Holly thought Mary seemed particularly confused about who she and Jake were and why they had turned up at her home. However, they helped her find her coat, handbag and old-fashioned mobile, ushering her into the driverless with explanations they weren't convinced she had understood.

Holly and Jake had already decided that they wouldn't drive all the way to Kennington. The inner southern neighbourhoods of London were the 'Wild West' to them, a case study in dereliction and despair. Significant parts of the Boroughs of Lambeth, Southwark and Greenwich had been virtually abandoned following repeated flooding and the breach of the Thames Flood Barrier. These climatic disasters came on top of severe economic downturns which had affected the poorer parts of London most harshly. To achieve the objective of their trip, they had to venture into these areas but to do so by driverless would be foolhardy. So, after they had docked the driverless at Clapham, they ventured down into the Tube for the last part of their journey.

"Wow! It's such a long time since I've been down here. I thought they were spending money on it. Can't see much evidence of that. It smells!" remarked Jake as they descended into the labyrinth of tunnels.

Holly, who was holding Mary's arm on the stairs, was focussed on their destination rather than their means of getting there. But Jake's observations reminded her that the London Underground was only a shadow of its former self which she could remember from her childhood. Large sections had been flooded. Some parts had been occupied by the 'left behinds' who had sought refuge and a place to live there when they lost their homes, jobs and prospects in the economic crash. Serious discussion had been given to abandoning the whole system but, eventually, in 2037, the Government of London had persuaded the central Government to allow the retention and improvement of about half of the lines on the network. Progressively and slowly, trains, tracks and stations were being upgraded.

None of this investment seemed very apparent to Holly as the three of them rattled along the Northern Line. The overwhelming impression was of a system still in decline with threadbare seats, chipped paint and faded, outdated adverts on the boards above the seats. As they went through the abandoned station at Clapham North, she spotted the makeshift tents on the platform and just glimpsed the shadowy figures now eking out an existence there shuffling along, apparently oblivious to the passing train. During the Tube journey, Mary had become animated, recalling in a way that made no sense to Holly, journeys she had apparently made by Tube in her youth.

The station where they got off was still called the Oval. As they reached the top of the steps, chipped their way through the recognition barrier, they emerged into the daylight. Instinctively, Holly looked to the left but the familiar entrance of a once famous cricket ground was no longer to be seen.

"What are we doing here, dear?" asked Mary as she held onto Holly's arm for support.

"This is where you met Colin, Gran," offered Holly but the information did not seem to register.

"Who, dear?"

"Colin, your husband," replied Holly using the terminology which had largely been rejected by most younger people but which was still widely used by the older generation.

As this unsatisfactory conversation continued between the two women, Holly could see Jake scanning the street for any lurking dangers. Holly suspected that media reports of inner city lawlessness were exaggerated, but she knew that Jake was still nervous about being there. Even Holly had to admit, it was a depressing area. There were very few shops. Lots of former shops had been converted into pretty unattractive looking housing units, many of which had themselves now been abandoned. There were hardly any vehicles, although further along the street she could see the remains of several cars long since deemed unroadworthy and not even valuable as scrap.

"This is where you met Colin, Mary, at the cricket match. Don't you remember?" interjected Jake trying to help out Holly.

"Colin? Colin?" replied Mary uncertainly, leaving Holly and Jake exchanging exasperated glances which signalled that further attempts at understanding were for now futile.

They walked a couple of hundred metres in the direction of where the cricket ground had once stood. Holly wasn't interested in cricket but enough of Jake's obsession with it had rubbed off onto her in the past that she recognised what came into view. Just ahead of them, still standing proudly in the midst of the abandonment all around, were the Hobbs' Gates, named in honour of Jack Hobbs, the Surrey and England batsman who, Jake had told her, had been one of the greatest in the game's history. This was a stadium that once held over 20,000 people and which had witnessed some of cricket's most famous moments. Now all that was left were the gates, a small plaque and beyond them the dilapidated ruins of the pavilion which had been scheduled for demolition but which was yet to take place.

Holly guided Mary across the largely deserted street and the three of them stood in front of the memorial to yet another lost theatre of English sport.

Holly tried again, "Gran, this is where the Oval Cricket Ground used to be. It's where you first met Colin back in the 1960s. You asked us to bring you here because you wanted to go back to the place where the two of you met. Do you remember?"

Still there was a vacancy of expression. Mary was looking around, as though searching for some physical sign which would trigger a memory.

"I don't know. I'm very confused," she eventually managed.

Holly led Mary by the arm around the memorial towards the remains of the pavilion. There was nothing stopping them walking round the other side of the crumbling structure and, as they did, an eerie vista opened up. The terracing and stands had been demolished about five years before when the area had been submerged under water. Part of what had been the playing surface had been covered with anonymous grey buildings intended as business units and serviced by a poorly laid roadway. Only a few seemed to be occupied. Even Holly felt a sense of history as she surveyed the abandonment in front of her.

But the remaining portion to the left of their view had pretty much been left as it had been before, no doubt awaiting a plan for regeneration which might never come. The foundations of parts of the terracing were still visible forming an incomplete arc near what once would have been the boundary line. But Holly's attention was drawn to several feral dogs roaming this urban wilderness. She felt distinctly uneasy, and she exchanged a nervous glance with Jake who, she was pleased to see, had clocked the potential danger.

"I know this place. I've been here before," piped up Mary, breaking the eerie silence previously interrupted only by the occasional barking of the dogs which now appeared to be heading in their direction.

"I remember that," she added, pointing across the expanse of open land and indicating the steel framework pointing out above the business units.

"They were for storing gas," she continued. "They were as famous as the ground itself. I think they were here the first time I was here. I'll let you into a secret, my dear. This is where I first met Colin. I didn't really know anything about cricket but my brother got tickets for a Test Match. I think it was against the West Indies and he had a spare one so I went with him with some of his friends. I don't know how old I was. Only eleven or twelve, I think. I was very young.

"It was a very hot day. Colin was sat next to me. He was one of my brother's friends but I'd not met him before. He was very well-spoken. Not a rough South Londoner like me. They had a very good player, now what was his name?"

Jake had researched the details of the match Mary must have attended.

"Gary Sobers, it was Mary, probably the greatest all-rounder in cricket history. Better than Ian Botham, better than Ben Stokes. You'll remember them. But Sobers didn't do that well in the match you saw. He was out for a duck in the second innings and England won by an innings. It was August 1966 – you must have been ten."

"He explained the game to me. He knew all about it. I didn't have a clue but it all seemed very clear once he put me straight," continued Mary apparently uninterested in the cricketing history just proffered by her granddaughter's partner.

"We had a lovely day. I think he bought me an ice cream. We didn't see each other for a while after that but I couldn't stop thinking about him. We called it a crush in those days. We were childhood sweethearts."

"When did you see him next, Gran? Can you remember?" asked Holly, still holding her arm and now feeling more anxious about the dogs. One was circling them and barking menacingly.

"I quite got to like cricket, you know. I think we came here some other times after we were together. Why has it all been knocked down? It was a lovely ground."

"There were too many clubs, Mary. They started playing cricket on football grounds so only a handful of big cricket grounds survived. Lords is still there but London didn't need two and anyway this place was too close to the river."

Mary appeared to be unconcerned about the menacing dog which had now been joined by two others.

"Come on Mary, I think we need to go back to the station. These dogs don't look too friendly," announced Jake.

Holly reinforced the urgency by guiding Mary in the right direction but the older woman resisted, turned back and looked across at the gasholder.

"Come on, Mary. We need to go," said Jake with more than a hint of alarm in his voice.

But as he did, Holly realised that Mary was rooted to the spot, her gaze fixed resolutely on the gasholder, and two small tears were running down her cheeks.

"Do you know he proposed to me here?"

Holly put her arm properly round Mary as the trickle of tears became a stream. The first dog was now standing only a few metres away from them barking more loudly. It looked evil. Its bones were visible. Jake stood firm while the two women remained joined in a hug.

Slowly, Holly sensed that her grandmother had finished the train of thought that had prompted the tears. Without saying a word, she guided her away from the dog, towards the remains of the pavilion. Holly saw Jake staring out the dog while the women retreated. Slowly, he also turned, his gaze still fixed on the dog and followed the others. Briefly, the dog looked as though it would follow as well but Jake halted, the dog halted and then Jake completed his careful walk towards the Hobbs Gate and the dog lost interest.

Just as Jake caught up with the others, Mary added, "I miss him. But he wanted to go. I didn't agree with it at first but he was determined to go. And he was in a lot of pain. So I helped him. But I wish he was still here."

Mary was still crying but silently with Holly holding her. As they walked back towards the station, Holly felt calmer. She could see that Jake was struggling to know how to deal with Mary's emotions. He walked alongside them without adding to the conversation. Holly just wondered what he was thinking. For now, though, she was more concerned with the immediate threat. Above all she was glad to be rid of those dogs and the air of menace which she had felt as they stood where the ground had once been. Jake, she thought, had also relaxed as they headed back towards the station.

"I can't believe it's forty years since I was here for that match," remarked Jake. "When England won the Ashes for the first time for years back in 2005. What a day, that was."

It all happened in slow motion. Holly never saw the first blow. The first she knew was Jake sinking to the ground. She tried to scream but couldn't. It took several seconds but it felt like an age before she took in what was happening and was able to respond. It must have been the second blow that enabled her to focus fully. This one was to Jake's back as the attacker emerged fully from the side alleyway. Holly had to choose between intervening to defend Jake or taking Mary further away from the threat. She chose the former, hurling herself at Jake's assailant as she let go of Mary's arm. She screamed loudly and wildly as she pawed at the man's face with her arms. It worked and he backed off cursing her as he fled back towards the cricket ground site.

Then, around the corner from the direction of the station, a group of people emerged, waving banners and shouting.

"The future's ours. The future's ours. The future's ours."

"Give us back our future. Give us back our future."

"A year extra for the old is a year lost for the young."

The group was still some distance away from them. Holly manoeuvred Mary into the alleyway and leant over Jake who was lying motionless on the ground. Despite the noise and confusion, she activated her I-COM.

"Ambulance. Police. To the Oval Station."

The protesters were getting closer and Holly knew that she and the injured Jake must still be in their view. She grabbed Jake under his arms and somehow managed to pull him into the alleyway. When she put him down next to where Mary was cowering, all she could notice was the smear of blood on the front of her new coat. But moving Jake must have made him regain consciousness.

"Where's Mary?" he somehow managed to muster as his brain kicked into gear.

Holly leant over him.

"An ambulance is coming. Gran's here. She's fine. They didn't touch her."

"What about you?" enquired Jake drowsily.

"I'm fine. Only a few bruises," replied Holly.

Then, just as his world had started to fall back into place, a young man suddenly towered above him screaming abuse at Jake.

"It's the older generation that has robbed us of our future. What the hell are you doing coming poking round here? And you're probably one of those campaigners who wants the age raised. Is this your parent? She looks more than ninety. Are you trying to hide away somewhere? Funny place to do it, mind you!"

Holly now realised that they had somehow run into a League of Youth protest. They were just unlucky enough to be in the wrong place at the wrong time. She started formulating a response but, before she could open her mouth, the young man disappeared, re-joining the other protesters who passed the alleyway without taking any interest in Holly, Jake or Mary. Then she heard the piercing sound of sirens as Jake drifted away again into unconsciousness. All she could do was wait as she hugged Mary, who had lived through the ordeal of the last few minutes without uttering a word.

CHAPTER EIGHT

Berwick, Northumberland.
Saturday/Sunday 11/12 November 2045

Wilfred found the politeness and apparent friendliness of their captors once they arrived in Berwick disconcerting. It was still dark as they were led out of the car in the yard of the police station, still in handcuffs but being treated respectfully and without any hint of aggression or impatience. They were taken in through a side door from the carpark into a dingy corridor which had clearly not seen any redecoration for many years. Tatty notices imploring officers about a variety of police matters adorned the shabby walls. Father and son were ushered into a plain room with a metal table and two battered leather chairs on either side. They were asked to sit down next to one another on one side of the table.

"Now before we do anything else, how about a cup of tea, gentlemen," announced Joe as he sat himself down on one of the two chairs on the opposite side of the table.

"And we might even be able to rustle up a biscuit or two," he added. "May I take your orders?"

"Tea would be nice," replied Wilfred but his son sat stony-faced, looking, Wilfred thought, deeply suspicious and avoiding eye contact with the man across the table from him.

"Eversley, are you tea as well? Not that I think we have much else on the menu," adding just a mild hint of sarcasm to his tone of voice for the first time.

Eversley looked down and said nothing.

"I'll take that as a yes," added Joe as he got up and walked purposefully from the room shutting the door behind him, leaving the two captives alone.

Wilfred had assumed they would be separated and he had hoped his son would have reached the same conclusion he had about their best hope of a plausible defence. Now he had the chance to speak to his son but for how long? Even more surprisingly, their I-COMs did not appear to have been disabled so was this an opportunity to communicate with the outside world?

During the car journey he had turned it over in his mind countless times. Eversley's I-COM must have been hacked and that had given them away. Or maybe the deception went further back and the earlier contact with the 90+ group members was in fact no such thing? Maybe Eversley had been communicating with infiltrators all the way along? How could they know and, anyway did it matter now? They had been caught pretty red-handed, it appeared to him, and paying money back in the farm cottage was surely the most damming piece of evidence against them. How could they possibly deny that they were trying to flee to Scotland to escape his imminent euthanasia?

"We are on a short break with me showing you where I did my Army training," whispered Eversley, taking Wilfred by surprise.

"Of course," replied Wilfred calmly as though without a care in the world, just as the door opened and Joe returned holding two mugs of tea which he placed on the table, smiling as he did so.

"And I've not forgotten the biscuits," he added, producing a packet of digestives from his pocket with a flourish.

"OK. I know it's still early and we've all been up all night but I'm due off duty now and I would very much appreciate your help in clearing up this matter as quickly as possible. I suppose there are two ways we can deal with this. Strictly speaking, what should happen now is that I should question you to determine whether there is a prima facie case against you both. If there is, I should hand you over for questioning to NARA who will then continue interrogations in their own distinctive way.

"As you know, the sentences are quite severe for those found guilty of deliberately evading the country's euthanasia laws. Incarceration in prison until your ninetieth birthday and then termination alone in the slammer. And for assisting someone to escape, the punishments are harsh – maybe ten years for you Eversley. Not a nice prospect for someone as young as you with all that life ahead.

"Now I need to ask you a few questions but, without prejudicing anything, it would seem to me that, at face value, the evidence will point all one way for you guys. Being on a remote footpath in the dark just a few miles from the border. Signing a document. Worst of all from your point of view, handing over a sizeable sum of money to finance your escape. I think it's fair to say that it doesn't look that good, does it?"

Wilfred noticed that, throughout this peroration, Joe maintained uncomfortable eye contact with both father and son but particularly with son. He reckoned that Joe had already worked out that Eversley was the main driving force behind his particular escape bid. Wilfred also knew that Joe would now from Eversley's behaviour earlier in the farmhouse that was impulsive and prone to outbursts.

"So, any thoughts gentlemen?" resumed Joe offering two men across the table from him an opportunity to minate themselves or maybe to plea bargain their way what appeared to him a pretty substantial hole.

ell, Joe," offered Wilfred tentatively. "I think you have erstood the situation and...."

e he could complete his sentence, his son cut across tiently.

"Dad, don't say anything. We're not obliged to say anything. And, what's more, I believe we are entitled to legal representation before we are questioned."

"You are of course right on the last point, Eversley. But this is just a chat and not a formal interview at this stage. So we don't need to worry about lawyers just now. But Wilfred to your point about misunderstanding the situation, I fear you are sadly mistaken. I have been working on this border for quite some years now and I know an escapee when I see one and, as I mentioned earlier, I think we will have all the evidence necessary for NARA to regard you as a pretty serious case."

Neither man responded. Joe stared at them both with a worrying smile.

"OK. Let's see if we can move this forward in a helpful way. Your prospects are, how shall I put it, grim. Here's what you have to look forward to: NARA interrogation, usually not that nice; multiple charges; court appearance; guilty verdicts; incarceration in His Majesty's places of correction; definitely not that nice, by the way; death by euthanasia without your loved ones present for you Wilfred and, for you, Eversley, a lengthy period in prison, the best years of middle age wasted all for the sake of trying to add a few miserable weeks to your father's life."

Still, neither father nor son responded. As Wilfred listened to Joe's predictions, he thought them to be a disturbingly accurate description of what might lay ahead for them. Even though he had at first been a reluctant convert to this escape attempt, Wilfred now realised that he was properly invested in its success. That was partly, he knew, for his own reasons but also because he knew that it was vital to his son that it succeeded. From their brief conversations, he knew that two powerful drivers governed Eversley's motivations. They were his fundamental belief in the justice of what he was trying to achieve for his father and the manifest injustice of a law giving the state the right to kill its own citizens. Wilfred suspected though that, if Eversley were honest with himself, he would feel a strong sense of shame and failure if his mission to save his father did not succeed. However, despite all this, Wilfred was struggling to know how to begin to mount a defence to the case Joe was presenting before them.

"You seem to have gone very quiet, my friends," said Joe. "Well, let me try to help you. I think there is an alternative to the rather unpleasant future I have laid out before you. If, as I hope, you both realise that your chances of coming out of this successfully through submitting yourselves to NARA and the processes of the law are limited, here's a suggestion.

"I'm a reasonable person and I have children and parents of my own. I know how you feel. In a way I sympathise with you. I don't wish to see you thrown into prison. If you would like to avoid that, I can offer a way out. For a suitable consideration, we could all forget that this ever happened. It's still very early on a Sunday morning and what doesn't appear on the record will not, as far as history is concerned, have ever taken place. You let me have a further 500 English. We drive out of here in the next half hour apparently heading for the NARA office but we drop you off en route and, to all intents and purposes, the last few hours will have been erased from the record. You go on your way, within England, I hasten to add, and I go home a little better off than I was before I came on duty last evening. The NARA are blissfully unaware that this particular escape attempt was ever undertaken and we all live happily ever after, well, until we are ninety. In a word, what's not to like about my eminently reasonable proposal."

The room fell silent for what seemed several minutes. The only sounds Wilfred could make out were the gentle tapping of rainfall on the interview room's only window and the distant noise of a police officer on an old-style laptop elsewhere in the building. Eventually, it was Eversley who broke the silence which was starting to become uncomfortable.

"I don't accept what you say. We haven't committed any criminal offences. I don't believe that the NARA would have enough evidence to put us in front of a court and, if they did, the case would not succeed. So why would we want to pay you a dirty little bribe to avoid something that is very unlikely to happen anyway?"

"Maybe because you know that basically they're zealots and bastards and they'll nail you one way or another even if you are innocent," retorted Joe who, after a few more moments of silence, continued.

"OK. Let's get on our way. I don't need to discuss this anymore with you. I have prima facie evidence against you by the bucket load and the NARA will take it forward. Just remember when you're languishing in prison, that you had the opportunity to take an easy way out and you turned it down. Come on, let's get in the car."

Joe's false friendliness had evaporated in an instant as he led them out of the room instructing Chris, who had reappeared, to handcuff them. They were bundled without violence but with a new sense of impatience into the yard and back into the car in which they had arrived earlier.

Dawn gave way to early morning as the car journeyed south on the A1 first hugging the Northumberland coast, past Holy Island, back through Morpeth and onward. The road was quiet and there were few drones overhead. Wilfred realised he must have drifted to sleep because he came round with a start and noticed plenty of people on foot, presumably heading for work. They were now in a large built-up area which he assumed must be the outskirts of Newcastle.

Nothing was said during the forty-minute journey but soon

they reached what Wilfred vaguely recognised from concerts he'd done here in the past as the city centre. They passed the brutalist Civic Centre built like so many English municipal buildings in the 1960s, and then they turned into a back street. Momentarily, their current dilemma was pushed from the front of Wilfred's mind by the sad sight of a derelict stadium which had once been the home of Newcastle United. He knew that St. James's Park had been abandoned some years previously when the club went bust after the economic crash leaving the ground slowly rotting and becoming overgrown. But his reverie was interrupted when the car slowed and turned into the car park of a shabby, anonymous office opposite the ground which he quickly assumed must be the NARA base.

They were taken inside, still handcuffed, by Joe and Chris who led them to a room which was dingier and more intimidating than the one in Berwick. Without a word, the two policemen left. The overwhelming feeling inside was oppressive, physically and psychologically. There was a stuffy warmth and the old-style light bulb wasn't powerful enough for the space. No drinks were offered and more than an hour then passed before anyone bothered with them. Then two police officers came into the room, instructed Wilfred and Eversley to follow them and led them, not handcuffed now, down another corridor and through a door which led to a flight of steps. The lighting here was even more unsatisfactory and Wilfred proceeded very gingerly down the steps fearful that he might fall. When they got to the bottom, he realised they were being taken to the cells.

One of the officers produced a bunch of keys, opened a metal door and a clanging sound of metal on metal filled the subterranean space. Wilfred was ushered inside knowing that he was about to be separated from his son but he was relieved that Eversley appeared calm and was making no

attempt to resis
asked him to
given a rudi
and trou
retre

t. Once Wilfred was inside, the police officer
and straight and raise his arms. He was then
tary body search and asked to remove his coat
and then left on his own. The police officer
e, taking Wilfred's coat, belt and backpack.
cked. After ten seconds or so, he could hear,
d by the thickness of the doors and walls, the
as another cell door was opened. Then the
o sets of boots clomping past his cell door,
up the steps and then falling silent as the door
stairs was closed. Then silence.
mined his new, spartan surroundings. A bed
ntly clean bedding. A bucket in the corner. No
ght. Just a weak single bulb recessed into the ceiling.
t down on the bed. He thought about calling out to
ersley but decided it might bring the police back downstairs
with unwanted consequences. He suddenly came over very
tired, and the pains in his hips, knees and now also ankles,
came back with a vengeance. He lay down on the bed and
closed his eyes.

In his next conscious moment, a police officer was standing
next to the bed towering above him. He was momentarily
alarmed in the few seconds it took him to remember where
he was and what had happened to them. He had no idea how
much time had elapsed since he had been taken to the cell.
Then he realised the police officer was holding a tray. Wilfred
sat up and took it from him. It contained a glass of water and
something which he thought was probably porridge. Without
saying a word, the police officer left and locked the door
again. Over what must have been half an hour or so, Wilfred
picked at the food in front of him and drank the water whilst
turning over in his mind what might happen next. He was
surprised that Eversley wasn't calling him. Maybe he was but

he couldn't hear him because the walls were s̶o̶ ̶t̶h̶i̶c̶k̶?̶ after rejecting the remaining porridge, he wa̶ ̶o̶v̶e̶r̶c̶o̶m̶e̶ ̶b̶y̶ tiredness again and lay down on the bed. He w̶a̶s̶ ̶physically and emotionally drained. There was part of him ̶t̶h̶e̶n̶,̶ to resist, to find a way out and to help his son ̶w̶i̶t̶h̶ ̶t̶h̶e̶i̶r̶ mission. But the overwhelming feeling in him was o̶n̶e̶ of their escape attempt and all the doubts he'd e̶x̶p̶r̶e̶s̶s̶e̶d̶ beforehand resurfaced. On top of all this, there was t̶h̶e̶ ̶p̶a̶i̶n̶.̶ He was finally admitting to himself that it was worse t̶h̶a̶n̶ ̶h̶e̶ had acknowledged until now and must be a sign of some̶t̶h̶i̶n̶g̶ sinister.

The same procedure must have been repeated at least on̶c̶e̶ again over the coming hours – a silent visit, unappetising food, the drift in and out of sleep. Other than that, silence. He even wondered at one point if Eversley was still in his cell. Perhaps he had already been taken for interrogation? For the first time, Wilfred felt actively frightened but fortunately sleep overcame him again rescuing him from his fears.

The next interruption to his slumbers was more invasive. This time he heard the door being unlocked and came round in time to see a protesting Eversley being bundled past Wilfred's cell roughly and led towards the stairs.

"Get up Wilfred," was the simple command.

He complied, straightened his clothes and was led out of his cell, up the stairs, along a different corridor and into the same room where they had been taken when they had first arrived there. Eversley was sat looking wan and defeated. Wilfred immediately assumed he must have been beaten up.

"What have they done to you, son?" he said as he moved instinctively towards Eversley.

"Nothing Dad, I'm fine, just tired. I couldn't sleep down there. Do you know it's Sunday now? We've been here almost a day."

Eventually, a man and woman walked in. He was probably about forty, dressed in a fairly sharp suit. She was younger and quite casually dressed in jeans, sweatshirt and trainers.

"So, you are on a short holiday, father and son, revisiting the part of the country where you did your army training – that's your story, I gather? To cut to the chase, it sounds like the tallest story we've heard in a long time. Any comment?"

The two NARA agents, who had by now introduced themselves as Ryan and Cara, used ridicule as their first line of attack and it was Cara who took the lead.

"You expect us to believe that this was some sort of nostalgia trip to the wilds of Northumberland to show your dad where you did your army training. A bit of father and son bonding, eh? Very touching but I don't believe a word of it."

Wilfred was increasingly taking a lead role, partly because he feared another outburst by his son.

"We've talked about this for years. Eversley enjoyed himself up here and it was an important turning point in his life. He often said he'd bring me here one day so that I could understand what he was on about. It's taken us a while to get around to it but we did in the end."

"Why did you set out on a remote footpath in the afternoon as it was getting dark and walk for several hours well into the evening?" interjected Ryan. "That's not exactly normal holiday-type behaviour, is it? Most normal people would have gone for a walk during the daytime, wouldn't they?"

Wilfred was momentarily alarmed when Eversley took up the baton to respond.

"Well, I did slightly misjudge the distance and I couldn't quite remember where things were but I wanted to find the fields where we did a lot of our training and I knew roughly where it was. And we used to do a lot of it at night and Dad had said he wanted to know what it must have felt like to be under fire in the dark. So that's why we came here and why we went walking when we did."

"In which case," shot back Cara," why did you use your I-COM to try to contact someone at the dead of night on a lonely footpath? This was a private moment for the two of you apparently so why did you want to invite others? And why use some code words? Come on, just admit it."

"There's nothing to admit," replied Eversley calmly and confidently, winning new respect from his father who had always thought his son too impetuous and impulsive.

"I had told an old friend that I was coming up for this trip and that I might get in touch if we had time. I was also a bit lost so I thought I'd call him for some navigation advice and also to see if he wanted to meet. And I don't know what you mean about code words. We have a bit of banter sometimes."

"By the way officer, I thought the contents of I-COM communications were confidential," added Wilfred, "even though I've never believed that the encryption is secure."

Everyone knew that evidence obtained from I-COMs was usually inadmissible in court but sometimes they nevertheless tried to put the frighteners on suspects by quoting from their intercepted communications.

"Souness runs half the length of the pitch, evades three English defenders and scores from twenty-five metres. What does that mean, then?" asked Ryan.

"It's just an old joke we've got about our footballing loyalties – it doesn't mean anything really," responded Eversley.

This exchange was one of many between interrogators and captives over an hour and a half, punctuated only by a few periods of silence and a shuffling of papers by the agents. But, gradually, their frustration became more obvious. Wilfred had noticed how both had remained polite and cognisant of the rules that had been introduced a couple of years previously about the conduct of these sorts of interrogations. That had followed exposure of some of the more lurid allegations about what had apparently happened in interview rooms like this one. These included allegations of intimidation, of humiliation and degrading treatment and even of some physical violence.

Now though, Wilfred hoped, both agents knew that he and his son weren't going to be a walkover.

"Cup of tea?" asked Cara with a tone reminiscent of someone out for a pleasant afternoon visit to a café.

"Yes, please. Thank you," replied Wilfred, equally friendly in his manner.

Cara glanced towards Eversley with an interrogative look.

"No, thanks. Not for me," he grunted, relapsing into his default demeanour for this sort of occasion.

Cara and Ryan left the room. Wilfred and Eversley visibly relaxed but said nothing for several seconds before Wilfred announced,

"I think we're winning. Just stick to the story and we'll be fine."

As this brief exchange concluded, the agents returned to the room bursting through the door aggressively, taking their seats roughly and resuming the interrogation. The promised tea was nowhere to be seen. Wilfred immediately noticed that Cara had a ruler with her which she lay down very animatedly on the table. As she did this, Ryan fetched a pair of handcuffs from his pocket and placed them deliberately on the table next to the ruler.

It was Cara who picked up the thread of the conversation.

"We are getting bored and fed up and we have plenty of other work that needs doing. All of us in this room know that you, Eversley, were trying to help your father get over the border into Scotland to avoid his legally required termination in a few weeks' time. The simplest thing would be for you both to admit this. We would charge you but we would point out that you had cooperated with our investigation and we would put in a special report for the prosecutor and the judge recommending lenient treatment. Alternatively, if you refuse to admit it, there is another route open to us. That's to use the special preventative powers we have to take you both into protective custody. If we reasonably believe that you are likely to commit offences under the Age Regulation Laws, even if you haven't done so already, then we can detain you indefinitely and you will have no recourse to the courts. It's pretty straightforward, really. Understood?"

As she finished her description of the options facing them, Cara picked up the ruler and brought it down heavily on the desk between the two suspects causing them both to flinch and withdraw their hands from the table.

Cara resumed with a new more animated tone of voice.

"I think you have both forgotten why we are all here. I have grown up in a world that was completely screwed up by your generation, Wilfred. You screwed up the economy, the climate, the response to the Great Pandemic, the care system and you made it well-nigh impossible for most young people to be able to afford a decent education or a home and you kept all the goodies for yourselves. Baby boomers, you were called and you never realised how lucky you were. Too young to have to live through a world war like your parents and too old to have to make a living in a rubbish economy. And you expected us to pay for your care in old age. 'Social care' you called it. Well, you wouldn't pay any more tax and the system collapsed. Well, fortunately, enough people saw sense to say that something radical had to happen to stop the old leeching off the young and, it should be said, to stop the old rotting away in their final years. Ninety is a very decent age to live to – way beyond the dreams of earlier generations and even now beyond the expectations of people in many other parts of the world. You may think you're conducting some libertarian crusade against the excesses of a totalitarian state. But actually you're defying the law of the land passed by Parliament elected on a manifesto promising to do exactly what you are trying to avoid – bringing life to a dignified end at a predetermined date."

Even though he disagreed with her analysis of the situation, Wilfred had grudging admiration for, and considerable surprise at, Cara's lucidity. However, now probably wasn't the time to engage in a political or philosophical debate about the morality of the age regulation laws. And Wilfred could sense Eversley's anger rising. He had got much better over the years at controlling himself but still sometimes his sense of injustice, his dislike of being cornered and his sheer bloody-mindedness got the better of him. Neither father nor son said anything in response to Cara's peroration.

It was Ryan's role to deliver the final warning.

"I am taking your silence as a sign of defiance. Unless you admit your guilt in the next minute, we will charge both of you with a variety of offences and we will not be recommending any leniency to recognise your cooperation given that you haven't in any way assisted this process."

Clocks were a rarity. They were unnecessary as everyone could see the time on their I-COMs or on screens and the value of clocks as antiques or even objects of desire had waned. But, somewhere through the walls of this unloved building in the silence, Wilfred could hear the noise of a clock, no doubt only still there because nobody had bothered to remove it. It was ticking, as if helpfully counting down the minute of thinking time.

Wilfred was using the time to try to think logically. He

suspected that the agents knew that they would struggle to get a watertight case against them. The laws were badly worded and proving intention was very difficult so their story, however implausible, would, he calculated, give them a reasonable chance of success in court. He knew they knew that. So, what best to do? As the minute ticked away, he had pretty much concluded that silence was probably the best option.

He suspected that his son, meanwhile, had spent the last sixty seconds in a fog of internal indignation and rage. He would have done the exact opposite of his father and spent the time responding to his feelings rather than trying to come to a rational decision. But, thankfully, he said nothing. However, Eversley's silence didn't save them from what happened next.

The two agents rose to their feet, moved quickly around the desk and, at the same moment, two others burst through the door. Three of the four agents pinned Eversley to the floor while the fourth restrained Wilfred who, despite his age, was trying to intervene to protect his son. Wilfred, observing the assault on his son, was disturbed and surprised to see that it was Cara who struck the first blow, picking the ruler from the table and bringing it down hard on the back of Eversley's head. This was an action repeated several times and accompanied by other blows with the hands from the other two agents. Pinned head downwards to the floor, Eversley was unable to manage any meaningful resistance. It was left to Wilfred, still stunned by what was happening, to try to bring the violence to an end.

"Leave him. Leave him. You can't do this," pleaded Wilfred as the natural instinct of a parent to protect his child kicked in.

With a strength he didn't know he had, the eighty-nine-year-old broke free from the agent restraining him, and lunged at Cara, grabbing the ruler from her hands. Cara spun round, wrestled the ruler back from him, and without as much as a breath, visited the same treatment on the father as previously

delivered or
a third and
By now Ev
happening
expletiv
that c
off
in

the son. The first blow was followed by a second,
a fourth with increasing force on each occasion.
ersley was handcuffed but his rage at what was
o his father erupted instantly with a series of
rected at the agents. Whether or not it was this
er to stop, Wilfred didn't know. But Cara backed
Wilfred lying face down on the ground, no longer
straint. Eversley also was lying, still handcuffed,
r offering resistance.

ur agents rose to their feet, straightened their
stood over their victims, it was, as now expected,
oke first,

ope you get the message. The NARA will not
determination to root out people who wish to
aw and try to frustrate the will of the people as
through Parliament. Unfortunately, our lily-livered
don't always back us up so taking you to court is just
much trouble. We could bang you up in protective custody
t it's too much hassle with all the paperwork. But we will
be watching you and one false move and we'll bring you in.
Just try to enjoy the last few weeks, Wilfred, and don't let that
angry son of yours lead you astray. Now go."

At this, the other three agents guided father and son to their
feet, checked that there was no blood from their beatings, and
walked them through the building, handed them back their
possessions and guided them out into a Newcastle back street.
At the door, Eversley's handcuffs were taken off. Without a
word, the agents went back into the building and Wilfred and
Eversley were left blinking in the autumn sunshine.

For quite some seconds, they stood there processing what
had just taken place. It also took a while for the pain to kick
in as the adrenaline died down. Wilfred, in particular, was
starting to feel a dull ache and the beginnings of a headache

as well as his pre-existing pains.

"Sorry, Dad," Eversley said as he put his hand on his father's shoulder, probably, Wilfred thought, for the first time in over thirty years." We should probably get a do r to look at you but let's get a drink first."

And they headed off, slowly, towards the ci Wilfred visibly hobbling and needing to be support son.

CHAPTER NINE

Robinson House, Cambridge, Cambridgeshire
Sunday 12 November 2045

During the journey north from London, Edward Watson must have dozed off because the Prime Ministerial helicopter was now already hovering above its destination. As he emerged from his slumber, he realised that the pilot was about to do what he hated and land right in the grounds of the Robinson. He disliked arriving like this. His humble origins still made him squeamish about the trappings of high office. What's more, he liked to arrive unannounced, spend time with his father and then slip away quietly.

"Rory, can we just head a further minute or so up the road and land on the sports field like we've done before. I don't like landing right in the grounds like some royal potentate."

"Sorry, sir, but security say we must land here. They don't want you walking down the road anymore."

His private detective reinforced Rory's view, "It's not a good idea to have you walking the streets, I'm afraid, Prime Minister, even in Cambridge."

The Prime Minister didn't have the stomach for an argument, reminding himself that even though he held the highest office in the land, he was often not master of his own destiny, particularly in everyday matters like his own personal security.

"OK, whatever you think," he offered weakly as the chopper lowered itself onto the lawn of the residential home where his father had lived for the past four years.

Outwardly, the Robinson still looked very much as he remembered it from his student days, a brown-bricked 1970s block. It had been the newest Cambridge college when it had been founded in the late 1970s, but had been the first to be converted to a new use after the University was dramatically reduced in size in the late twenties. The helicopter came to a standstill. His detective got out, surveyed the surroundings, judged it to be safe and invited Edward to step out. As he walked the short distance to the main entrance, the Prime Minister steeled himself for the reception committee that he knew would greet him at the door.

"Good afternoon, Prime Minister. So nice to see you again," said the Chief Executive of the group running this home which was part of a conglomerate that had pretty much cornered the market in top-end residential care.

Edward was privately amused by the fact that she always seemed to be here to greet him whenever he visited, even if it were on a Sunday.

"Hello, Rachel, nice to see you too," he replied trying his best to convey the impression that all was well despite his inner portents of difficult times ahead personally and politically.

Rachel accompanied him along the corridor towards his father's room. Photographs on the wall bore witness to the times when the building had housed bright young things at the beginning of their lives rather than those approaching life's end. Edward couldn't help noticing that, despite the fees paid to stay here, paint was peeling from some of the skirting boards. But at least the place smelt OK and somehow managed to exude an atmosphere more akin to a hotel than a care home.

"Sorry to hear about the vote earlier," chipped in Rachel with a weak attempt to convey a sense of sympathy in her tone. "But I'm sure there's a long way to go before things are settled one way or the other."

Edward thought it the height of hypocrisy for the well-paid boss of a care home group to appear to take the PM's side

when he knew that her company stood to benefit massively
if the euthanasia age were raised thus increasing her potential
customer base quite considerably. But he chose to hold his
fire for more important influencers and, anyway, he was now
focused on his father whose accommodation was just metres
ahead.

"Thank you, Rachel," was all he proffered in reply as
he walked into the room where the late afternoon autumn
sunshine was silhouetting his father against the window.

"Hello, Dad, how are you today?"

His father, who had been looking out into the well-
manicured gardens, turned and smiled at the sight of his only
surviving close relative.

"Hello, Edward, very good to see you. I know you're very
busy and it's very good of you to make the time to come and
see an old man."

"I will always make the time, Dad, however busy I am.
Anyway, it's good to get away from the Westminster bubble."

"I saw you on the news earlier. I thought you were pretty
persuasive but that Evie Smith is quite impressive, isn't she?
I think you've got a fight on your hands there, Edward."

Edward was close to his father despite the many battles he
had fought with him when he was younger. As a single parent,
Andrew Watson had found it difficult to combine effective
parenting with his job as an engineering manager. Even though
both shared a common cause of grief, somehow it had divided
them. Edward seemed to blame his father for the death of his
mother. Sometimes, Andrew seemed to blame his late partner
for leaving him with such a difficult son.

"Well I might have lost a battle today but I'm confident
I'll win the war," replied Edward to his father.

His decision to go into politics twenty years before had
been another cause of conflict between them. Edward had

been told by his father that he thought his son was throwing away the benefits of his Cambridge degree. He'd be sacrificing his earning prospects as a lawyer and he'd be entering a nasty bear pit for which he was ultimately unsuited. On both counts, Edward now thought that his father was probably right. However, he had never conceded anything in discussions with his dad and he always maintained an optimistic outlook about his career, whatever he was feeling inside.

"Anyway, Dad. Let's talk about you, not me. What have you been up to?" said Edward cheerily.

"The usual stuff. It's all very pleasant in here. The food's OK. The people are nice, well most of them, anyway. But there's nothing much for the mind in here. I'm bored. I've had enough. I would like to slip away now."

This was a plea Edward had heard many times before. His father had been diagnosed with a form of dementia a few years earlier but its effect was intermittent. Sometimes he was confused and rambling, occasionally aggressive but often lucid and apparently entirely rational. He also had a range of physical problems, mainly debilitating problems in his digestive system, for which advances in medical research didn't appear to have found any solutions.

"We've discussed this before, Dad. I'm not sure two doctors would agree that your condition merits it. I have power of attorney and I'm not prepared to sign anything to start this process. I'm sorry but I'm sure Mum would have felt the same if she was still here."

Evoking the memory of his mother was sometimes a mistake with his father and so it was today.

"Edward, please don't bring your mother into this. She had no choice about when she died and she died a horrible violent death. She wouldn't want to see me here wasting away."

His father's reference to the circumstances of his mother's

death brought Edward up sharply. Forty years had elapsed, but he still found it difficult to talk about it and he had not really achieved closure. When he was a mere backbencher and still travelling on the Tube, he would avoid the Piccadilly Line and Russell Square. He had never been able to bring himself to go to the memorial there to the victims of the bombing. What he did know, though, was that her death was one of the main factors that led him into politics.

"Mum's not here, Dad and I'm afraid you've only got me to advise you."

For a moment there was silence in the room. Edward knew full well that getting two doctors to sign wouldn't be a problem given that his Dad was already eighty-seven and diagnosed with dementia. His reluctance to sign as attorney was not really about the chances of it succeeding or not. It was because he didn't want it to happen. If he was honest about his attitude to his father's wish to undergo voluntary euthanasia, he knew he had a mixture of motives. First of all, he had to admit that there was a political dimension to the matter. However much his father's health should be a private matter, the fact was that it would not go unnoticed by the media if the Prime Minister signed a form allowing his father to be put to death. He could see the headlines now 'Heartless PM signs death warrant for his own dad'. This would be manna from heaven for those wanting the age raised and those growing numbers who were opposed to the idea of state-sponsored euthanasia at all at any age. But he also knew deep down that he didn't want his father to die, not now or even when he was ninety.

After a few moments the silence was broken by a knock on the door and a care assistant entering the room.

"Would you like some tea, Andrew? And Prime Minister, tea for you as well?" he asked.

"That would be nice," replied Edward on behalf of both

of them.

It seemed to Edward that the assistant took an unnecessarily long time to pour the tea while he offered opinions on the weather and the state of his father's health, as though he felt that he needed to savour being in the presence of greatness. Edward still found it odd how some people behaved in front of him just because he had the title 'Prime Minister'.

Once the tea was served and the assistant departed, Edward resumed with his father.

"Dad, do you remember the time we went to those homes in Leyton to look for a place for Uncle Bob?"

Bob, who had been dead several years now, was Andrew's elder brother and Edward's uncle. He had been single throughout his life and it had fallen to Andrew to sort things out when he got in poor health.

"We must have visited at least six places over a few days and they were all without exception dirty, badly staffed and degrading. No human being should have had to live in places like that, whether or not they were a member of our family. The thing that I remember most vividly was seeing a man, probably about the same age that you are now, sitting cowering in a corridor dressed in threadbare trousers and a dirty vest with holes in it. He was dishevelled and speaking nonsense. Nobody was paying him any attention. Of course even in places like that, there were staff that did their best but they were few and far between. Only the rich could afford to find places that were anywhere near decent for their relatives."

It occurred to Edward that even with dementia, his father might feel he was being preached at. He might think his son was using him to rehearse a political speech. But today, after the experience earlier at the conference, he needed to justify his actions to his parent.

"Things had got so bad in the twenties that people just

threw their relatives into places like that. But there was no money to run them properly. People couldn't afford to pay much. The Government's plan to 'sort out social care' came to nothing. Most people didn't want to keep their elderly relatives living with them because it cost them money they often didn't have and they had their own lives they wanted to live. And anyway, people had come to realise that it simply wasn't fair that young people were having to pay the price for the burden caused by the growing, ageing population. Plus all that money spent during the Great Pandemic to save elderly people has left a massive debt still being paid for by the young. Enough was enough and we had to do something about it."

Edward's dad listened, looking out into the garden but then, from time to time, staring straight at his son with an expression that suggested to Edward that his father had never heard this speech before.

"I still believe that was right. Human history has been about our struggle to control things to make life more bearable, more pleasurable and more just. All the great inventions of the industrial revolution, the developments of the digital revolution, the innovations of the medical revolution more recently have all been about having greater control over our lives. We learnt to control disease, to control birth, and with the euthanasia law, we have controlled death. We have brought certainty where there was uncertainty. We have improved dignity in old age. We have reduced suffering. And we have improved fairness between the generations by freeing up resources and distributing them more fairly.

"And it's not just my party that believes this. Other countries are now starting to follow our example. And the vast majority of our people still support the principle of a fixed lifespan because they remember. They remember how awful it was after the Great Pandemic. They don't want to go back to that. They want certainty. They want dignity. Life is not about the number of years lived. It's about the quality of years lived. Thank goodness even most of the great religions now accept that. This is progress."

It was as though Edward had been using the tranquillity and privacy of his father's room away from private detectives, free from advisors, and, hopefully, out of the earshot of media, to rehearse his next speech. His father spoke quietly once his son had finished.

"You know my view Edward. You describe how bad things had become very accurately. Yes, you're right. We had betrayed our old people condemning them to pain, suffering and lack of dignity in their final years. And we had betrayed our young people, snatching their hope from them. Cutting back on education. Shutting universities, taking resources away from schools, pricing youngsters out of the property market. Things were bound to come to a head. Where you're wrong is the solution. How can it ever have been right for the state to decide when its citizens should die? How can it ever have been right for the state to decide that everyone should die when they reach a certain age irrespective of their state of health, irrespective of their wishes? How can it have been right to create the apparatus of a police state to enforce this and cause people to try to flee their own country to try to escape a law which should never have been passed in the first place?"

Edward had never previously heard his father spell out so unambiguously and lucidly his opposition to what his son had done. His dementia seemed at that moment not to exist. Edward was about to respond when his father continued.

"But voluntary euthanasia is quite a separate thing. If people choose to end their lives in old age or even younger if they face severe health issues. Then, providing they are not coerced into doing so, why shouldn't they be allowed to do so? And that's what I'm planning to do, provided you'll allow me."

"No, I won't," retorted the younger man just a bit too sharply and in a raised voice. His father's rejection of what had been his political raison d'etre for the previous quarter of a century had hit Edward hard.

"Everything I have done in my political life has been about achieving justice, about improving fairness and about giving people dignity. My Government is often portrayed as heartless, as authoritarian and as scared by the League of Youth with whose violent support, it is claimed, we came to power. Wrong on every count is my response. Yes, we very definitely prioritised the young after years of governments, particularly Conservative ones, favouring the old believing that this would win them the most votes. I make no apology for changing that. But I strongly refute the idea that we have treated the old callously. Far from it. We have given them dignity, certainty and a better end to life. You must be able to see that?"

His father stared straight at his son but didn't respond, a silence which spoke a thousand words. At this moment, Edward Watson was no longer the Prime Minister. All the protections, all the façades, all the positioning which came with political office were, temporarily at least, stripped away. Now he was just his father's son. He realised that, even as mature adults, all children still want to please their parents.

Whether it was the accumulated pressure of the last few days in the political spotlight or whether it was solely about family, he couldn't know. Maybe it was both. But, for the first time for several years, the Prime Minister was in tears. At first, just watery eyes, then a flow but then a convulsion of his upper body as he sat in front of his father.

"Dad, I just can't do it. Mum was taken from me, taken

from both of us. I'm not going to be responsible for losing you. Not now anyway."

The older man said nothing in response as his son composed himself. But, after ten seconds or so, he laid a hand on his son's shoulder.

There was a gentle knock on the door. Edward recognised it as his private detective's.

"Just a moment. I'll be out in a minute."

Father and son remained for a full thirty seconds or so looking straight at each other but with nothing needed to be said.

"I'll see you next week, Dad," said Edward as he stood up.

"Thanks for coming, son," the older man replied.

Edward took a tissue from his pocket, checked his eyes in his Dad's mirror and walked out into the corridor, once again assuming the persona of Prime Minister.

"Prime Minister," said his detective as they walked. "There's a bit of a demonstration developed outside while we've been here but, as you'll see, I think we can regard it as a friendly one. How do you want to play it? We could leave via the back or you may be happy to be seen with the protesters."

Having run the gauntlet of his political opponents earlier in the day and still feeling emotionally destabilised by the meeting with his father, Edward felt attracted by the idea of being among friends as it were. Even though he was uncomfortable with some of the more extreme antics of the League of Youth, he thought it would do him no harm to walk out of the front door and get on the news surrounded by those who agreed with him.

As they neared the entrance, he stopped. Even though he had read it many times before, he paused to take in the plaque in the foyer of what was now his father's home.

'This building was formerly part of the University of

Cambridge. Robinson College, Cambridge occupied this site from 1977 until 2028. During that period, more than 25,000 students from all over the world were educated here and then went out across the globe to help improve the lives of their fellow human beings.'

He refrained from turning to the wall opposite because, somehow today particularly, he didn't want to have to look at the picture which showed that he was one of the most illustrious alumni among those 25,000. Instead he walked confidently out of the door where cameras flashed and a crowd of probably a hundred or more were chanting,

"Death at 90. Justice for the Young. Don't raise the limit."

Even though they were on his side, Edward still felt somehow threatened by their anger and venom and was relieved as he got into his helicopter and was soon up and away above them looking forward to getting home to his family for what was left of Sunday. He must have dozed off again for a few minutes of oblivion which were rudely interrupted by the vibration of his personal mobile which, after a few seconds of hesitation, he decided it was best to answer.

"Good afternoon, Edward. Just seen you on the news. Shame about the vote earlier. Close thing but you're going to need to try a bit harder, I think. Let us know if you need any help. Have a good evening, Edward. Goodbye."

It was typical of the calls he was now getting on a more regular basis. No small talk. No pleasantries. No chance to respond. He tried to put the call out of his mind, spent the rest of the journey dozing and before he knew it, he was sat in the first-floor lounge of his elegant Edwardian house in East London.

Edward and Sophie had decided early in his Premiership to make a statement by continuing to live in their family home and forego the Downing Street flat which had been the norm for his predecessors for almost 200 years. Edward would have been happy to give Chequers a miss as well but his partner couldn't resist the lure of a country home, although they didn't go there as much now as they had when he was first in office. Tonight he was glad to be in his real home and the imitation log burner inside and the warm glow of the streetlights through the curtains were a comfort. For the first time that day, he felt he could relax, albeit briefly, helped it had to be said by a pleasant meal made by Sophie. Edward's pledge to himself to cook for them at least once a week was being honoured more in the breach at the moment.

"I'm afraid I didn't watch it all but I think you were unlucky. It was very close. Who knows if the e-voting devices really work properly? It's anybody's guess," pronounced Sophie as they sat down. Edward was still in his work suit and Sophie in a designer tracksuit – running had recently become her latest passion.

Edward wasn't concerned about the accuracy of the vote, just its implications.

"Yes, it was close but they won and I think it's going to be an uphill struggle to see them off."

"But you have to, Edward", replied Sophie somewhat wearily. "I've told you before. It's all opportunistic politicking by that woman trying to advance her career. She doesn't represent public opinion."

Edward had hardly ever heard his partner refer to Evie Smith by name. Some years ago, when Edward had promoted Evie soon after she had become an MP, Sophie had accused him of having had an affair with her. He hadn't but the mention of her name seemed still to be uncomfortable for Sophie.

"I'm afraid you've got it wrong, Sophie. I think the truth is that she does represent a sizeable chunk of public opinion. And, whatever you think of Evie, she's got energy and momentum and she's formidable. You shouldn't underestimate her."

"And you shouldn't bow down to her. Just think about all the people you represent. All the battles you've fought. This country should be very grateful to you for what you've done."

"I'm not sure I have enough energy for all this anymore. It's a young person's game. Ironic really given that I stood up for the young."

Edward's voice tailed off as he rapidly lost interest in having a political conversation with his partner. For a while they chatted about family matters. Sophie reported the latest about their three children, two of whom were off on trips around the world. The youngest still lived with them, although, Edward thought, you'd hardly know it as she seemed rarely to be at home. Sophie's news about the children made Edward feel even more depressed. It felt like Sophie was reporting on someone else's offspring. Even though they were his, he sometimes felt he hardly knew them. He'd been close to them when they were younger but he seemed to have lost that connection now. But he refrained from sharing these inner thoughts with Sophie. When he'd done so before, she'd said it was all his fault that his children weren't that interested in him and that he needed to work harder to have meaningful relationships with them. He didn't want another lecture on this today.

Eventually, Sophie brought the conversation back to politics. Edward knew that, even despite all the problems high office had brought to their relationship and their family life, she was still attracted to power and she often gave herself away.

"Edward, don't forget who helped you into power. Don't lose confidence in your own ability. Relax a bit and get back your old fighting spirit. There's a lot to lose for us if this all goes wrong."

As she uttered these words of warning, she moved across

and sat close to Edward. But he was just too tired and wound up. He stood up, announcing that he would clear up the meal and went to busy himself as therapy to force his political dilemmas from his mind.

CHAPTER TEN

King's College Hospital, Southwark,
Greater London
Tuesday 14 November 2045

The logo at the entrance hadn't changed and it might still be called the NHS. But, as she rushed through the hospital doors, Holly was reminded that the system created back in the middle of the twentieth century was only a shadow of its former self. Even the ruling English Conservatives still professed to believe in it, but they had presided over a 'rationalisation' which had drastically reduced the number of services which were still free at the point of use. Fortunately for Holly and Jake, emergency treatment after a beating in the street still qualified and so she found herself visiting King's College Hospital to visit her partner, now recovering two days after the attack near the Oval.

However, Holly's overriding thought as she walked through the long corridor with her coat flapping and bulging laptop bag weighing her down, was not of Jake but of the last time she had been here. The memories of her mother came flooding back but they were disturbing ones so she immediately suppressed them. Instead she concentrated on finding the ward where Jake was recovering amongst the labyrinth of buildings which now made up one of London's biggest hospitals.

"How are you feeling?" asked Holly as she finally arrived at Jake's bedside, throwing her coat on the bed and dropping her bag onto the floor.

She was hot and bothered after rushing from a meeting. She was squeezing in a visit before heading off to meet up with her father and grandmother for another important pre-death day ritual. She wasn't looking forward to it at all.

"Drugged up to the hilt but I'm OK," replied Jake. "It's much better than yesterday. It's down here which is worst."

He pointed to his ribs and, as he did so, he let out a cry of pain accompanied by a sharp grimace.

"Twelve out of twenty-four broken, apparently. Some sort of record, I'm told!" he remarked with heavy sarcasm.

The broken ribs were the least of his injuries and there was little that could be done about them anyway apart from pain relief. He had taken several heavy blows to his head which was bandaged in the style of an Egyptian mummy. He'd broken an arm in the fall and there was lots of bruising everywhere.

"I've spoken to the police and they said they'd come and get a statement today if you're fit enough," added Holly.

"I suppose so but I'm not sure what use that will be," responded Jake.

They fell into intermittent conversation for a while. The events of the weekend had brought them closer together. Even though it couldn't have come at a worse time for Holly who had a crucial week at work, she realised how much she cared about Jake. Their rows about money and the like seemed now to be trivial and unnecessary. She could also sense that their joint concern about Mary's imminent legally-mandated death was giving them a shared purpose.

"I'm sorry but I'd better go, so I'm not late for the shopping trip," said Holly. "And I need to get changed. I can't go in these things," announced Holly after a while.

"You look alright to me," replied Jake, a comment which made Holly think he must be feeling better.

She gathered up her things but, as she did so, noticed a policeman talking to one of the nurses who was directing him towards Jake's bed.

He came over and introduced himself as PC Parkinson.

"If you're feeling well enough, I would like to ask you a few questions about the incident on Sunday at the Oval," announced the policeman, his question directed at Jake.

Holly expected Jake to make a confrontational response. She thought that it was pretty poor that it had taken two days before the police had bothered to start a proper investigation into what was, by any reckoning, a serious attack in a public place.

"Fire away," was Jake's unexpectedly conciliatory reply.

Holly interjected, "I was there as well. Will you be wanting to question me?"

The policeman turned to her with an air of mild irritation and replied, "That won't be necessary."

All of which reinforced Holly's growing belief that the police wouldn't be devoting any significant resources to this investigation.

Her first instinct was to walk out but she contained her irritation, sat down on a chair next to the bed and listened, keen to make sure there was a witness to this conversation.

"What were you doing walking around the Oval area on Sunday with an eighty-nine-year-old woman?" was the policeman's opening gambit.

"I'm sorry, officer, but I don't quite understand the relevance of your question. I was there with my partner and her grandmother whom we were taking to see the remains of the Oval Cricket Ground. This has a special significance for her as it was where she met her late husband."

Holly observed that the policeman's body language gave away an almost complete lack of understanding of either the sporting or emotional significance of the location and he ploughed on.

"Did you not realise that the area around the Oval is one of the most dangerous in London? It's a well-known haunt of dropouts, left-behinds and the advice is not to go there."

"I was aware of that but we decided that it was a risk worth taking in order to give my partner's grandmother the opportunity to visit somewhere special to her just weeks before her death and, as far as I am aware, that is not against the law," replied Jake.

"The fact remains that you deliberately went to an unsafe part of the city, probably trespassed on private land and deliberately put yourselves and others at risk. Now we are having to tie up valuable police resources on something which could have been avoided had you not behaved foolishly."

Holly felt she should intervene but, before she could, Jake shot back at the policeman.

"Officer, I'm struggling to comprehend what is going on here. I was the object of a vicious assault in the street on Sunday whilst going about my lawful business. My partner and elderly grandmother were terrorised in the same incident. I am now lying in a hospital bed with, as you can see, multiple injuries, and yet your line of questioning seems to suggest that you regard me as the criminal and not as the victim. Or I have I misunderstood something?"

The policeman offered neither explanation nor response but resumed his questioning.

"Can you describe the person who you say attacked you?"

Jake decided that further questioning of the assumptions that appeared to underpin this interview was pointless. So, he made an effort at describing what had happened although he hadn't really got a proper look at the man who had attacked him. The interview continued for a few moments with neither person seemingly believing that it would achieve very much. As abruptly as he had arrived, the policeman brought the conversation to a close.

"Thank you. That'll be all for now. We'll be in touch."

With that he got up, walked back through the ward and left leaving Holly with the distinct impression that very few, if any, resources would be devoted to tracking down Jake's attackers. Jake slumped back onto his pillow and grimaced, confirming how much pain he was still feeling.

"What a waste of time!" Jake hissed angrily as Holly stood up, moved towards the bed and carefully touched Jake's arm, conscious that she mustn't cause him more pain.

"Don't get bothered about it," Holly replied "That's the way things are. The most important thing is that you get better soon."

Jake was unimpressed.

"The most important thing is that this country has completely and utterly gone to the dogs. The police won't investigate a serious assault properly. I'm not going to let that rest."

"You'll have to for now. Just try and go to sleep. We'll talk about it when I come tomorrow. Sorry, but I must get going."

She swept up her coat and bag, squeezed Jake's hand and walked out of the ward. As she made her way back through the hospital's winding corridors, Holly's mind was in turmoil. She wasn't looking forward to what lay ahead for the rest of the day, another episode in the pre-death-day ritual for Mary. She was shocked, even though unsurprised, by what had just happened with the police. But it was those memories from the past, more than ten years ago now, that were really troubling her. Then she was brought up with a start.

Ahead of her, coming towards her down the corridor, she saw a woman in a wheelchair who seemed familiar. She seemed scarily familiar. By the time she got closer, she had convinced herself it was her. And what was even more disturbing was the woman pushing the wheelchair. She could have been looking at herself in a mirror. The couple were now almost level with Holly. Instinctively she reached out.

"Mum, Mum," she called out as she crouched down to be less than a metre away from the woman in the wheelchair.

Just as Holly started opening both arms to frame an embrace, the woman pushing the wheelchair exclaimed, "Excuse me!" in a voice loud enough to attract the attention of other people.

The next few seconds were a blur for Holly. She could feel two people restraining her on the floor as her increasingly frantic cries of 'Mum, Mum' carried down the hospital corridor vainly following the woman in the wheelchair who was being moved away at speed from the danger. Holly's shouts turned to sobs as she crumpled into a foetal position on the floor. She can only have been there for a minute or two before two security guards appeared, hauled her abruptly to her feet and led her down the corridor towards the hospital exit.

An hour later, ten miles to the south, Holly was sitting with her father in her grandmother's lounge. They were looking at images on the screen of dresses, coats and hats suitable for women of mature years.

"'Dying for Dresses?' What sort of warped mind came up with that name for a business?" asked David. "I'm a strong supporter of the present law but the whole point is about dying with dignity and that's a bit tacky, don't you think, Holly?"

Holly's brain had not yet focussed on the matter in hand and it took a few seconds for her father's question to register.

"Yes Dad, I agree about the name but let's have a proper look and see what would suit Gran. What do you think, Gran, what are we looking for?"

The events at the hospital had shaken her badly. The security guards had accepted her explanation that she had mistaken the woman in her wheelchair for someone else and had concluded that she didn't constitute a threat. She had been politely escorted to the main doors of the hospital and sent on her way. For Holly, though, that was far from the end of the matter. This had been happening more and more often to her. Seeing people who looked like her mother. In her mind she was seeing people who were her mother. But she had never gone as far as she had today. She knew why it had happened. It was there that it had happened, there in that hospital, more than a decade ago and she could never erase that from her memory. But, for now, with a supreme effort, she pushed it from her mind.

Holly knew that it was going to be down to her to make a success of the next couple of hours for her grandmother. She wanted to help make Mary's last days of life as pleasant as possible even if she was harbouring increasing doubts about the wisdom of a law which meant that a country gave itself the right effectively to kill its own citizens just for being old. She knew that her father, on the other hand, had few doubts that the law was a good idea and no doubt whatsoever that he would make sure his mother had a good send-off. But the fashion industry and clothes buying generally bored him, so she would have to take the initiative.

A whole industry had sprung up in the ten years since the law was passed and it was now apparently worth billions. Holly was a bit uncomfortable about it but she had worked on PR campaigns for companies involved in it, so she couldn't be too precious about it. Terminations had almost taken over from weddings as the occasions when people went on a spending spree. There was a large element of keeping up with the Joneses. People tried to outdo each other with their pre-death parties and with the surroundings in which they chose to die.

"That's a nice dress," remarked Holly as the images of garments, deemed suitable for women of ninety to wear on their special day, flashed on the screen.

She pointed to a cream knee-length dress with a suggestion of padded shoulders. "Very eighties, I'd say. Your era, Gran."

"Looks like the sort of thing Maggie Thatcher used to wear," interjected David whose sartorial opinions were few and far between but whose views on politicians, living and dead, were frequently voiced.

Mary didn't respond. The strange thing, thought Holly, was that the events of the previous Sunday seemed not to have left much of an impression on her. Perhaps this was the silver lining of having dementia. She had been caught in the middle of a noisy and violent demonstration and had witnessed Jake being beaten up in the street. However, it wasn't clear whether she could now remember it or indeed whether she could appreciate the gravity of what had occurred.

When David got the call from Holly after the attack, he had immediately set off by drone to come and collect his mother from the hospital where she had been taken for a check-up. Since then, she had hardly mentioned the incident and had resumed her shaky grip on reality, as though it had never happened. But then, as the pictures of clothes were offered up on the screen, she had one of her moments of lucidity.

"How is Jake? Is he OK?"

Holly was surprised, both that she had remembered and also that she had got Jake's name right.

"He's alright, Gran," replied Holly. "He's going to be in hospital for a bit. He's got a few broken bones and a lot of bruises but he'll be fine before long."

David, who'd told Holly he thought it had been a foolish idea to go to the Oval, clearly wanted to steer the conversation back to clothes.

"Now then Mum, we are going to visit the shop a bit later and it would be good if you had an idea of what you'd like to get. There'll be a load of things to choose from and it would be good to have narrowed it down a bit."

Making choices was not Mary's strong point now. Holly did her best to guide her grandmother but she knew they'd probably have to make the choice for her. After about thirty minutes of scrolling, zooming and studying the plethora of clothes available, they seemed to have alighted on a couple of fairly safe dresses, a long wool coat and some low 'court shoes'. It could be described as 'retro' but, Holly hoped, in an appropriate way for a ninety-year-old. She was fairly certain that her grandmother would not want to do what some of her contemporaries had taken to doing and recreate the fashions of their youth. Stories were legion of women terminating, dressed in sixties and seventies clothing reminiscent of their teenage and young adult years.

David messaged through the choices so that they would hopefully be ready to be tried on when they arrived at the shop later that afternoon.

"Come on Mum, let's get on our way. We need to get there before it gets too late," said David in the patronising tone he often used for his mother.

Holly helped her with her coat. They gathered what they needed and went out to the garden and boarded the drone. It was a short flight to Chislehurst where they were able to land not far from 'Dying for Dresses'. It was one of the leading deathday fashion retailers but, unlike most which conducted their business completely online, this upmarket concern had shops or 'showrooms', as they called them. These tended to be concentrated in small enclaves of shops aimed at the well-to-do and were usually in the posher parts of towns and cities.

It was only a short distance from the drone park to the showroom and, when they arrived, they were ushered in. Holly immediately felt that they were being treated in a rather unctuous manner reminiscent of undertakers. The place was furnished luxuriously, was very warm inside and was filled with a powerful scent emanating from the many vases of flowers placed liberally around. There were several other groups of people there browsing the clothes rails. But most, like Mary, David and Holly, were being ushered towards the changing rooms.

A woman introduced herself as the manager and took them through to a private dressing area. The two dresses they had chosen earlier were hanging up.

"Which one would you like to try on first ?" she asked, very particularly addressing her comments to Mary, although she was unsure if she would get an answer.

"That one," replied Mary straight away, leaving Holly surprised but, as often was the case, when she was in the company of strangers, something in her diseased brain seemed to kick in and bring her clarity and social skills back to the fore.

A gently patterned cream dress was removed from its hanger by the manager. Holly was pleased that her father took this as a cue to beat a retreat to the more public part of the showroom. Holly and the manager helped Mary into the dress and invited her to admire herself in it in front of a mirror. She offered no opinion and said nothing when the others enquired. The manager suggested trying on the court shoes 'to get the full effect'. Mary walked around, looked at herself in the mirror and then, as though she were many years younger and free of a debilitating brain disorder, asked Holly with a chuckle in her voice,

"Does my bum look big in this?"

The manager smiled at this. Holly let out a belly laugh.

"Oh, Gran, you look lovely in it."

For a moment the three women were united by the humour of the situation although Holly was fighting back the tears, overcome as she was inside by the profound sadness of the occasion. For the next ten or fifteen minutes, Mary appeared to be fully engaged with what was happening as she tried on the other dress they'd chosen online as well as a coat and some more shoes. David's opinion was sought and Holly felt that they were getting somewhere close to being able to make a decision.

Mary then wandered out into the showroom, now apparently perfectly understanding the purpose of the visit. She even started chatting to fellow customers.

"So, when's your special day, then?" she enquired of one slightly taken aback woman who offered only a feeble reply.

"Oh, in a few weeks' time."

Holly observed that, like many things in life, some people were blunt and to the point and others very circumspect and it was no different when it came to discussing termination.

As Holly and her father tried to steer proceedings back to the changing room and towards a decision, Mary stopped in front of a display and stood admiring the outfit on offer. The wording above it said it all. 'The Mary Quant Look – the Style of the Sixties.'

"That's what I'd like to die in," said Mary without any hint of doubt as she pointed to a 1960s mini-skirt and matching patent shoes.

CHAPTER ELEVEN

Harrogate, North Yorkshire.
Wednesday 15 November 2045

Wilfred had never enjoyed being driven by his son when cars needed a driver. Even now, as they took a driverless out of the centre of Harrogate in search of another old haunt of Eversley's, the older man's nervousness in the passenger seat was obvious.

"It's driven by a computer, Dad, so stop looking so worried," said Eversley.

"I'm not worried about the car. I know it'll be a safer driver itself than you ever would be!" shot back Wilfred.

"I'm worried about what we're going to do next. OK, it's nice having a few days with you but we can't carry on wandering around forever."

They had booked into a small hotel not far from the middle of the North Yorkshire town a couple of days after their ordeal in Newcastle. Beaten up during their NARA interrogation, they'd stayed one night in Newcastle. Wilfred had initially resisted his son's insistence that he should be seen by a doctor. So, they'd booked a video consultation which had resulted in a trip to a private clinic for a scan and examination of his head wounds. It was an expensive visit but the payment guaranteed that no questions would be asked as to the origin of the injuries. A visit to an NHS hospital or clinic would not, Wilfred judged, be wise in the circumstances.

As they'd sat in an unremarkable pizza restaurant in the knowledge that Wilfred's head wounds were relatively superficial, father and son had argued about their next move. Wilfred, convinced the NARA had hacked their I-COMs, suggested they were effectively being followed wherever they went. Another escape attempt to Scotland was, he argued, futile and dangerous. The truth was that Wilfred was losing the will to see through another mission.

"I'm getting too old for this sort of adventure," he joked.

After much debate, Wilfred had been persuaded by Eversley to agree to hiring a driverless and head to Yorkshire. He was genuinely keen to visit some more places which were special to his son, particularly the Army Foundation College where Eversley had first trained as a new squaddie. Wilfred suspected, though, that the idea of a nostalgic return to Harrogate was really a delaying tactic by his son designed to buy him time to try to organise an alternative means of evading the law.

So, here they were heading past the boarded up remains of Harrogate's former Convention Centre en route to the Army College.

"I remember it was a Nightingale Hospital during the Great Pandemic but, when it reopened after that, it limped on for a few years but the conference trade had slumped and it shut. I wonder if they'll just knock it down, it's an eyesore now," remarked Eversley.

Wilfred's attention was focussed not on a derelict conference hall but, as they turned the corner, on a building he recognised and which still seemed to be functional.

"Stop, Eversley. I remember this place. I had a concert here once. Yes, the Royal Hall. That's it. Very grand inside. Let's park and take a look."

"This isn't a good idea, Dad. Anyway you won't be able to get inside. And we need to get on before it starts getting dark."

It was obvious to Wilfred that Eversley wasn't keen on an unscheduled stop.

"It'll be fine. No one will know who we are and I just want a few minutes."

Eversley's resistance crumbled. He overrode the sat nav and brought the driverless to a standstill in a side street. Wilfred was out of the car almost before it had stopped. He could sense Eversley rushing after him as he made to cross the street in front of an oncoming driverless. Having safely negotiated crossing the road, he stood on the steps of the Royal Hall.

"Wow, this is it. Yes, I don't know when it was but they performed my first symphony here. Let's go inside."

"Dad, it's not a good idea," retorted Eversley. "You're an old man with a bandaged head drawing attention to yourself in the middle of a town."

"Don't fret so much, Eversley. It'll all be fine."

The doors of the Royal Hall were open and a large truck was parked nearby unloading padlocked crates, presumably containing sound equipment or maybe musical instruments. Wilfred ignored all this, walked straight ahead and started engaging the security guard at the door.

"There was a concert of my music here some years ago. We just happen to be passing by and I saw the place. I'd love to go inside just for a minute or two. For old times' sake."

After just a few seconds, a broad smile lit up the face of the security guard.

"I know you. It's Wilfred David, isn't it. I think I have pretty much all your pieces on my favourites' list. You've done so much to make 'our music' mainstream. Be my guest. Have a good look round and take as long as you like."

Wilfred touched the guard's arm.

"Thank you. Thank you."

Wilfred strode into the Hall with Eversley following behind. They ventured through into the main auditorium where technical equipment was being unloaded from boxes, presumably for a concert that night. From the look of the stage, this wasn't to be a concert of classical music. Neither that nor the banging and clattering of technicians at work bothered Wilfred. He walked down the aisle looking all around with the years almost visibly falling off him.

"I can remember it so clearly, Eversley. It was packed that night and they loved it. I got asked up on to the stage at the end. I think I might have made a short speech. Those were the days."

Wilfred was transported back to the time, long since passed, when he was at the height of his powers. He remembered how he had been an icon of Black British culture embraced eventually by the English establishment. He surrendered to the beauty of this moment, clearly oblivious to the rather faded glory of the Edwardian building. It looked rather unloved and its expensive rescue and refurbishment, nearly forty years earlier, was a distant memory. But Wilfred was seeing it as it had been when he was last there.

Then, as the random sounds of preparation continued, Wilfred was propelled by an inner force to climb the small flight of stairs onto the stage. There, ignoring everyone working all around him, he sat at a piano already in place for the concert that evening. Immediately he started to play. At first the sound of his playing barely cut through above the surrounding din but gradually the noise subsided and the music of Wilfred David took over. Technicians and stage hands, even though they were rushing to meet a deadline, downed tools. They listened as an eighty-nine-year-old man with a bandaged head, whom most had barely noticed when he walked onto the stage, held their attention.

Wilfred was entirely focused on the keyboard, apparently oblivious of his surroundings. He did look up to scan the scene in front of him and spotted Eversley standing in a gangway a few rows back from the stage. After a few seconds there were smiles of recognition between them. Wilfred knew that Eversley had recognised the melody of the piece that he was close to finishing. It was the tune he had been humming on their night-time walk in the wilds of Northumberland. It was the tune he had whistled in the driverless as they headed south from Newcastle.

By now, the work to build the set for the night's event had come to a complete standstill. Thirty or more people stood in silence, some leaning against the boxes they were unloading, as Wilfred improvised on the piano seemingly unaware of the audience he had attracted. He would play a section, stop, talk to himself about it, play it again and then move on. This continued for five minutes or more until, it seemed, he suddenly became aware of those around him.

"Sorry, I'm so sorry, I'm holding you up. How very inconsiderate of me," he said.

Wilfred looked around as though seeking permission to continue to interrupt their work. As the people on the stage reassured him that they were very happy to be stopped, Wilfred's attention was drawn to the back of the hall and to the security guard who'd let them in. He stood with an even wider smile on his face than that which had greeted them earlier. With Wilfred still at the piano, the guard broke into enthusiastic applause, a gesture that was immediately taken up by the assembled crowd including Eversley. The clapping continued for several minutes and a number of the impromptu audience started chatting to Wilfred. He was explaining breathlessly how he now felt that he could get the piece right after so many struggles with it.

Wilfred noticed that Eversley had come up onto the stage, but that he was making no attempt to stop the conversations. But eventually, after many more minutes, the son was able to extract his father. As the work constructing that night's event restarted, they walked towards the exit, thanking the security guard once more as they emerged into the autumn sunshine.

"They liked it Dad. So did I. It's very good."

"Thanks son. Thanks. I know I can finish it now."

"And thank goodness they seemed just to be interested in your music and not on why your head was bandaged!"

They got back in the car. Wilfred felt a new sense of togetherness between them.

"So what would you like to do now, Dad?" asked Eversley, surprising Wilfred with this question but confirming for him that his son now understood a little better how important completing this final composition was to him.

Wilfred felt a renewed sense of purpose to their wanderings and was happy to resume Eversley's itinerary.

"Shall we head to the Army College, then? Thanks for letting me do that. I've not enjoyed myself so much for ages."

Eversley reprogrammed the satnav and the driverless drew away. Less than ten minutes later, they were close to their next destination.

"That's it, Dad. Over there."

As the satnav announced their arrival, Eversley took control of the driverless and they cruised along the outer perimeter road of the barracks. Wilfred had a pre-existing image in his mind of what this place would look like. It was based on his conversations with his son all those years ago when Eversley had enlisted. In fact the reality of what was in front of him was rather less grim and foreboding than he had imagined. When Eversley had joined the Army more than forty years ago, every recruit, apart from officers, came here for their initial six weeks training. Eversley slowed the driverless as he glanced through the fence to get a better view of the place.

"Yes, it's all coming back to me now. I think my room was over there. I was only here for a few weeks but it seemed like an age at the time. It was hard, a bit of a rude awakening. But I met all sorts of folk from very different backgrounds. And by the time I left here, I knew I'd done the right thing joining up."

These recollections made Wilfred remember the phone conversations with his son from that period. This was the first time he had ever seen this place but he could still remember how he felt back then. His extreme disappointment, largely veiled at the time, that his only child had chosen to join the Army, came flooding back.

"I didn't want you to come here," Wilfred remarked as Eversley drew the driverless to a halt just a few metres from the main entrance.

"I know you didn't, Dad," he replied. "And, yes, I suppose it was partly a rebellion against you and Mum."

"What were you rebelling against? What was it that we had done that upset you so much?" asked Wilfred, realising that he and his son were on the brink of having a serious conversation, something that had happened only rarely over the years.

However, he wasn't to get an answer as their nostalgic visit to the Army Foundation College was brought to an abrupt end by two armed soldiers advancing on the driverless from either side. They were pointing their weapons at the vehicle and ordering the two men to get out and stand with their hands on their heads.

"This is a protected high security site and you are not allowed to stop here. What are you doing here?" barked one of the soldiers as father and son complied with his order.

Wilfred couldn't help thinking how such an abrupt tone from a soldier would have been unthinkable even twenty years before. But that was another legacy of the Pandemic when police and military had been given draconian emergency powers to control the population's movements. The powers had never been properly repealed and, thought Wilfred, England now resembled a police state.

Eversley's explanation of the reason for their visit seemed not to convince their interrogator. ID cards were demanded, examined and returned. A short lecture followed during which Wilfred imagined their locations and identities were being input into the national database. Then, just as abruptly as they had been ordered from their driverless, they were instructed to get back in and drive away from the area and not return.

Wilfred was pleased that Eversley hit the random button on the satnav just to get them away from the unpleasant encounter. So, the driverless moved forward heading past the entrance of the College, along the remaining length of its perimeter and straight ahead on an open road heading west further away from Harrogate.

For a while, they travelled in silence. Wilfred was humming again, composing in his mind and, for the moment at least, unconcerned about their next move. He knew that Eversley would have already formulated a plan which no doubt he would reveal soon. Despite, maybe because of, the experience they had gone through, Wilfred was now more determined to achieve an escape, and he sensed that Eversley was as well, if only because the need to demonstrate to himself and to his father that he could deliver on a promise.

"Have you ever been to Brimham Rocks?" Eversley asked. "It's nice there. We can have a bit of R&R and decide our next move."

Wilfred wasn't keen on the military idioms that often crept into his son's language. However, he knew that they were best ignored as they were second nature and not designed to rile him. Eversley reprogrammed the satnav and the driverless took them to the National Trust beauty spot, an outcrop of millstone grit formed into weird shapes on the moorland of

Nidderdale. They parked up and set off walking between the towering rocks. For a while Wilfred allowed himself to enjoy the tranquillity of the place. A mixture of children supervised by anxious parents and serious climbers with ropes and safety gear were enjoying the afternoon sunshine.

"Dad, I have another plan for escaping. You've only a few weeks left and I've made contact with 90+ again about getting into Hunstanton."

Wilfred was unsurprised by this suggestion. He knew that his son was determined, some would say stubborn, when he set his mind to something. But he also suspected that Eversley's motives weren't entirely altruistic. He knew that, for the younger man, it was almost a matter of honour that he succeeded in this mission. Wilfred, normally one to avoid difficult conversations, nevertheless decided that now was the time to get to the heart of the matter.

"What's this all about, Eversley?" he said, pausing briefly, half hoping for an answer that would spare him the need to continue.

None was forthcoming so he had to press on.

"Is this about me, or is it really about you?" he added trying not to sound judgemental.

Eversley appeared momentarily taken aback by his father's uncharacteristic directness.

"It's about you and it's about the fact that we can't just sit back and accept an unjust law that means that perfectly healthy people are murdered by the Government just because they're old and apparently expendable. I'm not going to allow you to be the victim of this and, however difficult it might be, I'm going to try to beat a system which should never have been set up in the first place. All this arguing about whether it should be 90 or 95 or even 100 is irrelevant. It shouldn't be anything. That's what it's all about. Nothing less. Nothing more."

Wilfred mulled over his son's words which were the most succinct explanation of why they were spending this time together roaming the North of England in what he still believed to be a mission with a low chance of success. He was tempted to drop the discussion there but something made him persevere.

"I don't think this is about me or even particularly about injustice. I think it's about you. You've always been a rebel ever since you were young. You rebelled against any sort of authority including parental. A lot of what you did was motivated by getting back at me and your mother. Now there's nothing unusual about children rebelling against their parents. In fact, it can be a very healthy thing. But I suppose the rather unusual thing in our case was that you seemed to reject us not because we were too strict, too authoritarian or too restrictive but because we were the opposite. Bleeding heart liberals, you once called us. And for most of your adult life you've supported the politicians and factions that have led us to where we are today. We are living in a repressive state that believes old people to be a burden and favours a forced redistribution of resources from the old to the young. I hate this Conservative Government. I despise their policies including a law requiring me and others to die at ninety. And the truth is that you know that this is wrong. But this is about your guilt at voting in the past for a party that proposed this. Now, rather at the eleventh hour, you are trying to make amends."

Wilfred paused briefly to allow a group of other visitors to pass them on the narrow path. It reminded him of how people had behaved during the pandemic. Once the group had passed, he resumed,

"Of course, there's a strong part of me that wants to stay alive. I'm reasonably fit for an eighty-nine-year-old. I still have some family and friends left. There's still much I'm interested in. And, above all, I still have more music in me. I must finish my piece. And I'd like to write more. I'm perfectly happy that my name is no longer that well-known. It's easier. There's less pressure. But I've still got so much I'd like to do if I get the opportunity. But actually, I've had a good life and what is sometimes forgotten is that, it sounds a bit trite to say it like this, but all good things must come to an end. Pleasure and happiness, in a sense only exist because they are fragile and temporary. You can only appreciate happiness if you have also experienced sadness. Pleasure means nothing if you haven't also felt pain. Limitless lifespans, like a piece of music that never reaches its finale, or a holiday that never ends, is meaningless and actually the poorer for not being finite."

Wilfred observed that his son was uncharacteristically quiet. They walked on.

"Yes, the idea of a fixed lifespan mandated by law introduced by a government that does not believe in what I would call real democracy is anathema to me. But the idea that people might choose to end their lives at ninety or any other age because they've had enough, because they want to avoid the degradations of old age or because they recognise that they've had their go and now it's others' turn is a perfectly rational and liberal thing to decide."

Wilfred had more to say but did genuinely pause hoping for a response. For probably two minutes they walked on in silence each absorbing the impact of what had just been said. Eventually, Eversley broke the silence.

"So, why did you agree to come up here with me then? It sounds like your heart's not in it."

"A good question," replied the older man. "And I've analysed that a lot myself. I suppose partly because I wanted to see if it were possible to live a little longer. It's not really any different when you're eighty-nine, to when you're twenty-nine, or forty-nine or sixty-nine. You have a basic sense of self-preservation. But I think it was more that I knew that we hadn't spent enough time together. Despite a lifetime of opportunity, we had never really got to know each other properly and I wanted to put that right before it was too late. And now I do want more time, definitely, to finish this composition. Going in the Royal Hall earlier has absolutely made up my mind. I need time."

Wilfred paused. High up above them on the highest rock formation at Brimham Rocks, he noticed a young man, probably in his twenties, part of a group of climbers who were tackling a sheer rock face. However, the young man wasn't concentrating on his climbing companions. Instead, he seemed to be looking straight at Eversley who had stopped several paces behind Wilfred. Wilfred turned to discover the reasons for the young man's attention. Eversley was weeping, very quietly but very obviously. Wilfred moved towards him. Then, for more than a minute, father and son embraced, an embrace that was much more than a formality, more than a regular familial greeting out of habit. Both were weeping as they held each other.

"There's a lot you don't know about me, Dad. I'm sorry for how I've been towards you, going back to when I was much younger. But I'm still so angry now, not with you or Mum but with the system."

"We can all be angry with the system for one reason or another. It's what we do about it that matters," replied Wilfred.

He sensed that there was more to come from his son.

"I've never told you and you've never really asked. But Afghanistan was much worse than I've ever let on to you. Emma knows. The kids don't but they probably should. I did things I should never have done. Every time I see your face close up, it brings it back. He can't have been eighty-nine but he looked like he was. He looked a bit like you. In my head, now, he almost is you. I didn't need to do it. I was scared. The Taliban were all around us. Two of my closest mates had disappeared as we went into the village. I thought they'd been shot. We were shooting at everything that moved. That's how it happened. He was defenceless and not a threat. It will never go away."

Wilfred could see that Eversley's weeping had subsided. His breathing had steadied. The disclosure appeared to have brought calm. What he had just been told wasn't a great surprise but the telling of it was. Wilfred couldn't think of the right words but hoped that none were necessary. Then, he noticed, up above Eversley's head, that the young man was still watching them, his attention completely diverted from helping his climbing friend by the unusual sight of two older men behaving like this in public. Wilfred thought to himself that what the man on the high vantage point would never know was that this was the first time they had hugged like this for almost half a century.

"OK, where to next?" said Wilfred attempting to bring the emotional temperature back nearer to normal as they released themselves from the embrace.

As they walked back to the carpark, Wilfred was told by his son that he was hoping to get a call anytime which he hoped would confirm that they could head to Hunstanton. They just had to be patient.

CHAPTER TWELVE

Media City, Salford, Greater Manchester
Wednesday 15 November 2045

Edward Watson and Evie Smith were sitting on opposite sofas in the green room of BBC Media City in Salford. Producers, researchers and other BBC staff flitted in and out constantly asking them if they were OK. Edward would have preferred to be in his own room but, given that the two protagonists in the forthcoming debate had to share, he was grateful for their interruptions and fussing. At least it reduced the amount of time he had to make small talk with his opponent.

Even though linear television was now largely a relic of the past, there was still an appetite for these live set piece duels at elections and to debate individual hot topics, like the euthanasia law. Edward had resisted a head to head debate with Smith for several weeks since the BBC had first suggested it but he had relented for two reasons. Firstly, fear of bad PR for refusing to take part but also because he still believed he could win the argument about the 90 Law and this would be a good platform to do so.

"How's your father doing, Edward?" asked Smith ignoring the BBC people buzzing around them.

As ever, thought Edward, his opponent looked elegant, her hair expertly coiffured, wearing a cream suit and, perhaps surprisingly, shoes with a heel instead of her normal flats. Edward was pleased he had worn one of his sharper suits today, even though he knew it didn't quite disguise his increasingly noticeable weight gain.

"He's getting by OK, thanks Evie," responded the Prime Minister in a tone of voice that suggested that he didn't want this line of questioning to go any further.

"It's very sad, this degeneration in old age, Edward, which of course is precisely why we all support the idea of legally mandated lifespans," offered Evie in a tone which gave every impression of sympathy.

But Edward interpreted the tone differently, believing that Smith was trying to wind him up before they went into the studio. He went on the offensive.

"Just remind me how you're doing with the power supply problems, Evie?"

As Business Secretary, she was taking the flak for the frequent power cuts which had been a feature of life for many people in the previous few months. Edward already knew the answer but asking the question represented the assertion of Prime Ministerial authority.

"We're getting on top of it, I believe," replied Evie without so much as a flicker of doubt. "I'm fully confident things will be back to normal by the end of the month."

"Glad to hear it," replied Edward.

"I trust you won't be promising that in public."

"I will sound optimistic but avoid making specific commitments," came back Evie, adopting a tone that sounded to Edward more than a bit condescending.

Theirs was a complicated relationship. For Edward, Evie was now the pretender to the throne, the young upstart whom he'd helped earlier in her career. In his view, she was repaying his help with ingratitude and vaulting ambition. He still recognised her achievement given her tough and tragic early life. But, despite all this, there remained a powerful sense of betrayal and the difficulty of accepting the passing of the baton from one generation to the next. And that meant he now disliked her and wanted to find the means of putting her back in her place.

"And how are things with Lizzie?" enquired Edward a little tentatively.

"She's fine, thank you," responded Evie maybe a bit too quickly.

Edward didn't pursue this tack but he was pleased with himself to have pierced the substantial layer of emotional armour erected around herself by the Business Secretary. The problems in her personal life, poured over salaciously in some of the newspapers, were clearly more difficult for her to handle than any challenges presented by her ministerial portfolio.

"We're getting on well now again," she continued offering a brief and rare admission that Edward had not heard before which confirmed that there had been troubles.

"Well I'm jolly glad to hear that," replied the Prime Minister sounding slightly triumphal.

"Edward, I know you think I'm an ambitious upstart. Contrary to what you think, I'm not after your job. This issue matters to me personally. I'm not going to let it go."

"Let's save this for when we're live, Evie," said Edward managing to make this sound like a Prime Ministerial instruction.

The two politicians fell into silence and their private thoughts for a few moments until Edward broke the silence by opening his folder of notes to consult his crib sheet. There in bold letters were the three key points upon which his advisers had recommended concentrating. He was wrapped up in his notes for maybe a minute before his attention wandered to the room, to his opponent, to his father and to his private doubts about just about everything.

Fortunately, his potentially dangerous reverie was interrupted by the call to the studio and the two protagonists followed the debate producer down a corridor, through several sets of double doors, through the dark extremities of the studio and then into the bright lights of the deceptively small space in which the contest would soon take place.

Edward had been through so many of these types of media event over the years that he felt a sense of déjà vu as he sat, strangely relaxed, waiting for battle to commence. By contrast, Evie was fidgeting nervously in her seat even though she should perhaps have felt in the ascendancy after her victory at the party conference just three days previously.

Then the title sequence was playing, the floor manager was counting down and, before they knew it, the familiar tones of the country's best-known political interviewer, were filling the studio.

Edward was calm enough to let his thoughts drift. Twenty-five years previously neither Laura Kuenssberg nor the BBC would have believed that they would still have been occupying centre stage in the media landscape. In the early twenties, a Conservative government had seemed set on a course of dismantling the BBC. And the BBC's then Political Editor had been the butt of criticism from all sides of the political spectrum accused of pro-left and then pro-right bias during the fevered political times surrounding Britain's exit from the European Union.

However, the BBC had survived and Edward was secretly pleased. He'd shared in the BBC bashing of the past. He'd supported changes to its funding - it was now paid for by a levy on broadband charges but it had essentially survived pretty much intact despite repeated skirmishes with the government about its alleged political bias. Kuenssberg, likewise, now in her sixties, had been a great survivor and was now the grand inquisitor of English television. She launched into a brief and pithy introduction in her distinctive Scottish burr.

"Good evening. Welcome to this BBC Special Debate on the great issue of our day, the future of our euthanasia laws. It is an issue which has divided the country, which has divided generations and which has divided families. And, of course, it is an issue which has divided the Government. And that division is what we are going to explore tonight in what is the first head to head debate on this issue between the two people leading the two factions within the ruling English Conservatives. They are, of course, the Prime Minister, Edward Watson, who supports the status quo and the Business Secretary, Evie Smith, whom many regard as the de facto Leader of the Opposition. She, I know, rejects that title, but she is indisputably the voice and face of those wanting reform.

"Let me start with you, Evie Smith. You won a vote at your party's special conference last weekend to increase the termination age from ninety but without stipulating a new age. How can you expect people to support a reform of the law if you don't decide what age the law should be changed to?"

Edward was pleased that the spotlight was thrown first onto his opponent and also that Kuenssberg had gone for the jugular with her first question by focussing on what he believed was the central weakness in the reformers' case. Smith, though, looked completely unruffled and unsurprised by this line of attack.

"Well Laura," she started in her normal rather ingratiating tone. Edward was always particularly irritated by politicians who tried to sound over familiar with their interviewers by addressing them by name.

"It's really important to make it clear right at the outset that the Prime Minister and I actually agree on many aspects of the euthanasia issue. We all remember why our country took the decision it did back in 2035 to create a fixed lifespan and the arguments that were valid then are still valid now. Anyone over the age of thirty or so will remember the horrors of the Great Pandemic in 2020-21, but they will also remember the terrible price we all paid for the economic depression that followed it. And it was the young who suffered particularly as they picked up the bill…"

Kuenssberg was unlikely to allow Smith the opportunity to deliver an historical perspective and, as Edward expected, cut in sharply.

"Business Secretary, please spare us the history lesson and answer my question if you would. We all know how we got here but the issue now is this. If you want us to increase the termination age, what age are you proposing?"

"Forgive me, Laura, I'm coming to that but I do think it's important to understand that this is not an argument between those in favour of compulsory euthanasia and those against it. This is an argument about what age is appropriate for termination to take place."

"OK – what age then?" interjected Kuenssberg sounding slightly irritated.

"As I was about to explain," responded Evie still maintaining her air of unflappability but this time refraining from namechecking her interviewer, "we believe the correct way of determining the age is to convene a Citizens' Assembly to come up with a recommendation about that. As you know, this course of action has been used on a number of occasions very successfully in recent years about various tricky issues – climate targets, closing airports, pension reform, for example. And we feel this is what should happen here rather than the Government stipulating at this stage what the age should be. The important thing is agreeing the principle that ninety is too young and then, as a nation, we can take time to work out what the new age should be."

Edward listened to this familiar line of reasoning and was formulating a riposte in his mind expecting Kuenssberg to turn to him for a response but he, and clearly also his opponent, were both rather taken aback by where the debate went next.

"Come off it, Business Secretary," challenged the BBC's first-choice political interviewer, still on top of her game even after all these years in the limelight. "The precise age limit is a bit of a red herring, isn't it? Your real objective is to get rid of compulsory termination altogether, isn't it? But you're frightened to say that because of the League of Youth and losing the young people's vote?"

Edward noticed a slight hesitation in Smith's response. Clearly, she hadn't been expecting this, well, certainly not at this stage.

"What on earth gave you that idea, Laura?" she replied sounding slightly breathless and also giving a very clear impression of playing for time.

Edward, rather than enjoying his opponent's discomfort, found himself wandering in thought. He found it very difficult to banish from his mind the fact that he had always admired Kuenssberg's style and that he always looked forward to being interviewed by her. He also found himself thinking how much easier being the interviewer was than the interviewee. After a few dangerous seconds, he was brought back to the matter in hand by the rapidly escalating tension of the exchange between Smith and Kuenssberg.

"I have a tweet here that you sent in 2038 in which you said, and I quote, euthanasia at ninety was a necessary political response to a particular set of circumstances but morally, in the long-term, we will never be able to justify it." For effect, Kuenssberg repeated the words which she clearly felt undermined Evie Smith's position rather fundamentally.

"Euthanasia at ninety was a necessary political response to a particular set of circumstances but morally, in the long-term, we will never be able to justify it."

Kuenssberg leant forward, fixing her gaze on Smith and

waited for an answer which was only forthcoming after a longer than ideal pause from the Business Secretary's point of view.

"Well, I don't recall that particular tweet…," she began unconvincingly.

"The 21st October 2038, from your MP account, that's when it was sent," offered Kuenssberg.

"I'm not disputing that I sent it, Laura, but context is everything. I don't recall the precise circumstances in which I sent it but I'm pretty sure it was at the point when people were calling for a repeal of the remainder clause. The idea that we might cull vast numbers of over nineties with a retrospective change to the law was quite repellent to me and I think to most reasonable people. But that's not the issue now. The issue now is whether or not the state should put its own citizens to death at the arbitrary age of ninety irrespective of their health or other circumstances. That's the question we need to address and I would be very interested to hear what the Prime Minister has to say on that point."

Edward of course realised that Evie's invitation was not an act of generosity designed to ensure equal airtime but an attempt to turn the spotlight away from herself, albeit temporarily. But Kuenssberg was having none of it.

"We will hear from the PM shortly, of course, but I just want to pursue this a tiny bit further with you, Business Secretary. I have asked you two important questions and you've failed to answer either of them so I'll have one more go. What's the new termination age you're proposing or are you really saying – scrap the whole euthanasia law completely?"

Edward quickly reminded himself that Kuenssberg would have plenty of ammunition to throw in his direction shortly so any schadenfreude was misplaced. After what seemed an eternity, but was in fact just a couple of seconds, Evie responded.

"I appreciate you're only doing your job, Laura, but I'm not going to be bullied into answering hypothetical and irrelevant questions. For such an experienced and consummate interviewer as yourself, I am surprised that you appear to have failed to grasp some of the basic issues of this debate."

This line of attack surprised Edward who knew that questioning the integrity or intelligence of such a popular and respected interviewer as Kuenssberg would not go down well with viewers. Evie persisted.

"No one is suggesting at this time that the idea of a fixed lifespan should be abandoned. We have moved on as a society from our outdated views of twenty or thirty years ago when prolonging life at all costs got us into terrible trouble – a wrecked economy and a collapsed care system. I think you're being mischievous in suggesting that this is my plan because it isn't. And, with respect, I think I have already answered the other point. A citizen's assembly taking evidence from a range of experts will recommend what age above ninety is appropriate. What we are trying to achieve here is an end to the state killing perfectly healthy citizens just because they're ninety. However, at the same time we want to keep all the benefits to society and to individuals of a set lifespan. I really can't see anything that controversial about this approach."

Emboldened by Smith's discomfort, Edward hoped that Kuenssberg would turn to him now. In fact he had momentarily considered interrupting anyway but he didn't need to.

"Prime Minister, there we are, a perfectly sensible reform of the law that will achieve the best of both worlds. That's the view of the Business Secretary and indeed, since your special conference, the view of your Party. Why are you standing in the way of this?"

"I'm not standing in the way of anything. I'm just trying

to make sure that we don't rush headlong into reform without proper consideration of all the issues and I'm grateful for the chance to set them out today. But first, I do have to follow up what Evie has said just a moment ago in answer to your question about raising the age limit. Citizens' Assemblies have their place but it would be a complete abrogation of leadership for the Government not to make a specific proposal on a new age limit. So let's hear the Business Secretary give us her own personal view on what would be a suitable new age limit. She must have thought about it. She must have an idea. She can't seriously expect us to believe that she's never discussed it with others. So come on Evie. What's it to be – ninety-five, 100, ninety-two and a half, ninety-seven and three quarters? Or perhaps the real answer is that you don't want a specific universal age for everyone but different ages for different people depending on their health. Or, as Laura has suggested, no age limit at all. Come on, tell us?"

Edward surprised himself with the confidence with which he had just delivered an uncharacteristically direct attack on his opponent. The suggestion of a smile showed itself on Laura Kuenssberg's lips. But, for Evie, this was like a red rag to a bull.

"Now, Edward, OK, let's get real about this. The only reason you ever supported the introduction of euthanasia laws and the only reason you support them now is because you fear, you not me, Edward, you fear the political consequences of upsetting the League of Youth. You would never have got into power without them. You wouldn't have stayed in power without them. You have appeased them. You have given into them. And you've listened to those false prophets, some of them claiming to be religious leaders, who've somehow forgotten some of the principles on which Western civilisation has been built. All people are created equal. Everyone counts irrespective of race, irrespective of faith, and most importantly of all, irrespective of age. You've allowed yourself to be convinced that somehow bringing life to an end at a point the state decides is enough is OK. Hitler would have been proud of you."

Smith was on a roll. She was hardly pausing for breath so Edward couldn't interject. Kuenssberg was happy to let the two run the show for now. Evie continued.

"But it's worse than that, Prime Minister. What many of your fellow citizens don't know is that you are a hypocrite. At the very same time that you are telling us that we must all die at ninety even if we are perfectly fit, contributing to society and still enjoying life, you are pursuing a completely different approach when it comes to your own family. Your own father, in his late eighties, wants to die apparently, which of course he is perfectly entitled to do voluntarily if his immediate family consents. As I understand it, you are blocking his wishes and refusing to sign the papers. So it feels to me that many people will look at that and say – one law for you and another for everyone else. Euthanasia at ninety for everyone but not for your own father. OK, he's not yet ninety but what this shows to me is that you don't really believe in compulsory euthanasia or indeed any euthanasia. You know in your heart of hearts that it's immoral and unnatural. You often talk about certainty, about control. Well life isn't meant to be like that all the time. Uncertainty and unpredictability and fear and pain are part of what life is about. They provide the spur to action that keeps humans going. Yes, we're right to try to make life decent and comfortable for our people but we are wrong to pretend that we can eliminate all the bad bits of life. And anyway, who are we to judge what are the bad bits? Out of adversity comes strength. Out of challenge comes resolve and ingenuity. Out of fear comes love. If we leave our law as it is, history will look back and condemn this country."

Edward hadn't expected this. The situation with the Prime Minister's father was one of those open Westminster secrets that political journalists had kept out of the public domain. It was widely known in the corridors of power but talking about it in public or publishing or broadcasting it was regarded as a breach of confidentiality, even in 2040s England.

"I am not prepared to discuss the private medical details of a member of my family on national television, Evie and I hope, Laura, that you would support me on that. I would never dream of revealing anything of such a private nature about you and I'm shocked and surprised that you have stooped so low today. But let's move on and let me address your other points.

"It really is very clear in my view. We seem to be in danger of ignoring several things that this country has learned the hard way over the last twenty or so years. First of all, it's not the League of Youth alone that has led us to the realisation that the value of life should be measured not by its length but by its quality. Of course, no one wants to see lives cut short at a young age but we have done much to reduce that possibility through technology. Medicine can repair most things now and things that killed people in the past, road accidents, other accidents, are much, much reduced. But what we haven't done is to eliminate the degradation that so often accompanies old age. Dementia and other conditions are still rife.

"Despite our efforts in the past, we can't afford to throw unlimited resources at caring for the old when the young have to suffer in an unacceptable way. Schools and universities shutting, job prospects very limited, and taxes rising on the young working population while the older baby boomers live in comparative luxury. This isn't just a question of politics, it's a moral issue. And what has happened over the past generation is that the majority of people, including the old, have come to accept that actually it's fairer if life is fixed. Also, they agree that it's actually better to live a good life but to die before it all starts falling apart. And, in fact, the certainty given to all of us in knowing when we will die brings clarity and a sense of calm."

Edward stopped. Evie looked straight at him. Kuenssberg allowed the significance of the last exchanges to sink in.

"OK. I think it's clear that we have two very clearly opposed views here – maintain the status quo or abolish the termination law. Neither the Prime Minister nor the Business Secretary have said this in so few words but I'm sure everyone watching will draw their own conclusions."

As ever, thought Edward, Kuenssberg had summed up the situation very accurately. This was a watershed moment and, in a way, although there was still a further forty-five minutes scheduled for the programme, nothing else could be said that would illuminate the issue any further. The debate continued and Laura Kuenssberg led them through other aspects of the issue. Evie and Edward were very polite and respectful of each other. Audience questions came in via video link but somehow, Edward knew, that there was now no turning back. The course was set.

PART TWO

CHAPTER THIRTEEN

Hunstanton, Norfolk.
Friday 17 November 2045

Once the call had come in, Wilfred and Eversley had known they needed to move quickly. Wilfred had to admit that they could not go on wandering around the country without a plan. He knew that they had probably been lucky so far, particularly with his impromptu concert in Harrogate in front of quite a few people. He had even thought that the young man high up on the rocks at Brimham Rocks could have been suspicious. But too much speculation wasn't helpful. What was helpful was that he felt that he and Eversley were now on a genuinely shared mission. It was a mission designed to build their relationship and to allow his creative work to be completed. Most importantly for Wilfred, he believed that his son now appreciated and understood just how important this last piece of music was.

However, to realise their objective, they were now having to make their way in the early morning chill along a deserted stretch of the Norfolk coast to meet the people who had promised to spirit them away to safety. After the failure of their Scottish escape plan, Wilfred was convinced that Eversley's I-COM was compromised. His son disagreed, arguing that they could have been betrayed by someone in the resistance group.

"I'm dealing with a different group of people here. It's going to be fine. And this is a much easier means of escape," insisted Eversley.

"I'd love to believe that," answered Wilfred "But somehow this all seems pretty risky to me."

Pulling his battered overcoat tighter around him, Wilfred

struggled to keep up with his son as they walked along a country lane after leaving their driverless in a remote carpark the evening before and staying overnight in a run-down pub not far from Sandringham. Wilfred had thought the whole arrangement extremely foolhardy. They'd arrived late after driving from Yorkshire, had to have somewhere to sleep before the planned early morning rendezvous and Eversley had overridden his protestations. The publican didn't blink an eyelid when they walked in but, as with the taxi driver in Northumberland, the tip may have helped.

Having survived the night, Wilfred was now full of foreboding about the hours ahead. He was cold. It couldn't be much above freezing, having been over 20C only the day before. Wilfred had found him a woolly hat from deep in his backpack and he had gloves and proper walking boots but he could still feel the chill cutting into him. He was in considerably more pain than even just a few days ago, something he wouldn't admit to his son. The replacement knees and hips he'd had a few years before at considerable cost didn't seem to have done the trick and, worst of all, even fairly moderate walking now made him feel breathless very quickly. He probably should have consulted a doctor some time ago, particularly about the breathlessness but he didn't really want to know exactly what was wrong with him. And he was determined to underplay his ailments to his son and anyone else. On top of all this, he was now genuinely frightened about what lay ahead. The fact that Eversley had produced a previously hidden handgun from his bag heightened rather than lowered Wilfred's concern.

"I'm not happy about you with that gun," protested Wilfred once again, as they trudged along the lane in the pitch black, having crept out of the pub before six in the morning. "How did you get it?"

"Don't ask Dad, you don't need to know. We just need it to make sure everything goes alright, Dad. Stop worrying."

Wilfred remained unconvinced but Eversley went through the plan, as he had several times during their drive the previous day.

"We get to the beginning of the sand dunes. We follow the left-hand path onto the dunes and when we get to where the dunes open out onto the beach, we wait. They'll be looking out for us and we'll call and use the codewords. It's a well-tried and tested arrangement. Hundreds of people have got into Hunstanton this way. It'll work."

After a further fifteen or so minutes, and with the first glimpses of daylight emerging, they reached the end of the road. Concrete bollards to prevent vehicles getting onto the beach and faded signs warning of the dangers of swimming were all that greeted them. The only sound Wilfred could hear was the gentle lapping of the sea away in the distance at what must be low tide.

He had rarely felt more in need of a rest and slumped against one of the bollards causing Eversley momentary alarm. The younger man offered his arm and helped Wilfred onto the sandy path which was cradled between the looming dunes.

"Right, Dad, this is where we need to wait. Not a sound please. Not even your music."

Wilfred, who was glad of the chance to take the weight of his legs, willingly complied.

Although no sound emanated from his son, Wilfred knew that Eversley would be calling up his contact on his I-COM. He hoped it would work. He even found himself praying that it would work. It was many years since he had done that. He had thought that he had left God behind a long time ago after he'd fallen out with the elders of the church he had attended. But now, in an hour of need, frightened and cold on a lonely beach, he seemed to be welcoming God back.

After a couple of minutes Eversley half turned his head and, without saying a word, gave his father a thumbs up sign followed by a finger to the lips to remind him of the need to keep quiet. Eversley appeared to be checking things in his pockets. He slipped off his backpack and readjusted the contents. Then he took up his gun, started moving forward, indicating to Wilfred to do the same. Wilfred could hardly move, frozen by the cold, by pain and by fear. He was shivering and his teeth were starting to chatter. He actively thought to himself that he had probably never felt as frightened at any previous point in his eighty-nine years as he did at this moment. But he felt compelled to follow his son and he edged forward crouching low, almost crawling in the sand rather than walking.

Twenty metres or so further forward, Eversley paused. Even though the sand dunes must still be providing some cover, Wilfred felt exposed. He was convinced that they must look like two conspicuous ants on a clear, light-coloured floor just waiting to be squashed. Wilfred watched as Eversley moved forward again, this time passing the last real dune and almost sliding down a gentle sandy slope to the expanse of firmer beach below. He knew it was his turn to do likewise. Everything was telling him it was unwise. They would be seen, captured, and it would all be over. But something, his love of music, his love of his son, propelled him awkwardly down the slope. He landed next to Eversley but he couldn't help let out a muffled cry as a sharp pain shot through his ankle. Eversley almost smothered him as if to drown out the noise which had reverberated around the vast beach whose pools of water were now glinting in the early morning sunshine. Then, out of the nothingness, a voice.

"We can see you. Look to your left at about 10 o'clock

and we're near the edge of the dune."

Wilfred froze. Eversley shot his hand into his pocket to try to locate his hand-held. Wilfred realised his son must have inadvertently left it turned on so the message had come through there rather than to his I-COM. Then, just as Eversley was turning his gaze in the suggested direction and tapping his father on his shoulder to do the same, the shot rang out, shattering the misleading tranquillity of the morning. It was a gunshot like no other that Wilfred had ever heard. It felt quite close and both men instinctively dropped fully to the ground, burying themselves as tight to the sand as possible. Wilfred expected more shots but none came. Not a word was spoken between them. Wilfred assumed that they were now in a stand-off. Once again they must have been duped. Wilfred imagined that the NARA agent who'd fired the shot would not be in any hurry and would simply wait until fear, desperation or even boredom forced the two to break cover.

Wilfred and Eversley remained rooted to the ground for several minutes. Beating a retreat into the dunes didn't seem an option to Wilfred and he imagined his son would be thinking the same. A moment later, the decision was made for them. Wilfred could hear voices not that far away, maybe fifty metres from them, in a direction consistent with the I-COM message and then he saw them. Two men were walking slowly but almost upright towards them. They didn't look like NARA agents or police. In an instant Wilfred's brain processed the information in front of him, concluded these were friends not foes and clambered up onto his knees which sunk down into the sodden sand.

"Here. We're here," he called out before Eversley grabbed his father issuing an angry rebuke at the same time.

"Stop it Dad, stop it."

Wilfred, cowed and shaken, froze again and watched as

Eversley took his gun from his pockets, aimed in the direction of the two men and fired. First, a single shot. Then a second. Wilfred tried to shout but no sound came out. But, summoning a strength he didn't know he had, he managed to pull Eversley towards him, down onto the sand where the gun slipped from Eversley's grip and lay harmlessly next to them.

"Don't be so stupid, Eversley."

Wilfred realised his son was sobbing, but his attention quickly changed to the two figures advancing towards them with one of them pointing a gun directly at him. As he struggled to take in the situation, Wilfred instinctively put up his arms as the two figures pushed through the dune grasses and came to stand over them.

"He's right, your mate, you shouldn't be so stupid," uttered the man with the gun.

"You're assuming we're NARA agents. Perhaps that's understandable. But you know as well as us, that they rarely get up this early. We fired the shot just to make sure you were rooted to the spot for long enough for us to find you and check you. Do we look like NARA agents? A bit too old for a start?"

Wilfred realised that it was he who would need to respond. Eversley was completely still, staring straight ahead and clearly struggling to comprehend what was happening. He was about to say something but the younger man did his work for him and offered a single word, "Klopp."

It was now Wilfred's turn to be confused but the mention of the name of one of Liverpool Football Club's greatest-ever managers jolted Eversley from his trance.

"Paisley," whispered Eversley, a single word which elicited a weak suggestion of a smile from both the men stood over them. Wilfred could feel the tension dissipating.

"Right, I'm Tom and this is Jimmy and we need to get off this beach fast."

Tom swept up Eversley's gun from the sand while Jimmy helped Wilfred to his feet. The four men retraced the route through the dunes that Wilfred and Eversley had made a little earlier. Wilfred was still shivering but the pain in his feet and knees had lessened, albeit probably temporarily. Once they were off the sand, back at the end of the country lane which had led them from the pub, the small clandestine group stopped and drew breath.

Wilfred, mindful of the Scottish experience, was still not entirely convinced of the bona fides of their apparent rescuers. On the other hand, rather like a person given a break while being tortured during interrogation, he was just glad to be off the beach and apparently, for now at least, safe. Tom was clearly the leader of the rescue party.

"OK. Sorry about that little upset on the beach. It's just our way of double-checking things. Show me your ID cards please."

Wilfred and Eversley complied. Tom examined them closely and then handed them back.

"Right, we're going to need to get moving quickly now because our dear friends from the NARA will be starting work anytime and we don't want to run into them. Just do what we say and you'll be fine. In half an hour, you'll be tucked up in a nice warm flat away from prying eyes and all will be well. There's just one more formality before we set off. The money we discussed, would you be able to let us have that now?"

Wilfred had suggested to his son the previous day when they had talked about money, that it might be sensible not to pay everything in one go. Eversley had dismissed the idea as impractical. So, now when the request for 500 English was made, Eversley counted it out quickly and handed it over.

"We need to take this path, get back onto the beach at a different point and then it's a shortish trudge into the town away from any important roads. OK?"

The four set off in the direction indicated but, after less than five minutes, Wilfred was struggling. His pains had returned and he was still feeling chilled to the bone even though it was now almost fully light and sunshine was forcing its way through the clouds.

"My Dad can't go at this pace. We'll have to slow down," implored Eversley.

Wilfred was pleased when, after a brief chat between the two rescuers, Jimmy offered to carry his backpack for him and also produced an extra fleece jacket which Wilfred put on under his overcoat. They set off again and Wilfred was happy to see Tom look back every minute or so to check that he was OK. They reached the next way onto the beach quite quickly, cut through a thin gap between trees and soon they were among dunes again. It was hard going for Wilfred as the sand slipped away beneath him with every step he took but Jimmy offered him his arm at steeper sections. For the first time since they'd left Yorkshire, Wilfred felt a bit more relaxed.

He started assessing the two men as they walked. Both looked younger than ninety. Maybe they had themselves been smuggled into Hunstanton before? Or, more worryingly, was that they weren't rescuers at all but disguised NARA agents? Wilfred felt he had no choice but to assume the former. Tom looked very fit and a bit of a rogue, he suspected. Maybe it was his cockney accent but, fairly or unfairly, Wilfred had cast him as a man with a bit of a colourful history. He smiled a lot. Jimmy, on the other hand, looked rather gaunt and wiry and gave off the impression of being worried and put upon.

Wilfred was surprised to hear that Tom had responded to Eversley's probing questions about how the colony worked.

"The maintenance of law and order in remainder colonies is a complicated matter. There are security checkpoints on the two main approach roads. Rather like the Berlin Wall in the last century, they are partially successful in discouraging remainders from venturing outside their colony. The rules about this are complicated. Remainders aren't banned from leaving colonies but there's a list of permitted reasons - visiting family members, getting specialist medical treatment and other exceptional circumstances. However, enforcement is sporadic and somewhat arbitrary so remainders determined to venture out often can.

"But, in recent years, the emphasis of the police and Government has been more on stopping people who weren't registered to live in colonies from entering. We've been pretty good at smuggling in people in their late eighties. Every few months the NARA has a crackdown. Like many things in our country, these crackdowns are often a bit half-hearted and very short-lived and seem to be designed for PR purposes rather than genuine law enforcement. But, as you'll know, they have had some high-profile successes where people, sometimes just weeks or even days short of their ninetieth birthdays, have been caught trying to secrete themselves in here. Do you remember Sara Jones? She was caught, sent to prison for a week before being euthanized on her ninetieth birthday in gaol without her family around her."

Wilfred noticed approvingly that Tom was able to keep alert, looking from left to right and sometimes behind, as he delivered this summary of the state of the colony.

"What you probably also know is that some people here believe that the checkpoints are a good idea because they discourage the eighty-somethings from trying to get into the town. They reckon that the uneasy truce between Government and police on the one hand, and the remainders on the other, will be upset if their colonies became seen as safe havens for those trying to evade the 90 Law. But they're a minority."

After maybe twenty minutes on the beach, Wilfred was feeling just as bad as he had an hour or so before.

"I'm sorry but I need a rest."

"Sorry, Wilfred, but we need to keep moving. Here, have some chocolate. That'll help."

Wilfred, who never normally ate chocolate, gratefully accepted. They carried on, veering now off the beach and joining a grey residential street. This must be the real beginning of the town, thought Wilfred.

"Is this it? Are we here?" he asked.

"Yes, we're here. We've avoided the checkpoints but we still need to go a bit further."

Wilfred turned his collar up against the drizzle which had started while they were on the beach. It was now getting heavier. The chocolate had served only to remind him of his hunger. They were now on what a sign announced as 'South Beach Road'. It wasn't so cold now but the irritating rain was blowing into his face. To the left, large safety notices warned of the danger of erosion and collapse. Then, to the right, the largely abandoned remains of what looked like a holiday camp stood as an eerie testament to the original raison d'etre of the place. Wilfred could remember when this stretch of the Norfolk coast had been a place where people flocked for holidays or days out.

Wilfred's fascination with how the place had changed was enabling him to forget about his aches and pains. He realised that he was looking out across what was still called the Wash, once a clearly defined inlet but now largely indistinguishable from the North Sea whose rising levels had refashioned this and many other parts of the coastline. He had some vague memory that he might have come here on a summer holiday once as a child with his parents. For a brief moment, he remembered his parents, both long dead, and the memory of holidays with them now seemed unfathomably blissful.

Now, they must be getting nearer the centre of the town. The streets were getting busier. It was breakfast time. But there were lots of people about. In fact there were far more people about than you would expect at this time of day, particularly in a remainder colony. And then he realised. Far more shocking than the impact of the physical changes to the coastline, the people walking past him were not like people he saw from day to day in the regular world. Many were shuffling. Many had walking frames. Many were sat on benches or under shelters out of the rain. Nearly all seemed to be out on their own. But more than a few who passed nearby him were talking to themselves. Often incomprehensibly. A couple even tried to engage Wilfred and the others in conversation but he couldn't understand what they meant.

Suddenly, though, Wilfred was drawn back from his wonderings, as Tom stopped walking and pointed to a blue front door halfway along a terraced street.

"This is it. Let's go in."

CHAPTER FOURTEEN

Manchester Airport, Greater Manchester.
Friday 17 November 2045

It was rare for them to travel together and unusual for both to be opening something in the same area on the same day. But, in straitened times, even the security services thought it made sense for Prime Minister and Monarch to share a helicopter trip from London. Edward Watson wasn't enjoying the ride. He wasn't nervous about flying but he knew the King was, and the Royal fear created Prime Ministerial tension. Today was no different. Edward could see the King visibly sweating and repeatedly rubbing his hands as they circled above Manchester Airport waiting for permission to land. He distracted himself by looking out over the familiar landscape below. On a crisp dry morning, he could make out the sun glinting on the Trafford Centre, now much smaller in size than in its heyday. He could also get a bird's eye view of Old Trafford football ground, still regularly welcoming over 75,000 fans.

He would be happy to travel by drone but the security services had decided that their reliability was suspect and so old-fashioned helicopters were still used by those deemed high security risks. Now that there was only one runway at Manchester, there was often a queue of aircraft waiting to land. Carrying the two most powerful people in the country on board did not seem to confer any priority for landing slots.

"I'll be glad when we get down there. I can't be doing with all this circling," complained the King.

"It'll not be long, I'm sure," Edward replied, glad if he were truthful to witness the Royal discomfiture. Edward knew that the King had taken up yoga recently but it didn't appear to have helped him deal with the stress he evidently suffered every time he flew.

Little had been said between the two men during the flight which was a blessing for Edward who had expected a further tirade from the King about the 90 Law. However, he was deeply worried about what the day might bring. He suspected that the real reason the King had been particularly keen to accept the invitation to open the new extension to the RHS Bridgewater Garden had nothing to do with a love of horticulture. He doubted it was mere coincidence that the Garden was situated in the constituency of the Business Secretary, one Evie Smith. Monarch and the effective Opposition Leader would be together and he wouldn't be there to supervise them. He, meanwhile, would be opening a drone corridor, a politically more significant event, he thought, but he still felt he'd be missing the main action.

The helicopter landed at a remote corner of the airport. Edward hung back allowing the King to walk down the steps first. When he reached his waiting car, the Monarch turned, offering Edward a cheery wave.

"Have a good day, Prime Minister. I'll look forward to comparing notes with you on the return trip."

"Thank you, sir," was all Edward could manage before he walked across to his car.

Once inside, he pulled up his briefing notes on his mobile screen as I-COMs, like drones, were deemed too much of a security risk for the Prime Minister. As he studied the pages in front of him with only minimal attention, it dawned on him, not for the first time, that he must have had hundreds of days just like this in the decade since he entered Number Ten. He would have to whip round a series of engagements, making several speeches, meeting scores of people face to face and being seen in the flesh by thousands more.

What he never found out was what they all really thought of him. His opinion poll ratings went up and down but he'd stopped paying much interest to them. All he did know was that the King's approval ratings were still sky high, partly still no doubt due to the tragic circumstances of his accession to the throne. He felt a pang of jealousy but it soon passed. Part of him didn't care anymore. For the remainder of the short car journey, he did his best to complete his homework for all today's engagements even though he was distracted and his mind was elsewhere.

The next few hours passed in a bit of a blur although he did enjoy them. He was pretty confident that everyone he met would have no idea that he was wishing the day to pass quickly. There were cheering crowds as he performed the ribbon cutting of the opening of the M60 drone loop which now circled Greater Manchester. The drone corridor roughly followed the course of the orbital motorway which once circled the conurbation and sections of which had fallen into serious disrepair. Edward thought one local politician, whose speech had accused the Government of bias in favour of London by prioritising the refurbishment of the M25, had abused his position.

A visit to a mental health charity and a tour of the recently reopened Manchester Art Gallery followed. As he was being led away from the Gallery to his car, his private hand-held rang. He waited to get into the car before answering it. He immediately recognised the voice which launched straight in without any pleasantries.

"Good work, Edward. You have delivered on a promise. The Manchester drone corridor ahead of schedule. Excellent. We need more of that sort of thing. My friends in business aren't greedy but they do want to make sure they get their agreed benefits for helping you. So don't forget who your friends are, Edward."

There was a brief pause on the other end of the line but, before Edward could respond, the voice continued.

"Just a little titbit for you, Edward. Something you probably won't want to hear but I think you need to hear. We've had someone trailing your friend Evie Smith today at the Bridgewater Garden and she had a cosy little private chat with the King after the formalities were over. I've got it all on tape. Let me play you a little bit of it."

Edward could feel his heart beating faster as, after a short pause, a slightly muffled recording of the King came down the phone line.

"You've probably already realised that my real motive in taking you aside today is nothing to do with the RHS, interested though I am in it and in this wonderful place. What I am about to do is to go against one of the most hallowed principles of our constitution. We all know that the Monarch should not get involved in matters of political controversy. I've thought long and hard about whether I should do this. I've also agonised about how to engineer this meeting. You might be relieved to know that I abandoned some pretty madcap ideas, including getting you smuggled into Buckingham Palace in the boot of a car.

"I believe we are at a moment of grave national importance. The decisions we make as a country in the next week or so will determine the course of our history for many years to come. I have to confess that it's really only in the last couple of weeks that my opinion has firmed up about all this. But now I have no doubt that we have to make sure the law is changed and I'm sure it's my duty, not just my right, to intervene to get the Government to change its mind.

"In my view voluntary euthanasia, if properly regulated with appropriate safeguards, is the correct way to deal with this. People who wish to end their lives to avoid suffering should be allowed to do so, as indeed they are under the law, irrespective of their age. But condemning people to die at ninety irrespective of the state of their health and irrespective of their wishes can't be right. I think the truth is, that in the wake of all the problems of the twenties, the Great Pandemic, the economic collapse, the climate crisis, the care scandals, we allowed ourselves to be persuaded that inter-generational fairness and so-called dignity in old age justified the state in killing its own citizens at a predetermined age. We have to reverse that decision and I have come to believe that history would rightly judge me a very poor occupant of the throne if I had done nothing to try to make that happen."

The recording stopped. The voice came back on the line.

"There's more Edward."

The recording resumed.

"I have of course heard all the debates about 90, 92, 95, 100. But do you know, I'm increasingly of the view that the debate is not about what age. It should be about whether there is any age. I understand why you and others wanting a change are being a bit circumspect about this but actually, I think you would gain a lot of support if you called a spade a spade. In your heart of hearts, what do you really believe? I suspect that you don't really believe that a law requiring euthanasia at 92 or 95 or even 100 would somehow be morally justified whereas a law requiring termination at 90 isn't"

Edward was at the same time unsurprised but indignant.

"It's completely out of order. Completely out of order."

"Spot on, Edward. Spot on," came back the voice. "Stop him. Stop her. Stop them, Edward. That's your task. Goodbye."

As the line went dead, Edward slumped in his seat, his

head hanging down on his chest. His worst forebodings about the day had come true. He was jolted back to the immediate by the slowing of the car and the realisation that they were at the security gate at the private back entrance to the airport.

"Can we just pull up for a few minutes once we're through security before we go to the helicopter?" he asked his driver.

The Prime Minister, fearful that the King would already be on board the helicopter, felt he needed a few moments to compose himself. Should he confront the King? Should he confront Evie? His mind was a mess. He didn't know how best to deal with this. But, as he tried to compose himself, a car sped into the compound just in front of him and the King stepped out and strode confidently up the steps and into the helicopter. Edward knew he couldn't delay, got out of the car and walked across. As he climbed the short flight of steps, the image of his wife imploring him to hold firm came into his head. Once inside, he sat down quickly in his assigned place across the aisle from the King and fastened his seatbelt. Before he could open his mouth, the young King started what he knew would be a difficult conversation.

"Good afternoon, Prime Minister. How was your day?"

"Very good, thank you, Sir," replied Edward. "Both events went very well. Everyone seemed very pleased to see the drone corridor open. People were using it straight away, soon after my short opening flight. And the art gallery refurbishment is impressive. It's very pleasing when you can see for yourself the evidence of how decisions we take on high improve things on the ground."

"Yes indeed," noted the King slightly dismissively.

"And how was the RHS Garden?"

"Absolutely splendid. They've done a great job there. It's spectacular. Sounds more fun to me than a drone corridor, I have to admit. But then I don't think you're a great gardener, are you Edward?"

Edward was rather taken aback by this. He was very sensitive to the criticism he'd often received that he had no hinterland. In the popular imagination he was just a politician without any other interests, something which was often portrayed as a failing. He wondered if the King, consciously or sub-consciously, was feeding on this perceived weakness.

"I'd love to, Sir, but, as you'll appreciate, I don't have much spare time."

Edward, definitely feeling riled at this point, decided to go on the offensive.

"And was the Member of Parliament for Worsley in attendance at the RHS, Sir?"

"Indeed she was and what an impressive public servant she is, Edward. She made a great speech. Her constituents obviously love her to bits and we had a useful chat afterwards."

"I'm glad to hear it," responded Edward through gritted teeth.

"In fact, Edward, we had a very useful chat, Evie and I."

The noise of the helicopter blades starting to rotate cut across their conversation. The King paused but, once they were airborne, he resumed.

"I'm going to come straight to the point, Edward. I am increasingly of the view that one should say what one really thinks. I know you won't like it and you may well say that I'm well out of order. But I have decided I can't sit on my hands any longer. I have told Evie that I support her efforts to reform the 90 Law."

For just a few seconds, the only noise was that made by the helicopter which was now moving at speed southwards taking Monarch and Prime Minister back to the capital. Edward had to decide how to respond. Polite rebuke or angry denunciation. All his political instincts told him to choose the former. He chose the latter.

"Sir, there is no other way of putting this. I too will call a spade a spade. You are indeed well out of order. Never in my lifetime has the constitutional Monarch interfered in politics in the way that you appear to be doing now. Never has the Monarch tried to oppose the policy of the elected Government, a policy voted for in an election, a policy still with widespread public support. I know you mean well. I know you are looking for a meaning for your role. Your father and grandfather before you were very much the same. But they were wrong, just as you are wrong. The role of the Monarch is to be a ceremonial head of state. Yes, offering advice to the Government is fine and indeed welcomed. But this is way beyond that and is utterly unconstitutional. We have a constitutional crisis here. I don't know quite how we resolve this."

CHAPTER FIFTEEN

Bromley, Greater London
Monday 20 November 2045

"Come on Gran, it's time to go now. Let's find you a coat and some shoes. We are just packing a few things for you to take. But we've not a lot of time so we need to get moving"

Mary was slow to respond, and Holly could tell that she seemed confused as to who had disturbed her from her sleep. But she complied with Holly's instructions, got to her feet unsteadily and allowed herself to be guided across the room. Even though they were familiar, the abundance of instructional notices around her grandmother's home depressed Holly profoundly. 'Toilet', 'Cupboard with Plates', 'Remember to have lunch' rang out as insults to her former intelligence.

"Would it be a good idea to use the toilet before we go, Gran?" suggested Holly.

"Who are you? I don't remember you from before. Are you a new carer?" was Mary's unwanted but not unexpected response.

"It's Holly, Gran, your granddaughter. And Jake is here as well."

"Where's David, is he still here?"

"When was he here, Gran?" enquired Holly, feeling a little alarmed.

"Just now. He must still be here. He never said goodbye."

"I'm sure he will have done, Gran."

Holly guided her grandmother towards the bathroom. While she was there, Holly hurried to the bedroom and threw a random selection of clothes into the case they had brought for the purpose. It was difficult to know what to take. They weren't going on a holiday. They were taking Mary on a trip of indeterminate length and with an uncertain destination.

When Holly returned to the lounge, Jake was helping Mary into what Holly thought was a surprisingly well-chosen winter coat. He'd found her some shoes and was helping her with those. Holly noticed the death day clothes they had bought a few days before lying on a chair across the room. She shuddered at the thought that Mary might have been trying them on. She hoped that they would remain unworn.

"Now Mary," said Holly, "Jake and I are taking you away for a few days. It's all been arranged just to give you a special treat before you leave us. It's a bit of a surprise but we think you'll enjoy it. So, we can't be late. Are you good to go?"

Mary's confusion had reached a new level of intensity.

"I've just seen you on the TV, dear. You were very good."

It was now Holly's turn to be confused.

"It must have been someone else, Gran. Maybe someone who looks a bit like me?" suggested Holly as she ushered Mary towards the door.

Jake picked up the case and clothes and opened the door. Holly could see that he was still in some pain after his beating only a week ago. He was walking awkwardly.

They helped Mary into the driverless, selected a pre-programmed destination having muted the sound and the vehicle set off. It was almost ten o'clock at night.

"Why are we going by car? We normally go in the drone," asked Mary in a matter of fact way.

"We thought a car would be more comfortable in the dark, Mary. You can have a rest if you like. We've a little way to go. Why don't you try to get some sleep?"

But Mary didn't appear interested in sleep.

"It was definitely you, dear," persisted Mary. "It offends human rights. That's what you said."

Holly felt she couldn't simply ignore her grandmother.

"What offends human rights, Gran?"

"The 90 Law, of course. You said that it was an immoral law and that was why you were taking your grandmother away."

Holly glanced at Jake who was in what was still called the driver's seat as the driverless eased along Mary's driveway to the security barrier.

"I'm not following what you mean, Gran. Were you watching the news before we came?"

"Yes, it was about that court case, you know the one."

Holly had a flash of recognition. For a moment she thought that her grandmother might be having some curious premonition of what was happening to her – an elderly woman on the eve of her termination being spirited away. But she remembered the case that had been in the news a lot in recent days which bore an uncanny resemblance to the situation she and Jake were trying to bring about. Holly decided not to pursue the matter but she was pleased her grandmother seemed to have understood something she must have seen on the news.

"Gran, we're taking you away for a few days to have a little break before you leave us. We'll take good care of you. Do you understand what I'm saying?"

"Sounds lovely, dear."

Holly was thankful when Mary apparently accepted what she was told without further explanation. She was unprepared for what was about to follow.

"I was thinking about my job today. I loved my job. I probably spent too much time working when you were all young. But I couldn't help myself. There was so much to do."

Holly wondered why her grandmother sometimes had flashes of clear and vivid memory like this but could never work out what, if anything, sparked it.

"I'm so glad that you took me back to Herne Hill the other day. It was great to see everyone again. And just to be there in that part of London. That was where I was happiest, you know. I had a mission. I had purpose. It was all about helping people. Not just as a doctor but helping them sort out all sorts of other things in their lives. Do you remember that time when we organised all those Christmas food parcels? You helped. We stayed up half the night packing everything into boxes and then we took them round. I remember climbing up all those stairs in the high-rise blocks. On Christmas Eve, I think it must have been."

Holly couldn't actually remember distributing Christmas food parcels but she probably had been involved as a very young child. But she did remember her father talking about it. They were just one of many acts of altruism dreamt up by Mary when her son was young. She had apparently sold them as fun activities and he was expected to be a willing helper.

"People round there needed things," Mary continued. "They needed practical help but they also needed encouragement. They were tough times for many people in Southwark, in Lambeth, in those areas. London was often portrayed as a moneyed paradise, a great financial sector that powered the economy. Well, there was lots of poverty in the less fashionable parts. So, I had to do what I could."

Never before had Holly heard her grandmother being quite as lucid as this since she had been diagnosed with dementia several years previously.

"This is all very nice round here but there's not the same spirit as there is round there. It's a nice house and it was very good of you to help me organise everything when we moved out but my heart is still back in Peckham."

This was a theme that Mary had often dwelt on before

she became ill - the move to the leafy suburbs, as she used to describe it. Holly knew that she had never quite taken to living in outer London with, in her view, its suburban values and right of centre political leanings. This dislike had been masked when her husband had still been alive. Holly had always assumed that, in their years of retirement together, her grandparents had settled into a comfortable contentment. She had also believed that her grandmother had finally released herself from the need constantly to be trying to change the world. Now this illusion had been laid bare.

"Don't worry. I'm not going to ask you to move me back there," she said with a little chuckle, a chuckle she rarely heard from her these days.

"I'm quite content here now. You all look after me well. And I know what's going to happen soon and I'm ready for it. I know I railed against it in the past. I told you, and lots of other people, how wicked it was. But now that it's upon me, maybe it doesn't seem so terrible after all. I've had my time. I've done my bit. It's time to move on."

Holly wanted to contradict her grandmother but thought better of it. Maybe it was cowardly on her part but she decided that sleeping dogs were best left undisturbed for now. After a few minutes, Holly turned round and confirmed that Mary seemed to have fallen asleep. The driverless was just negotiating the turn onto the M25. Holly was comforted by the number of vehicles still on the road this late into the evening. For a while she and Jake sat in silence as the driverless headed anti-clockwise. The Queen Elizabeth Bridge loomed out of the night sky ahead. As they headed up to the bridge, Holly noticed the bricked-up entrance to the old tunnel which had once carried northbound traffic but which had long since been abandoned. Mary was still asleep. Holly was surfing the news sites, using her handheld. There was nothing of great note and she googled her father's company name, as she did from time to time.

"I knew it. He never talks about this sort of stuff and thinks it's none of our business."

"What are you on about?" asked Jake.

"Flying High, one of England's earliest drone hire companies, has been served a court order over unpaid debts thought to total over one million English," read Holly.

"A preliminary hearing has been set for December 10th," she continued.

Holly scanned the rest of the short article which also contained a photo, clearly from a few years ago, showing her father with a beaming smile in front of his first fleet of drones.

"It's much worse than he's ever let on. I knew it. That explains a lot, don't you think?" said Holly with a bitterness in her voice which even she recognised as uncharacteristic.

"Well, it doesn't take a genius to work out that Mary's money would come in quite handy."

"Don't say that," shot back Holly, knowing even as the words left her lips, that she didn't really believe them.

"It's true, and you know it."

A few minutes of silence followed. The driverless was cruising through the flatlands of Essex. Away to their right lay the abandoned remains of the Lakeside Shopping Centre. The discussions and arguments between Jake and Holly that had led them to this moment had been heated and sometimes acrimonious. Although Jake agreed that they should do something to try to save Mary, it was Holly who had developed a steely determination for the mission they had now begun. At first Jake had wanted to try to involve David and other relatives to try to come to some sort of family agreement. But Holly had been sure that her father in particular would never agree to it. She argued that they had to act alone and they had to act quickly, as the days were ticking down to Mary's death day.

"So, just remind me, what's our story?" piped up Jake.

"You know what we're doing. We are taking Mary for a few days surprise trip away just before she reaches her death day. A relative of ours has a cottage in Norfolk and she's said we can stay there for a few days. It's fine. Stop worrying about it."

Holly knew it was a story that might do for now and which contained an element of truth but it omitted a vital detail, that the cottage was inside the remainder colony of Hunstanton. Although she thought it unlikely, the police did put roadblocks even on motorways and had powers to stop anyone with the flimsiest of excuses. She didn't fancy having to explain why they were driving through the night with an eighty-nine-year-old relative in the back of their vehicle.

The first objection that Jake had made to Holly's plan had already been overcome. How and when would they be able to spirit Mary away from her house? They had the entry code to her estate and to her house as part of an emergency plan involving many family members. So, they could physically get in but how could they pick a safe time to go there undisturbed? David went every day but not at a set time and a succession of neighbours and other carers went in to check on Mary.

"We've already successfully completed stage one," Holly reminded Jake. "I estimated the time Dad might visit and we gave him half an hour's leeway and it worked."

Jake's second objection was more difficult to answer. How were they going to get into Hunstanton? Holly herself didn't have a definite answer to this fundamental component of the emerging plan. But she insisted that what they had to do above all was wrest Mary from the clutches of David and get her as far away from him as possible.

Holly knew that Jake's commitment to the plan was still not wholehearted and he was still suffering from the physical and mental impact of the vicious attack he'd suffered at the Oval only a week ago. But here they were in a hired driverless, late in the evening, heading towards Norfolk on a journey that would take them well into the night. They were on their way and they'd figure it out. Holly momentarily relaxed and emboldened by the darkness, put her hand on Jake's as he rested it unnecessarily on the steering wheel. A weak smile crossed his face. Holly leant across and kissed him briefly on the lips.

"Well I am still worried about it. It may be technically true but I seem to recall that last time I looked, kidnapping was a crime. And, anyway, what are we going to do even if we get into Hunstanton? We can't stay there forever. Mary's absence will be discovered in the morning and then we'll be on the most wanted list!"

Holly knew that Jake was right. They were breaking the law and she didn't know how this plan was going to end. She knew nevertheless that it was the right thing to do.

"Do you know? I'm still a supporter of the 90 Law in a way. What's humane about letting people go on and on, particularly if they've lost their mind like Gran? But I just can't see her go. Not her as well."

"I know. It's not really about her, is it? It's about someone else. It's about your Mum."

"How do you know?"

"I've always known."

"What do you mean?"

"You helped her die. You've never told me as such but I just knew."

Holly looked straight ahead. She knew that nothing else needed to be said. As she sat buried in her thoughts, Mary punctured the silence.

"So where are we going?"

CHAPTER SIXTEEN

Cambridgeshire Fens
Tuesday 21 November 2045

It had been a night she wouldn't forget in a hurry, one of the most uncomfortable of her life. Holly had wanted to keep travelling into the small hours believing that driving there in the middle of the night would be the best way of getting into Hunstanton. But she had been forced to give up on her plan partly by Jake's protestations and partly by Mary's repeated and urgent need for comfort breaks. In the end they had checked into a chain hotel at a service station on the M11, booked a double room and smuggled Mary in via a fire exit. Holly had lain awake most of what was left of the night sharing a double bed with her grandmother, listening to Jake tossing and turning trying to sleep on the floor. She had been expecting the police to knock on the door at any moment during the night tipped off by the suspicious all-night receptionist but nothing had happened.

Now they were on their way again, deliberately choosing minor roads where possible across the Cambridgeshire fens, closing in on their destination. The weather was foul. Even though it was a driverless, Holly still found it disconcerting not to be able to see out properly as the windscreen wipers struggled to keep pace with the lashing rain. They were probably about an hour from Hunstanton and Holly was still uncertain about when, or indeed whether, to make the call.

"We have to call Dad. He'll be beside himself and, for all we know, he'll have already alerted the police. We just need to make sure we calm him down."

"It's madness, Holly," argued Jake. "I think you're

overestimating your ability to have influence over your father. He's stubborn, determined and, ultimately, a very selfish man. He won't be up for being persuaded. Anyway, what are you going to tell him?"

Holly was conscious that she and Jake were now having conversations about Mary almost as though she wasn't there even though she was sat just behind them in the driverless

"We'll just reassure him that Gran is safe," Holly replied feebly.

They drove on for a few more miles in silence as the rain eased a little. Holly was finding it difficult to judge what her father's reaction would be. Previously, there had been a few occasions when her grandmother had wandered out of the house and had been found in the garden. Holly knew that, on one occasion, a neighbour had called him at three in the morning to tell him that his mother was lying in the back garden calling out his name. But the security system at the house meant that she could not realistically get out into the street. So, none of the family had ever been worried that she would escape and be in real danger.

However, she was pretty certain that her father would have narrowed down the suspects this time. He would have gone and done a search, established that his mother must have been taken from the house by someone and that it must almost certainly have been a member of the family. The only people who had access to the codes needed to get in were two neighbours and about ten members of the family. The only surprise was that he hadn't already rung her. But maybe, thought Holly, he was just playing it cool because he was certain who'd taken her. Holly turned round, suddenly aware again of her grandmother sat just behind her.

"How are you Gran?"

But there was no reply and Holly was momentarily alarmed.

Mary's head had slumped onto her chest and it looked like it was only the seatbelt that was preventing her from rolling right over. Instinctively, Holly shook her grandmother gently. It was probably only a couple of seconds before she stirred but it felt much longer. Within a few moments, Mary seemed to Holly to have dropped off again. She decided now was the moment.

"I'm going to call him."

Holly knew that Jake didn't want her to make the call but she also knew that, in the end, he would acquiesce. She might be much younger than him but she saw herself as the dominant partner.

"Use the hand-held so I can hear what he says," was Jake's only request.

Holly took her hand-held from the inside pocket of her coat and called her father. She knew he would wait a while before he answered so as to create the impression of nonchalance. He was true to form.

"Hello Holly, always nice to hear your voice," he shouted above what sounded like wind noise around him, trying to sound as though everything was normal.

Holly could tell straight away where he was.

"Dad, are you in the drone? You shouldn't take the call if you are. Call me back when you've landed."

"Wait, Holly, don't hang up. It's perfectly safe for a quick call. I'm at cruising height."

"Just quickly then," grateful that the circumstances would probably make this an easier call than if her father had been on firm ground.

"Look, this is just a brief call to let you know that Gran is safe. We have her with us and we are looking after her. You don't need to worry. I can't talk for long and don't try to track us down. She doesn't want to come back."

Holly had decided to make the call for a mixture of motives.

Partly out of a sense of duty to Mary's closest relative, but also a hope, maybe a forlorn one, that her father might be appeased, or might see her point of view. She was to be rudely disappointed. David's calm immediately evaporated.

"Holly, I absolutely will try to track you down. You have no right to kidnap your grandmother and I will report you to the police if you don't immediately tell me where you are."

Holly surprised herself with the anger she vented on her father.

"Don't be ridiculous, Dad, you won't report us to the police. You won't want the family name in the limelight will you? Might be a bit tricky if people started asking too many questions about some aspects of your business, mightn't it?'

"Don't you be so ridiculous. You've no idea what you're talking about. And my only concern is Gran's welfare. I am her closest relative and I have to be involved in decisions about her health and wellbeing as her nominated power of attorney."

"But you've never asked her what she wants, Dad, have you? I'm sure you love Gran but you've made a lot of assumptions on her behalf."

Holly was about to end the call but before she could do so, her ears were split by a thunderous noise down the line. She moved the hand-held away from her, tensing as she did so. She wanted to end the call to shut out the noise and to avoid alarming Mary but something made her not do so. The initial noise was followed by a series of other strange sounds.

"Dad, Dad, are you alright?" shouted Holly.

There was no response. Holly shouted again and much more loudly as their driverless continued along the country roads of East Anglia. Even Mary realised something was wrong.

"What's going on? What's the matter with David? Has something happened?"

Holly's repeated and increasingly anxious shouts elicited no response. All that she could hear was a rushing sound and then nothing. The call had been cut at the other end.

"What are we going to do? What are we going to do, Jake?" she screamed, as Jake overrode the driverless and brought it to a stop in the next lay-by.

"Calm down, Holly. It's probably just interference on the call because he's in his drone and it's happened before when we've spoken to him. I'm sure he'll call back"

"That wasn't interference, Jake, that was a collision or worse. I've never heard a sound like it. We need to call someone. We could call his PA – he might know where he was going."

Before Jake could formulate a response to this suggestion, Holly had answered her own question and was calling David's PA. There was no response. She left a message.

"Try calling your dad back," suggested Jake who didn't fancy making the call himself.

Holly called David but there was nothing. She tried several times more but still nothing.

"We must call the police. We need to do something," announced Holly, increasingly agitated and alarmed.

"Don't be stupid. We have no idea where David is. We don't know what if anything has happened to him. What are you going to say to the police? I'm in the middle of kidnapping my grandmother to try to evade the 90 Law and, by the way, I've just been cut off in a phone conversation with my father."

Holly rarely lost her temper with Jake. Usually, she employed cutting sarcasm or a tone of moral superiority to try to undermine him.

"I'm calling 999", she announced, throwing any sense of caution about their own position to the wind.

But just as she was about to initiate the call via her I-COM, an incoming call interrupted her. It was her father's PA who was unable to confirm what David's diary was for the day. He seemed more concerned to interrogate Holly about Mary's disappearance.

"Mary is fine but do you know where David was going today? I was just talking to him and I'm pretty certain he was in the drone and there was a terrible noise and then silence. We've called him back but nothing."

Holly, deciding that there was nothing to be gained by continuing the conversation, ended the call. Then the reality of what might have occurred hit her.

"Dad, Dad, No, No," she said between sobs unable to process what she clearly feared to be the death or very serious injury of her father, following several days of intense worry about her grandmother.

"Holly, calm down, calm down," said Jake forcefully. "We don't know anything yet. But do you know where he was going today? We can't ring 999 without some idea of roughly where he might be?"

"I don't know. I don't know. I do speak to him most days since Mum died but I don't ask him very often and he's always going all over the place. I'm going to ring 999 now."

Holly made the emergency call, offering only the scantiest details of what she feared might have happened to her father. The operator assured her that he would check with the emergency services in London to see if there had been any reports of drone crashes and call her back. Even though her emotional turmoil was playing havoc with her powers of reasoning, she had sufficient presence of mind to know that a call back would probably not be that quick.

Holly slumped back in her seat in the driverless. She rebuffed Jake's attempt to put his arm round her.

"Look, I'll call the police non-emergency line and get

their advice. I know it'll be the local police here but I'm sure they'll help. You look at the web and see if anything is coming up about drone crashes," he suggested in a conciliatory tone.

They both set about their tasks without further discussion. Jake had to reveal a certain amount of information about his location and why he was calling the East Midlands Police but he was promised a call back. Holly scoured the internet for a few moments but there was nothing. Mary, who had initially seemed to be aware in a general sense that something was amiss and that it involved David, had reverted to her more normal modus operandi and said nothing.

Just at that moment, Holly's I-COM rang and a man's voice, without any pleasantries or preamble, pronounced a single word. Even though she was still stressed and overwrought, Holly's brain eventually kicked in and recognised it as a codeword. Somehow, she managed to remember the necessary response which seemed to satisfy the man at the other end of the line.

"Holly, it's Tom. Everything OK?"

"Yes, we're on our way. I'm not quite sure how far away we are. Yes, sorry. We've had to stop. A bit of a problem but we're OK and we'll be on our way soon and should be with you in less than an hour, I reckon."

"OK, but we might have a bit of an issue at our end. There seems to be something kicking off here with the police and military. There's been lots of activity, particularly around the colony boundaries. So, stop near King's Lynn and wait for me to call you."

Holly knew that news would come in sooner or later about her father. There wasn't anything else they could do for now and their attention turned back to the question of how they were going to try to get into Hunstanton. Jake resumed the Satnav and the driverless pulled out of the layby and re-joined the modest flow of traffic heading towards King's Lynn.

Holly had made contact several days before with the 90+ Group who'd accepted her request for help to smuggle them in. But she'd been told to think up some cover stories about why they needed to visit Hunstanton, a task they had not yet completed. As the driverless propelled them closer to the need for a decision, she and Jake kept their thoughts to themselves. And they waited nervously for word to come in about David.

After about twenty minutes, they saw signs for services and spotted an American diner, a number of which still remained on England's arterial roads.

"Let's stop and get something to eat. I'm hungry and it doesn't look too busy. And it sounds like we might need to bide our time before they can get us into Hunstanton."

Holly was initially reluctant but Jake overrode the Satnav and her objections. They made their way into the diner, guiding Mary carefully across the carpark, ordered some food and went and found a table which Holly judged would be good for a private conversation. For the first five minutes or so, everyone concentrated on their meals. Even Mary seemed to have some sense that conversation needed to be conducted carefully. It was Jake who broke the silence.

"I'm worried about our cover stories. I don't see why they can't just smuggle us in. I know that's what often happens. I've heard stories about people being helped into Hunstanton via the sand dunes but what possible cover story could we have? What reason could any of us have for wanting to go to Hunstanton particularly in the company of an eighty-nine-year old?"

"We need to think laterally," came back Holly. "People quite often get in, I'm told, on compassionate grounds to see relatives. Also, people are allowed in for work reasons. Between us, we can surely come up with some plausible reasons why we need to get in? The problem, I think, is that it will be easier for us two to get in. I know it's risky, but I think that we should have Mary in the boot of our car when we enter. Yes, there might be searches and we could get discovered, but there's a decent chance that they won't bother to search. Don't forget, the police are often very half-hearted about enforcement and the political climate is changing so they are even less likely to be vigilant."

The suggestion that she might have to travel in the boot had obviously passed Mary by. Jake, on the other hand, was quick to jump in.

"We can't stuff your grandmother in the boot. That's inhuman and anyway, they're bound to search the car if we get stopped. And from what your contact told you, it sounds like we will be stopped. Maybe we need to lie low for a day or two?"

"We can't do that unless 90+ ask us to. Time is running out. We need to secrete Gran, come up with two good cover stories and brazen it out. And there's always the possibility of bribing the police if they start getting awkward."

Several minutes of discussion followed about the pros and cons of bribery as part of the emerging plan but it was agreed that it should only be a fall-back option. As Holly and Jake had got more into the detail of what they were planning, they had temporarily forgotten their anxiety about David. Holly momentarily allowed herself to believe that maybe she had misinterpreted the scary noise on the line when she was speaking to her father. But she couldn't stop herself scanning news feeds on her I-COM for any untoward news about drone crashes in London.

All of this meant they were becoming less aware of what was happening around them. The diner was getting busier but actually that helped mask their conversation. It also meant, though, that they were initially oblivious of what was unfolding on the news channel relayed on screens at the other end of the room.

"Do you think Mary will actually go in the boot?" whispered Jake to Holly.

"It'll not be easy but I think it's our best option."

"But we need our cover stories," Jake reminded Holly.

A further several minutes of dangerously animated conversation followed with Holly coming up with ideas which Jake attempted to ridicule. In the end, Holly succeeded in browbeating Jake into submission with a story which had the advantage of being largely true.

"We're visiting my Great Aunt who's poorly and who has no other living relatives. I haven't spoken to her in years but I have an address for her in Hunstanton and I'm sure she'd be happy to see us. But Gran can't be visible. She'll have to be hidden."

Holly could sense that Jake retained many misgivings about the plan but he didn't have a better one. The conspiratorial conversation subsided and both Holly and Jake tried to engage Mary in some small talk with only limited success. They took in the surroundings of the diner again. It was at this point that Jake registered what was being said on the news channel. The BBC were reporting from outside the Parliament building in London.

"Our understanding is that there will be a vote on the 90 Law in Parliament as early as next week. We don't yet know exactly what the proposal will be. But it's clear that the debate, which has been building with increasing intensity over the past few weeks and months, is going to come to a head very soon."

"That's it," said Holly. "This will make our chances of getting into the colony easier. The police won't be as bothered to stop people if they think the age is likely to be raised."

"I'm not so sure," added Jake. "It could have quite the opposite effect. They may be even more determined to keep the status quo."

They would know soon enough. They finished their drinks, returned to the driverless, and set off. They were already out of the diner before a travel alert flashed on the news channel reporting major holdups near Heathrow Airport after unconfirmed reports of an accident involving a drone.

CHAPTER SEVENTEEN

Hunstanton, Norfolk
Tuesday 21 November 2045

It was only four days since their clandestine arrival in Hunstanton but to Wilfred, it was a lifeline in more senses than one. It felt to him like a safe haven and it had provided him with time. Time to compose. Time to practise. Time to complete. The 'safe house' they had been taken to on the afternoon of their arrival was perfectly habitable but unloved and chilly. It gave off a smell which Wilfred couldn't quite identify but which he knew he disliked. But he didn't really bother about these practical things. For now he felt safe and he felt creative.

His son, on the other hand, wasn't at all relaxed. Wilfred could see that he was bothered by not knowing exactly what would happen next. Eversley would pace around the house eager to engage their minders in a discussion about the future beyond the next few days. He kept telling his father that he couldn't stay there forever. He needed to get back to his own family before too long. When Tom had brought them to the house the previous Friday, he had told them they must remain indoors for a few days. Their meals would be brought to them. They would be fine if they kept a low profile. Very soon, Tom would return with a definite plan for how Wilfred could stay permanently and safely in Hunstanton.

Neither the conditions nor the waiting bothered Wilfred. In fact, he felt more relaxed than at any time so far on their escape journey. As far as he was concerned, they had reached a destination. Apart from eating meals and dozing in a chair, he had spent the hours working on his piece. He had set himself up at the kitchen table, extracted the old-style written sheet music from his backpack and continued composing. He hummed the tunes, paced the room and occasionally used the meagre collection of cutlery from the kitchen cupboard to improvise.

On the fourth morning, the two men sat at the stained kitchen table having taken their 'Tuesday Breakfast' from the fridge. They sat eating it unenthusiastically. Eversley was watching a news channel through his I-COM. He reported what he heard to his father.

"It looks like the debate in Parliament about the termination age will be next week but it isn't at all clear what exactly they'll vote on, raising the age or abolishing the 90 Law altogether. And nobody seems to know what would happen if the vote went in favour of raising the age. Would it come into effect immediately or whether there would be a delay?"

Wilfred's response was his usual one to the news.

"It's all speculation, Eversley. That's the trouble with the news. Too much speculation. We'll just have to wait and see."

His son appeared still to be interested in what his I-COM was telling him as he picked at the last unappetising morsels of his breakfast. Wilfred got up, unnoticed by his son, and went back upstairs to his room. He had been wanting to do this ever since they arrived but he feared his son's reaction and even himself appreciated that it might be unwise. Something, though, made him throw caution to the wind. He went to his backpack, reached down inside the main compartment and carefully lifted out the black case. He undid the hinges and there it was - his pride and joy. He took it out, pressed it to his lips and started playing, quietly at first, but then more boldly.

He couldn't have been playing for more than thirty seconds before Eversley burst through the door.

"Dad, you can't do that. Stop. Stop. The whole street will

hear you."

But Wilfred carried on, pretending he hadn't heard him, and so engrossed in playing the saxophone which he'd been carrying in his backpack throughout their journey but which he hadn't until then unpacked. He expected Eversley to come over and stop him but his son just stood by the door speechless. He could see that his son had recognised it - the same distinctive melody which had filled the Royal Hall in Harrogate the previous week. But played on the saxophone, the principal instrument for which it was intended, Wilfred believed it was even more captivating. Somehow, any worries that their hideaway would be discovered melted into the background.

"I've just about finished it, Eversley," panted Wilfred breathlessly as he momentarily broke off from playing.

Then, after another thirty seconds or so of animated playing, he made a request.

"I need some other instruments and some other musicians so we can rehearse it properly."

"We'll have to see about that, Dad. But for now, we need to make sure you're safe somewhere."

Their conversation was interrupted by a series of firm knocks at the door. This was unusually early for the daily delivery of food. Even Wilfred felt anxious. He knew that many in the colony were unhappy with the smuggling operations which brought evaders into Hunstanton. His impromptu early morning recital could well have alerted nosey neighbours. Perhaps, he thought, they should just ignore the knocks. Eversley, though grabbed his weapon, went downstairs and whispered at the door.

"Who's this?" Wilfred could hear his son ask.

"It's Tom, please let me in," came the reply in the distinctive South London accent which reassured Wilfred.

Eversley unlocked the door and Tom slipped quickly into

the house. Noticing the gun, he joked,

"Please don't point that thing at me again."

Their conversation was interrupted by the sound of music floating gently down from upstairs.

"What a fantastic sound! I knew your father was a famous musician and he's obviously not lost his touch."

"Yes, you're right about that," replied Eversley. "He's still composing and he's determined to finish this piece whatever happens."

"Can you ask your father to come downstairs and then I can explain to both of you what's going to happen next?"

Eversley went upstairs where Wilfred was persuaded to break off from his music and come down to speak with Tom. Over the next few minutes, Tom outlined a plan, explaining how they would need to move to another house but one where Wilfred could stay indefinitely. There'd be other evaders there and there would be a monthly cost to pay. But there'd be daily support and proper security arrangements. The move could take place within a few days when everything was in place but, for now, they would need to be patient and stay put.

Wilfred listened with interest and then repeated his thanks to Tom for helping them get into the colony. He knew his son would have a list of questions but, thankfully, thought Wilfred, Tom changed the subject.

"So, you're still composing, I gather?"

"Yes, indeed and I'm nearly finished with this piece. But I need some help, Tom. You've already been very generous to us with your time. You've taken great risks on our behalf and I hesitate to ask you for anything else. But I would love the chance to try out this piece with a few other instruments. A piano, a violin, some drums. Do you think there might be some people here who would be interested in helping me out?"

"We have plenty of musicians here in the colony. And there

are people who're interested in just about every sort of music. I love the sax. I'm into jazz. I'm not so keen on old classical stuff. So, what would you call your music, then, Wilfred?"

For the best part of the next half hour the two men discussed music. Wilfred interspersed the chat with snippets on the saxophone from the songs and other pieces that Tom particularly liked. Eversley sat in the background, hardly getting involved but his body language continued to radiate anxiety. Wilfred, on the other hand, wanted to find out more about the man who was happy to help them.

"So what's your story, Tom, if you don't mind me asking? I sort of feel I recognise you."

"Nothing like as interesting as yours, Wilfred, I'm afraid. But you might have seen me on the telly. 'Gangland boss gone straight,' was what they used to call me. I was a bit of a bad boy in my younger days. A few spells inside. But I gave all that up years ago. I did a degree in criminology and got involved helping youngsters keep on the straight and narrow. Some people here seem to treat me like some sort of angel. Others think I'm still a crook. But I suppose it's part of the reason I do this sort of stuff, helping people like you. Giving something back, I suppose, is what people would call it."

After a while, Tom brought the discussion to an end, promised to do what he could to facilitate the premiere of Wilfred's piece and started to bid his farewells. Wilfred was pleased to hear his parting shot.

"Look, don't worry so much, Eversley. It'll all be fine. We'll keep your father safe. And we'll get you back home to your family before long. And, by the way, if you want to nip out with your father to get some fresh air, that should be fine if you stick round these few streets. But perhaps try to keep the sax playing restricted to the daylight hours and maybe keep the volume down a bit, if that's possible!"

He made to leave but, as he did so, Wilfred called out,
"Tom, can I detain you for just a few more minutes? Let
me play you the overture. It's only a few minutes."

Tom answered by taking a chair again and, with Eversley
still standing and still looking agitated, Wilfred took his sheet
music, prepared the saxophone and began. For the next three
and a half minutes the eighty-nine-year old worked his way
through bar after bar, with a stumble here and there, but he
was pleased to see that both members of his audience were
transfixed.

When Wilfred finished, Tom broke into a round of applause
and then said simply,

"It's beautiful."

He headed for the door and let himself out leaving father
and son sat in silence for a few moments. Then Eversley,
reassured by Tom's words a few moments earlier, made a
suggestion.

"Dad, I think it'll be OK if we take a short walk. The
seafront is only a couple of streets away so how do you fancy
a quick stroll? It's raining but I think it'll do us both good
to get out."

Twenty minutes later, they were locking the door and
turning along the terraced street to the sound of seagulls flying
overhead. The wind had dropped and the rain had turned to
drizzle. As they turned a corner, they could see the sea ahead
in the distance and Wilfred felt a pang of contentment. It
was partly nostalgia. The smells and sounds of the sea were
a pleasant reminder of trips to the coast as a child and his
seaside holidays with Eversley and his mother from their
Manchester home, usually Morecambe, sometimes North
Wales. But it was also because, for the first time since they
had set out on this escape plan, he felt that success was now
within their grasp.

Just then, though, his attention, was caught by the sight of a hunched figure, a woman walking very slowly along the street towards them. She was wearing a threadbare coat and scuffed shoes and she was making painfully slow progress with the help of an old-style Zimmer frame. With every step she took, it looked like she might topple over.

"She looks very frail," observed Wilfred and, without waiting for Eversley's reply, he walked over to the woman and offered his arm to steady her.

Eversley tried to discourage him but Wilfred waved him away.

"Thanks very much. That's very kind of you," remarked the woman, as the two elderly people continued along the street together with the younger man observing the spectacle from a few paces behind.

"The weather's improved, so I thought I'd get out for a quick stroll," continued the woman.

Wilfred was thinking that this woman must be about the frailest person he had ever encountered and he was wondering to himself just how old she was. In the normal world, of course, you didn't see people like this anymore.

"How long have you been in Hunstanton?" he asked.

"Too long," she replied quickly. "I was 101 when the 90 Law came in. So, I was sent here. At first, I thought it was the right thing. But now I'm 111. 111, can you imagine that? I can still walk. I reckon my heart is still working fine. But I can't remember things. I get confused."

"We all do sometimes," offered Wilfred sympathetically.

"And do you know, it's not worth it," continued the woman. "I keep going but I don't know why. If I lived in the real world and not in this place, I could go for VE. But you can't get it here. We're condemned to a life seemingly without end and for what purpose?"

The woman had stopped to deliver this homily. Wilfred stood next to her, transfixed by her speech. He wanted to offer words of reassurance and of hope but he couldn't. Instead, he exchanged a few pleasantries, wished her well and she continued on her way. Wilfred re-joined his son and the two men walked to the seafront where they sat on a bench looking out to sea.

CHAPTER EIGHTEEN

Hunstanton, Norfolk
Tuesday 21 November, 2045

The torrential rain of the morning had given way to weak sunshine as Holly, Jake and Mary reached the King's Lynn ring road. Holly was now driving using manual override because she was looking for a suitable place to stop. Most vehicles would only allow override for five-minute stretches because, as Holly knew, the accident statistics showed that machines were much more reliable than humans when it came to driving safely.

They'd agreed to stop just beyond King's Lynn to await further instructions from Tom and also to transfer Mary into the boot of their vehicle. As they rounded King's Lynn, Holly and Jake were disagreeing about how to achieve this.

"We have to talk to her and explain why we're doing it," argued Jake. "If we don't, she'll probably make a right old racket in there and give the game away if we get stopped."

"I think she's less likely to make a fuss if we just stop, guide her out of the car and put her in without a great big preamble," retorted Holly.

The issue remained unresolved as they edged their way onwards, unable to identify a suitably discreet stopping place. A strange mixture of apprehension and excitement was gripping Holly. Apprehension about what had happened to her father but a rather disconcerting sense of nervous excitement about what might lie in front of them just a few miles ahead.

Holly's anxieties about getting into the remainder colony had now been largely replaced by a quiet determination. She was also being carried along by her belief that the fast-moving political developments were going to work in their favour. It was unlikely, she thought, that anyone would be too bothered about a few people coming into Hunstanton given what was going on in the wider world. She tried her father's number several more times and his PA's but without any response from either.

Holly was enjoying a moment of displacement from her pressing concerns, admiring the sun glinting off the sea away to their left. First, she heard the noise. It was a noise rarely heard these days. And then she saw it. A military helicopter sped through her field of vision visible for a just a few seconds before it disappeared behind them and away to the south. Jake seemed sure of the significance of what they'd just witnessed.

"That must be a senior politician or royalty. They're pretty much the only people using those things now. Interesting. I wonder who's being taking a look at little old Hunstanton. Excuse the pun, but no one in power normally wants to be seen dead within a hundred miles of the place, do they?"

Holly offered no response to this rhetorical question. She used the manual override again to slow the driverless and bring it to a stop in a parking area. The lay-by looked like it had been created by using the former course of the road before it had been straightened out and widened. Helpfully, there was a thick line of evergreen trees between the parking area and the road. It felt like as good a place as any for doing the planned transfer to the boot. However, until they heard from Tom, there was nothing they could do.

"Can't we call him?" asked Jake as they sat in the lay-by in the gathering gloom of the afternoon.

"No, I don't have a number for him, only for the original 90+ contact. We'll just have to wait," replied Holly whose mind was swinging wildly between the logistics of their mission to save her grandmother and her concern for her father.

She kept scanning the news feeds and then suddenly let out a scream. She transferred her I-COM output to her hand-held and thrust it towards Jake.

"M25 still closed after drone crash near Heathrow," he read out disbelievingly.

"That's Dad. It must be Dad," shouted Holly. "We'll have to go back to London. Now Jake, we'll have to go."

"Don't be so hasty," objected Jake. "You're jumping to conclusions. That could be anyone's drone. There are thousands and thousands of them in London. Try your dad's number again."

"There's no need. I know. I just know it's him."

"No Holly. You don't know anything yet," responded Jake, resisting her attempts to start reprogramming the satnav.

However, the developing argument was brought to an abrupt end as a call came in on Holly's I-COM.

"It's Tom. Are you at King's Lynn?"

"Yes."

"Right. You need to move quickly. Have you got a cover story?"

Holly briefly explained their idea and Tom indicated approval before telling her that they should drive in on the main road. Then he gave them an agreed rendezvous point inside the colony.

He added a final comment, "Make sure only two of you are visible when you drive in."

With that he rang off without any pleasantries.

The call from Tom saved them from having to make a difficult choice – whether to continue with their mission or head back to London to discover David's fate. Without any further discussion, Holly started reprogramming the driverless. However, there were a couple of other cars parked further ahead. Jake, always the more cautious of the couple, suggested they should sit tight and wait before transferring Mary to the boot. Holly disagreed.

"We need to do it now. If we wait for them to leave, someone else will probably pull in. Let's just get on with it. Once we've got the hatchback up, no one will be able to see what we're doing."

She didn't wait for Jake's reply but got out of the driverless, pulled on her coat to protect against the chill that was now blowing off the sea, and opened the rear door.

"Gran, let's get a bit of fresh air before the last bit of the journey."

Mary complied without a word, getting out and allowing herself to be led across to a rather battered picnic table alongside the roadway. Jake also came across and joined them. Holly looked straight into her grandmother's eyes.

"Gran, we are nearly at Hunstanton. When we get there, you'll be safe and there will be people there who will help us look after you and make sure you can live for as long as you want. But just to make sure that we don't have any problems, we'll need to hide you from the police for the last bit of the journey. It'll only be for about ten minutes and then we'll be safe."

Without waiting for a response, Holly guided Mary firmly back towards the car instructing Jake to open the hatchback. She glanced around, and then helped Mary climb into the boot, something she accomplished without protest and with remarkable agility. They then helped her into a foetal position on the floor, reassured her that all would be well, pulled the boot cover across and shut the tailgate. Just as they did so, another vehicle sped into the rest area causing her momentary alarm. But it slowed to a stop well beyond them only for a man to get out and dash in obvious discomfort straight to the small toilet block.

A moment later Jake and Holly's driverless pulled slowly away to re-join the road for the last leg of the journey. But then they encountered an unexpected problem. The system told Holly that the rendezvous address she'd in-putted didn't exist. She tried several other addresses but all produced the same result. She remembered that she'd once read that many map apps had excluded colonies from their directories, pandering to the widely held view that these were places that didn't officially exist. There was no option but to go to manual override which she did and the vehicle then pulled away.

The road seemed quiet as they passed signs for Dersingham, Snettisham and then Heacham. Holly had to reselect manual override twice as it reached its time-limit. Now they were less than two miles from the beginning of Hunstanton. Jake and Holly sat in silence as they travelled ever closer to the decisive moment of their enterprise. She was relieved that there was no noise coming from the boot. Mary seemed to be acting exactly as they had hoped she would.

Then, in a flash, Holly's anxiety levels shot up as she spotted something on the rear view camera, coming towards them at speed from behind. She soon recognised it as a small convoy of police vehicles. She counted three regular cars and two unmarked vans bearing down on them. She was literally holding her breath as the convoy approached. But then, in a matter of seconds, it had overtaken them, showing no visible interest in their driverless.

"What was that all about?" said Jake, breathing out loudly in relief.

"Who knows, but there must be something interesting going on in Hunstanton," replied Holly.

Less than a minute later, as Holly was still looking ahead just to check that the police hadn't done a 360 degree turn, they were suddenly at the colony boundary. All that indicated this was a dirty and damaged 'Welcome to Hunstanton' sign, the legacy of an age when the seaside resort invited and encouraged as many visitors as possible. And there were a couple of Portacabins which appeared to have been put there to accommodate police who carried out roadside checks. Today, though, there was not a soul in sight. It reminded Holly of abandoned border posts she'd seen on her treks in Asia when she was younger.

Disbelievingly, she continued into Hunstanton passing bungalows which would once have been described as 'neat'. Now, more often than not, they sported peeled paint and, in many cases, boarded up windows and doors. There were very few vehicles moving on the roads but plenty of abandoned ones, often missing a wheel or two, parked at the kerbside or on driveways. Technically, it was illegal for remainders to drive but few, it seemed, wanted to.

All this meant that Holly and Jake's driverless seemed quite conspicuous. Holly's relief at getting into the colony unchallenged was being replaced by anxiety that they must surely be attracting attention. However, there was little alternative but to plough on to the agreed rendezvous in the town centre. Holly, still driving in override, was nevertheless going more slowly than normally in the belief that this would make this uninvited vehicle less obvious.

Her mind even allowed itself to wander from the stresses of their mission to observation of the surroundings. English towns in the 'real' world outside the colonies were in many cases depressing and unloved. But Holly found time amidst her anxiety to be shocked by what she was seeing of Hunstanton. It was clearly in a different class when it came to decay and dereliction. The roads were badly potholed. Hunched figures walked through the streets in drab clothing passing shops that looked distinctly uninviting. Badly produced notices advertised cheap products as litter blew along the pavements. Most houses looked like they'd not had any work done on them for many years. Even modest attempts at improvement seemed to have come to nothing, with half-built extensions or new blocks mothballed, awaiting an unlikely resumption of work.

However, this observation didn't last long as Holly had to concentrate again on finding the rendezvous point which she did a few minutes later.

"I reckon this is it," she announced.

She looked around. There was no sign of anyone there to meet them. Holly slowed the driverless and brought it to a standstill. They both sat in silence for several minutes. Holly became increasingly anxious as the moments ticked by. Jake suggested calling the original 90+ contact. Holly disagreed.

As the conversation continued back and forth without a firm conclusion, they were interrupted by a man heading in their direction unsteadily along the uneven pavement. Alcohol consumption had reduced dramatically over the past decade as a result of legal restrictions on sale, greater acknowledgement of the health risks and rising cost. Holly had read about the alcohol problem in remainder colonies where a blind eye had been turned to the illegal mini-breweries and illicit drinking houses. At first glance, it appeared the man bearing down on them might well have been frequenting one.

"I'm going to see the King. I'm going to see the King!" he bellowed to no one in particular as he wobbled down the street.

Holly made the mistake of catching his eyeline which served only as encouragement for his verbosity which was now directed at them through the window of the driverless.

"I never imagined I'd see the King in Hunstanton. Reckon he'll get those MPs to raise the age and maybe free the colonies."

With which, he raised a mock glass to the air, shouting, "God save the King!" as he tottered away down the road.

Jake consulted his I-COM, browsed the headlines which confirmed that the King was indeed expected to be making a surprise visit to Hunstanton.

"It's true. That explains the helicopter and that police convoy. This will change things, surely."

"Maybe it will," added Holly cautiously. "Perhaps it also explains why it feels weird here. We just drove in. We've been here almost half an hour and no one seems at all surprised to see us here. Look, I will call the 90+ contact here that I spoke to months ago. I think it'll be safe now."

Holly had almost forgotten about Mary still secreted in the boot but, before she made the call, they went around to the back of their driverless. There was no sound from inside. Immediately they were worried and Holly opened the boot without hesitation. Mary stared up at them from inside.

"Hello dear," she announced, as though it was the most normal thing in the world to be huddled inside the boot of a car.

"Come on Gran, we can get you out now. We've arrived and I think it's safe now."

They helped the eighty-nine-year old out into the cold of a November afternoon and ushered her round to the back seat, with both Jake and Holly glancing around to see if they were being observed. But there was hardly anyone around and those few figures nearby wandered along the street seemingly uninterested in the new arrivals.

Holly walked away from the car and made the call, returning moments later to announce animatedly,

"I got straight through and I'm confident it's OK. They'll meet us here in half an hour and they've a house where we can stay tonight while we work out what to do next. But they reckon there's a momentum now building behind changing the law. They think the King would only be here with the Government's blessing, so it's a signal of a change of policy."

It was now late in the afternoon and they were all feeling hungry but they determined that wandering about looking for something to eat was unwise even if the world was changing around them. Holly reassured Jake that she was confident that the contact she'd spoken to was reliable so they stayed put.

The wind had dropped and the rain had turned to drizzle. More than half an hour had passed and there was no sign of the promised rendezvous. Holly was starting to worry although she kept her concerns to herself. Then their attention was caught by the sight of a hunched figure, a woman, walking very slowly along the street towards them.

"She looks very old," remarked Mary to the surprise of both Holly and Jake.

Without waiting for any response, Mary got out of the driverless and walked over to the woman and offered her arm. Jake jumped from the car but Mary waved him away.

"How long have you been in Hunstanton?" asked Mary.

"Quite a while," she replied quickly. "I can't quite remember exactly how old I am but I'm old, very old and I'm fine. I can still walk. I reckon my heart is still working OK. And I know who the Prime Minister is!"

"Who is the Prime Minister, then?" asked Mary jokingly.

"Edward Watson, of course," responded the women without a moment's hesitation.

Mary stood next to her but said nothing in response. Holly had no idea what Mary had understood from this conversation. The encounter appeared to have run its course. So, they ushered Mary back into the driverless and wished the woman well as she continued painfully on her way.

CHAPTER NINETEEN

Hunstanton, Norfolk.
Wednesday 22 November 2045

Wilfred had assured Eversley he would just walk to the seafront and be back within half an hour. He'd enjoyed their trip out the previous day and he had convinced his son that he didn't need accompanying. Wilfred knew that Eversley was getting a hard time from his wife back home. There had been a heated phone conversation the previous evening. Hearing one end of it was enough to demonstrate to Wilfred that all was not well and that Eversley would be needing to get back home soon.

"Talk to Emma. Sort things out with her. I'll leave you in peace. You don't want me listening in, do you?" Wilfred had suggested.

"OK Dad, but half an hour maximum and don't go talking to anyone."

This was a command that Wilfred had no intention of obeying. His appetite to discover more about the colony had been whetted by what he had seen as they walked into the town and then on the walk to the beach. He planned to venture further. When he left the house, armed with the walking stick he'd had since he used to climb mountains in the Lake District years previously, he headed in the direction of the seafront so as not to arouse his son's suspicions. Once he was safely out of view from the safe house, he doubled back through a maze of streets, following his nose with the vague intention of finding the town centre.

Wilfred could admit to himself as he walked that he didn't have the strength to go that far. His aches and pains had got a lot worse since the beginning of the escape attempt. Now the worst thing was the shooting pain in his right hip that appeared all too frequently and without warning. But it was the breathlessness that worried him most. But he was determined to explore so he'd have to put up with it.

There seemed to be more people out walking than he had expected. The numbers gave him comfort, offering anonymity and cover. However, he soon realised that, despite his pain, he was walking faster than most others on the street. Many were using frames. Some were being pushed in wheelchairs by people who looked to be in just as much need as the chair's occupant. A very few had motorised chairs. All looked old. Extremely old. This was the world of the very elderly, and a world whose age profile wasn't mitigated by even a few younger people. He walked past a building that he thought must have once been a school. It was boarded up. Then it struck him. In the normal world you wouldn't go far without seeing children or at least hearing the sounds of children playing in the distance. This was a childless community.

He looked at his watch. It was really only people of his generation who still wore them. He had been out almost half an hour. Eversley would be starting to worry about him. But he was drawn to carry on. And he realised there were noises not far ahead. People were being pulled towards them. He wanted to ask his fellow slow travellers what was going on but he thought he shouldn't. But he instinctively felt that something important was happening so he continued. And then it appeared.

Coming in from the direction of the sea, it reminded Wilfred of war films he'd seen in the past. But helicopters were a rare sight now. This must be something special. Wilfred stopped in his tracks and watched as, straight ahead of him, above the Victorian rooftops and only maybe 200 or so metres away from him, the chopper hovered. He could hear the noise of the blades but, more than that, could see trees below it being blown violently in its wake.

"It's the King," announced a man, bent over a frame, who had stopped next to him. "There were rumours about it yesterday. It's true."

The assertion of a royal arrival was repeated by other onlookers. Wilfred thought to himself that it was very unlikely but he was determined to find out. He walked on, noting after a few minutes that he had forgotten about his pain. To his astonishment, he turned a corner and there, not much more than 100 metres ahead of him, the helicopter had landed on a patch of grass that must have once been public gardens. As the blades slowed, a door opened and out stepped the unmistakable figure of King George the Seventh. Even Wilfred, no great Royalist, was impressed.

What was even more remarkable was that there appeared to be hardly any protection around the King. A handful of security guards in hi-vis jackets were making a half-hearted attempt to keep some space between the Monarch and the growing crowd pushing ever closer to him. Wilfred moved forward. He was faster than most of those around him. A small reception committee, apparently led by a woman wearing a dog collar, was trying to make itself heard to the King above the noise of the chopper. Wilfred moved to the front of the crowd and was practically within touching distance of the King. He could hear him talking animatedly.

"Well, what an interesting flight to get here. We flew over the remains of Sandringham. How sad it was to see it in such a state. I remember going there as a child. Well, I think I can but it could have been Balmoral – all those royal palaces looked the same to a young child."

"Yes it is very sad, Your Majesty," he could hear the vicar

saying to the King.

She couldn't have been a day over forty. Wilfred remembered that the churches had come to an agreement with the Government a few years before to allow a Minister of any age to work inside the remainder colonies. This woman, who'd introduced herself as the Reverend Zoey, must be one such.

"The weather on the flight can't have been that nice?" Zoey continued.

"Not at all. In fact I thought it might stop us getting here," replied the King.

That was probably what he had hoped, thought Wilfred to himself. It was well-known that the King was a bad flyer.

"Well, I'm glad you were able to get here," gushed Hunstanton's Vicar. "It is a great honour to welcome you to our town."

Wilfred wasn't that interested in politics although he still liked to call himself an ageing leftie. He feigned disinterest in the daily ebb and flow of politics but he knew more than he let on. He knew that the colony was a place without any formal leadership structure and, what's more, members of resistance groups based in Hunstanton were unlikely to be interested in being part of the protocol of a Royal visit. Into this power vacuum, he imagined, had stepped Zoey. Although she was very much younger than the colony's inhabitants and was almost certainly in favour of the existing laws, she would probably command a peculiar sense of trust among residents. It was, Wilfred supposed, a tribute not to her leadership qualities but more to the enduring respect for the authority of the dog-collar.

As the pleasantries of the welcoming continued in the wind and rain outside the old council offices just adjacent to the library, Wilfred's gaze was drawn to the remains of rather feeble municipal flowerbeds still lingering from an era when

Hunstanton had proper local government. But, as he waited for something to happen, he found himself imagining the conversations that must have gone on between George and his advisors before this trip was approved. Getting to this point would have required him to overturn centuries of Royal protocol in a matter of days. His advisors would surely have been adamant that this was a very bad idea. The notion that the King sat above party politics was crucial to the role of the Monarchy, never mind that it was a central pillar of the still unwritten Constitution.

But Wilfred was here, witnessing an historic moment, and that appealed to him, even if he was blissfully unaware of everything that had led to this. But it must be to do with the 90 Law. It surely was. It would help shift the debate in the direction he wanted it to go. And turning up unannounced in a 'remainder' colony was a pretty dramatic symbol. Never before, in the decade since the law came in, had the Head of State been to any of the colonies. With the Parliamentary vote now almost certain to be scheduled for next week, his intervention must be deliberately timed to influence public and political opinion.

"If it were done, it were well it were done quickly," Wilfred said to himself with a slight misquotation of Shakespeare.

"You said you would like to visit the clinic to see some of those injured earlier this week, Your Majesty. The clinic said it would be better if we went now, if that's OK with you."

"I quite understand that and I'm happy to be guided by you about the timings," replied the King, eager to get on with the visit.

"This way, Your Majesty."

Wilfred realised that the surgery was just across the road. Many of the assembled crowd moved away but Wilfred followed the Royal party and no-one stopped him. From the outside, the surgery looked rundown. There was still an 'NHS' sign by the door, although the 'H' was missing, perhaps appropriately as it was well known that health services, like most things in remainder colonies, were hand to mouth and a confusing mix of 'self-help' and government initiative.

"It's the only doctors we've got," someone shouted in the direction of the King as he approached the building. "Nobody cares about us. Sub-human, they call us sometimes."

Wilfred was now within touching distance of the King who appeared not to have heard the shouted comments. But Wilfred could hear every word that Reverend Zoey was saying as she briefed the King about what had happened a few days before, although sparing him a few of the more gruesome details.

"The League of Youth turned up in the town, riding in unchallenged on motorbikes. At first it was a peaceful protest. They walked through the centre, just across there where the main shops are, probably about fifty of them. They were holding banners with slogans supporting the current law. But then, as if from nowhere, it got nasty. A few of them broke away from the protest. The first I heard from my office was the sound of breaking glass. Then shouts and screams. They attacked colonists who were just unlucky enough to be in the area. I ran to help. It wasn't a pleasant scene. It was only some of the Leaguers who were involved. In fact some of the more peaceful ones tried to stop them. I did what I could. It took ages for the police and ambulances to arrive."

Somehow, this description didn't do justice to the horror of what had happened and the scene that greeted the King, and all those following him including Wilfred, came as something of a shock. The reception area had been pressed into service as a makeshift ward. It was packed with several beds and chairs, all occupied by people heavily bandaged, many with arms in slings and some attached to drips. Through the open doors of a small number of consulting rooms, Wilfred could see more people in similar states and also hear some raised voices and cries of pain.

A man, presumably the doctor in charge, stopped attending to one of his patients and came over to the King. Wilfred reckoned the doctor must be at least in his seventies, if not older. He wore a frayed and slightly soiled white coat. He looked tired and harassed.

"Good morning, Sir. What a surprise but thank you for coming to see us," he uttered, giving the impression that he had not been forewarned that the Monarch was about to pay a visit to his surgery.

It would have been a shock at any time but particularly now, thought Wilfred.

"Are all these people here with injuries from the incident the other day? These injuries look pretty serious."

"These are not the worst, Sir. They've gone to King's Lynn or Norwich. Some of these here probably look worse than they are. Lots of bruising and a few broken bones and quite a bit of blood in most cases. We did our best to work out which people might have had head injuries and got them to hospital. To be fair to the hospitals, they were happy to take them all. Sometimes, the Queen Elizabeth doesn't want to know if we ask them to take people from here."

The King was listening intently, clearly still trying to take in what he was witnessing. Wilfred shuddered to imagine what he would see if he went to the hospital in King's Lynn, given that these were apparently not serious cases. The King moved uninvited towards a man in an adjacent bed.

"Hello. It's good to meet you. What's your name?"

"Richard," the man replied clearly not bothered about observing Royal protocol.

"And what happened to you, Richard?"

"I was just walking along the street. I'd been to the shops and I was on my way home. I could hear a lot of commotion in the next street so I went round the corner to have a look. There was this group of people, mainly men, but some women, charging down the street shouting and cheering. Some had bats and sticks. Suddenly two of them headed straight towards me, screaming and bawling. 'Death to Remainders. Thieves of our Future. Give us what's ours!'

"The next thing I knew, one of them grabbed me and pushed me to the ground. They were both still screaming slogans at me right close to my face. I could feel their spit on me. They were out of control. Then another one appeared. He had a baseball bat. The last thing I remember was seeing him lift his arm and bring the bat down towards me."

"How are you feeling now?" asked the King, visibly shaken at the story of one of his subjects, presumably over ninety, being attacked in such a vicious manner in the street.

"I've got quite a bad headache but I'm alright apart from that. But do you know what's the worst bit about it? It's not the physical pain. It's thinking about why they did it. What has led these people to do this? I reckon they were in their thirties and that sort of makes it worse. How is it that they have become so angry that they feel able to go around on an orgy of violence against people almost three times their age? What have we become, your Majesty? What have we become?"

The King had no simple answer. Instead of responding to the rhetorical question still hanging in the air, he confined himself to a brief offer of commiserations.

"I'm very, very sorry to hear what happened to you. I'm sure the police will find your attackers. I hope you feel better soon."

This was hardly a convincing response, thought Wilfred, as everyone knew the police were notoriously reluctant to investigate any crimes in the colonies unless they were offences against the Age Regulation laws.

The King talked briefly to several more of the wounded. Wilfred noticed that at least a couple of those receiving treatment were much, much younger than everyone else, presumably League of Youth members hurt in the melee. Perhaps more moderate campaigners who were turned on by the hard-line Leaguers? Before the King had the chance to talk to them, Zoey was suggesting that they might move on.

As they left, the King was clearly still processing what he'd seen and heard over the past twenty minutes or so. As he turned back into the street, he was confronted by the need to respond in public to what he had just witnessed. Running across the street towards the clinic was a reporter with a camerawoman in tow. Wilfred recognised the face of the reporter. He thought he was a BBC Royal Correspondent although he couldn't remember his name. A cluster of other reporters with cameras and microphones arrived alongside but Wilfred didn't recognise anyone else. The rest must be local media or just interested onlookers.

"Sir, BBC News. What did you see in the clinic, Your Majesty, and what comment do you have about what has happened here in Hunstanton in the last few days?"

Wilfred was still surprised by the ease with which reporters would now shout questions at members of the Royal Family, so-called 'door stepping', something previously frowned upon but now common practice. What's more, royalty, like politicians, were generally the subject of opprobrium if they ignored such questions.

"I have just been inside the clinic to visit some of the people who were injured in the unfortunate incidents here in Hunstanton in recent days. Whatever the rights and wrongs of the arguments about our age regulation laws, there can be no justification for violence, particularly when its victims include the oldest in our nation who should be allowed to live out their remaining years in dignity as long as nature allows. Thank you."

Just two short sentences which might have sounded measured and bipartisan if uttered a generation earlier were now incendiary, perhaps, Wilfred thought, even more so than the King realised or intended. The BBC's follow-up question was lost in the media scrum as the King was ushered out of the rain back towards the old Town Hall building.

"Do you believe that Parliament should vote to raise the termination age?"

As the King disappeared into the building, the small security force barred the way for the throng of people who had by now attached themselves to the King. Wilfred stood in the street, leaning on his stick and still trying to process the enormity of what he had just seen and heard. He knew that once these images and the King's words were broadcast, many people would see the King's statement as a clear signal in favour of raising the age limit or even abolishing it altogether. The King was challenging the view, still held by many, that remainders were almost sub-human, people who had no right still to be around, people who should not have been spared back in 2035. Wilfred knew that the King had lit the fuse paper and he would now have to wait for the explosion.

Wilfred looked at his watch. He had been out of the house for over an hour. Eversley would probably already be out searching for him. He was about to retrace his steps when, sooner than he had expected, the King, still accompanied by Zoey, emerged from the old Town Hall. As he did so, a young woman suddenly emerged from the side of the building hurrying towards the King causing the King's bodyguard to move quickly to block off her path. But the King intervened.

"No, it's fine, leave her be," he instructed the bodyguard, as he offered his hand to the woman.

"Hello. How can I help?"

"Sir, I'm sorry to barge in like this but I just wanted to ask you something. I heard about half an hour ago that you were here and I decided I had to try to talk to you. I just want to make sure you're aware of two things. The majority of the Leaguers who came to Hunstanton on Saturday came here with one purpose in mind – peaceful protest. The violence that happened in the streets near here was not of our making. It was terrible. It should never have happened. I can tell you that most of us condemn it. It was the hooligan element that sometimes try to attach themselves to us that were responsible for the violence. I hope they're punished.

"But I hope that you don't allow this to affect your view of the 90 Law debate. If MPs put the age limit up or if they abolish it altogether, that will not be a good outcome for anyone. We seem to be in danger of forgetting why the law was passed in the first place. First of all, it was about fairness. The terrible damage that successive older generations, and the politicians that had elected them, had done to the young. They had ruined our educational opportunities, our job prospects and our living standards. But just as important was how the new law improved conditions for older people. People, young and old, realised there was a better way for everyone's sake. That's what we are trying to preserve."

The King listened intently, thanked her, walked from the Town Hall accompanied by Zoey and this time smiled at the waiting media. On this occasion, though, he waved away their persistent questions. As he walked to a waiting car, another determined questioner was able to penetrate the inadequate security cordon. This time it was a man and clearly a Remainder, surely well over ninety and looking a little frail.

This encounter was very brief.

"Good of you to come, Sir," said the intruder. "But it's not all it's cracked up to be, this living for ever, lark, you know. I've had enough. It just gets a bit boring, a bit pointless and I should have gone at ninety."

The King said nothing in reply and turned towards the car which would presumably be taking him back to his helicopter. But Wilfred noticed him hesitate. The King stopped just for a couple of seconds before getting in the car and looked straight in the direction of Wilfred who imagined a flash of recognition. Wilfred held the Royal gaze, smiled briefly and then the King bent down, got in and was gone. Wilfred set off to make his peace with Eversley.

CHAPTER TWENTY

Hunstanton, Norfolk
Thursday 23 November 2045

Twenty four hours later Wilfred was feeling chastened. When they had been eventually reunited the previous day after Wilfred's unscheduled royal encounter, Eversley had lost his temper with his father. Initially, Wilfred had laughed it off and had tried to enthuse his son about the significance of what he had witnessed. In the end, father had apologised to son and calm was restored. Today, however, Eversley was insistent that they would go out together for a walk and that his father must stay at his side.

It was a grey, blustery morning and, despite the excitement of the day before, Wilfred couldn't help but feel the depression that seemed to stalk the streets. It wasn't so much the physical decay, the unloved buildings, and the dirty pavements. It was, as before, the people. Yesterday, it had been their age which fixated him. Today it was their apparent poverty. Not all looked down at heel, but most did and they were predominantly going about their business alone, presumably left on their own after the death of partners. Or, in many cases, Wilfred assumed that they had fled to Hunstanton on their own in the first place.

He was still keen to explore and perhaps to talk to some of the colonists. He was a naturally curious man and needed to understand them better. Yesterday's excitement had spurred him on creatively and he had spent the previous evening composing, practising and almost completing his piece. Today he was feeling good and happy to wait for Tom to provide him with musicians. In the meantime, he could find out more about Hunstanton.

His attention was abruptly returned to the present moment by the sound of shouting which seemed to be coming from around the next corner. He felt Eversley's hand hold his arm.

"Wait, Dad. Let's turn back. It's not safe"

"No, no, let's take a look. I want to see what's going on."

He started walking again. Eversley followed. They turned left to see a noisy crowd waving banners and reciting slogans.

'Death for Murderers. Death for Evaders. End life at 90.'

As they got closer, Wilfred could see that some of the crowd's placards contained a face whom he recognised from the minimal news coverage he'd bothered to watch recently. It was a man who'd been accused of assaulting a League protester in the town a few weeks before. He soon realised that the protesters' attention was focused on a building just ahead of them.

"It's a court, I can see the sign. It must be a court hearing of some sort. Maybe the guy who beat up the Leaguer," speculated Eversley.

"Really," said Wilfred "Do they still have courts here?"

The protesters were converging on the building. Even Eversley, seemingly curious to find out what was happening here, moved tentatively forward following his father's lead. Wilfred saw the sign above the entrance. It was indeed a magistrates' court. So, in one of the curiosities of 2045 England, justice was still being dispensed in the colony, even though many other institutions of the state had largely abandoned the town.

They slowed as they got closer, appreciating that this was not just a peaceful demonstration. The crowd, nearly all men, probably fifty strong, suddenly surged forward towards the entrance where a single security guard stood with mounting fear in his eyes. Wilfred had occasionally heard from his son about the exceptional violence and brutality he'd witnessed in the Army, but somehow this angry mob on the streets of an English seaside town was more shocking. They pushed forward again, shouting their slogans more loudly still.

Within moments they were surrounding the lone guard who, Wilfred observed, wisely offered no meaningful resistance. He could see onlookers and passers-by trying to move away. Then he heard the first screams, saw the first scuffles and then, all in a flash, people were falling to the ground. Those in the vanguard of the mob briefly looked round at the scene they were leaving in their wake. Few hesitated, though, and the surge carried on up the steps of the court and into the building. Wilfred was rooted to the spot, scared and fascinated at the same time. Then, as he looked round, he realised that his son was no longer at his side. Real fear took over. He scanned the mass of humanity ahead. He turned and looked behind. Something was telling him to get away. Something else was telling him not to abandon his son.

"Eversley, Eversley," he called in hope rather than expectation of a reply, still unable to locate his son.

As he continued to call out, he could see that several people had been injured. It appeared that some of them were being tended to by onlookers. Others, he imagined, looking at the ages of some who were helping, by the protesters themselves. Then he saw him, near the top of the steps. Eversley was grabbing a man, probably half his age, who was shouting and waving a placard. A struggle ensued culminating in Eversley landing a punch which sent the protester falling backwards down the steps.

"Eversley, Eversley," Wilfred called out again.

His son, briefly pausing in the middle of the orgy of violence, caught his eye.

"Dad, move away. Move away. Get away from this"

Eversley turned back, throwing punches and kicks at more

protesters and then, to Wilfred's horror, disappeared into the building, following the protesters who were cramming into what must surely be a court hearing. The protesters, some just inside the building and others crammed together outside, restarted their chanting with new slogans.

"Attempted Murder. Attempted Murder. More than Assault. More than Assault. Uphold the Rule of Law. Justice for the Young. Justice for the Young…"

Then the chanting stopped and Wilfred could just make out another voice struggling to make herself heard above the din.

"The job of this court is only to consider the charges before it. It is not our job to decide what charges should or should not be brought against an individual. This is a public hearing and members of the public are welcome to witness the proceedings but only if they do so peacefully."

Wilfred assumed the voice must belong to the chair of the magistrates who sounded remarkably calm despite the fact that her court had been invaded and the workings of the law interrupted. Several protesters shouted questions at the chair who replied patiently. The exchanges continued for several minutes but the Chair's patience ran out and she instructed the protesters to leave the court. Wilfred imagined that she had little force to back up her authority and he was proved right. The protest turned angry and violent again. They stormed the room, their target the man in the dock. Pandemonium broke out. There were shouts and screams and the sound of boots clomping over the loose fitting floorboards of the court.

"Eversley, Eversley, come out of there," called out Wilfred in the vain hope of getting his son to extract himself from the madness in front of him.

He knew only too well that something inside Eversley would be propelling him to get involved, to try to stop the protesters, to try to take a stand, as he would see it, against the iniquitous termination laws. Most of the protesters were now inside the building. On the steps of the courtroom entrance several injured people were still being attended to. Wilfred could hear the sound of sirens in the distance. He moved forward towards the steps thinking that he might be able to offer some help. Then, the sharp pain in the hip, which had been increasingly bothering him in recent days, returned with a vengeance causing him to grimace and let out an anguished cry. He felt light-headed. The world around him lost its reference points and then he could just make out the stained concrete of the courtroom steps flying towards him. Then nothing.

Wilfred had no idea how much time had elapsed but all he was now aware of was a throbbing in his head and a voice. A voice that got louder. Then louder still.

"Dad, Dad, it's Eversley. Stay with me, Dad. The ambulance is coming."

Wilfred couldn't process any of this and drifted away. Again nothing. For how long, he would never know. Later he would remember thinking that it wasn't fair that he had died before he was ninety. And he'd been cheated of a painless death with an injection in a comfortable, warm room. Dying on a dirty courtroom step wasn't how it was supposed to be, even in this most cruel of countries. Then another voice.

"Wilfred, it's Tom. It's Tom Blatchford. You'll be fine. You've just had a bump to your head. Talk to me, Wilfred."

Wilfred could make sense of this. The throbbing was still there but he could also hear sirens. They sounded very nearby. Was he going to be arrested for hiding in Hunstanton?

"Tom, where are we? What's happening?"

"You've had a bump on the head, Wilfred. Eversley, your son, is here as well. It'll be alright."

"Dad, we need to move you away from here. Can we help you up?"

"Eversley, what's happened to you?"

As some sort of clarity returned to his vision, he could see a bandage round Eversley's head, a blooded bandage.

"Don't worry, Dad. It looks worse than it is. Somebody hit me. I'll be fine."

Wilfred had no memory of what had happened to him and couldn't offer a clear explanation but, as they helped him to his feet, Eversley and Tom started guiding him away from the area.

"We'll get you looked at later, Wilfred," said Tom "But for now we need to get away from here. We don't want to be around when the police show up."

Tom led them through the streets away from the town centre and the noise of sirens faded into the background. Wilfred had no idea where they were heading. The bang to his head had at least had the effect of suppressing his painful hip. But it needed both Tom and Eversley to hold him up and almost carry him to make any progress.

"This isn't the way back to the house," Eversley said suddenly, looking anxiously in the direction of Tom.

"You're right, Eversley. But there's someone I'd like you to meet, also an evader and I think your dad and her would get on well. Don't worry so much, Eversley. It'll be fine. Trust me."

A couple of minutes later, they stopped in the middle of a row of sad looking shops, many of which were boarded up. Tom unlocked a door and led them inside and upstairs to a flat over the shop. They guided Wilfred to a sofa and lowered him down onto it. For a few moments, he felt very light-headed again and thought he was about to pass out. A glass of water was put into his hand. He sipped from it. Then, realising just how thirsty he was, drank the rest quickly. Then, for the first time, he surveyed the room. There were three people. Two women shared a sofa opposite him. One looked quite young.

The other was much older, perhaps around his own age. There was also a man, maybe in his fifties, sat on a chair by the window. Wilfred felt particularly drawn to the older woman, smiled at her and held out his hand towards her.

"I'm Wilfred, nice to meet you."

"Hello Wilfred. I'm Mary, nice to meet you. Please let me have a look at your head. I'm a doctor."

Mary got up and moved across to sit down next to Wilfred and conducted a thorough examination of his visible injuries before questioning him about his aches and pains. All the others in the room stood back, allowing Mary to do as she wished. Mary enlisted Holly as a nurse to help dress Wilfred's wounds using some clean tea towels Jake found in a drawer. She told Wilfred he should take some strong painkillers which, she assured everyone, was all that was required plus, of course, some rest. Wilfred was pleased when Tom produced some from his pocket and he swallowed them quickly with another glass of water fetched by Holly. He looked straight at Mary and smiled broadly.

"Thank you so much. You are very kind".

Within minutes the two eighty-nine-year-olds struck up a conversation and started telling each other their life stories. Tom interrupted this only to do some formal introductions. Then the two people, practically nonagenarians, continued their chat as though they were old friends reunited for the first time in years.

Tom whispered to Jake, Holly and Eversley in a conspiratorial tone,

"They'll be swapping phone numbers in a minute!"

Wilfred was so engrossed in his conversation with Mary that he hardly noticed that the younger generation, upon whom the burden of responsibility for the elderly bore heavily, returned to matters of practicality.

It was Holly who spoke first.

"Tom, we're very grateful to you for finding this place for us but what are we going to do now. I still don't know if my father is alive or dead. If he's alive, he's probably on his way here determined to find his mother and take her home before her birthday next week. He will get the police to help him track us down. Don't we need to get out of the colony before he gets here? What can we do?"

"We can take care of that, Holly," replied Tom. "I think the best place for you at the moment is right here. The Leaguers out there on the streets are a bigger danger than your father. The police have apparently given up on knowing what to do here since the King made his visit yesterday. They've never been that interested in restraining the League of Youth and they're probably not going to do much about evaders given the way the wind is blowing. So, sit tight for now. Stay indoors. We'll look after you. And we'll find a place where all five of you can stay together, so you'll have a bit of company."

Jake clearly unimpressed, added, "You make it sound like we're all going to have a nice holiday by the sea. With sirens wailing in the distance and with a wounded eighty-nine-year old recuperating in front of me, the reality could not be further removed from the idea of a seaside break."

Eversley signalled his agreement with Jake's scepticism. But, while the logistical discussion continued, Mary and Wilfred were still deep in conversation. They had even worked out that they might have met as small children.

"I lived in Brixton when I was young after my parents came over," remarked Wilfred.

"I was in Peckham but we used to go to Brixton Market a lot."

Their chat rambled on and Wilfred, though still waiting for the painkillers to work, felt much better.

"They can remember what happened eighty years ago but not earlier today," observed Holly.

Next they got onto music. Wilfred was naturally modest but couldn't resist telling a suitably self-deprecating version of his life story to Mary.

"Well that's fascinating," replied Mary "I thought I recognised you."

Tom then addressed the group as a whole.

"Look, I understand that you're all under a lot of pressure. But our aim in 90+ is not just to help people escape termination but to assist them in continuing to follow their dreams once they're safe. Wilfred is a great musician. I hadn't realised when I first met him just how important he has been in the musical history of this country. There was a time when so-called 'Black Music' was seen as niche and not mainstream. I'm no musical expert but I know this man is an icon and he's one of the reasons why 'Black Music' is now just as English as Elgar or the Beatles. And I have also had the benefit of hearing him play and I can tell you, he knows how to write a good tune!

"The one thing Wilfred wants to do as soon as possible is to get his latest composition performed. He's just about finished it in the last few days since he arrived in the colony. It's a chamber piece for saxophone. He can play the sax but we need a pianist and a violin and a drummer. Then we can put on a concert and Wilfred will be a happy man."

As Tom made his announcement, Wilfred glanced at Jake, Holly and Eversley who were all clearly struggling to grasp how Tom could be so focussed on the idea of this concert when there was an existential struggle to be fought all around them. He was delighted, though, by their response.

"It's a few years since I have, but I can play the drums," offered Jake tentatively.

"Brilliant, that's a great start," said Tom. "Any other hidden musical talent?"

"I'm afraid I haven't followed in my Dad's footsteps when it comes to music," apologised Eversley. "One of my daughters can sing beautifully. I think it's skipped a generation."

"I gave up violin lessons after a term," added Holly.

"Not to worry. We have a start. I used to be able to knock out a mean tune on the piano so we might have to make do with that but I'll see if I can recruit some other musicians. We'll try and do it in the next couple of days. Now, though, the priority is to get you all to a new house. Just give me a couple of hours and we'll sort it."

As Tom made to leave instructing them all to stay in the flat, Wilfred noticed a sudden look of alarm on Holly's face.

"It's Dad, he's calling me."

"Dad, Dad, where are you?" she shouted as she reached across to grab her hand-held from her coat pocket. She switched from her I-COM to her hand-held but the line went dead.

She tried calling him back. But there was nothing. Wilfred didn't understand what was going on.

"Is there a problem with your father?" he asked tentatively.

Between them Holly and Jake explained what had happened, how they believed that her father must have had a drone crash but that they still didn't know for sure.

"I think we should leave. It's not going to be safe here. I've got to find out what's happened to Dad. I caused the crash by ringing him. But we've got to keep Gran away from him whatever happens," was Holly's summary.

For a few minutes more, the group of conspirators, huddled in an upstairs flat with sirens still sounding outside, resumed their discussions. Eventually, they were persuaded by Tom to stick to his plan and hunker down in the flat before moving later to a new house. Not for the first time today, Mary's lucidity suddenly surprised them all.

"Where's David? Will he come to see us?"

This temporarily paused the discussion until Holly responded.

"Gran. Dad will try to find you so that he can take you back for your termination. Now, we know you don't want that so you need to stick with us for now. Trust us."

Until that point, Wilfred hadn't appreciated Mary's condition. Her lucidity over the past hour had completely disguised her dementia. There was no response from Mary but Wilfred was unsure if that signified acceptance or lack of comprehension. Somehow, though, this helped bring the discussion to a close. Tom left, promising to return within two hours. Meanwhile, the two groups of evaders, thrown together fortuitously only hours earlier, sat and waited.

CHAPTER TWENTY-ONE

Hunstanton, Norfolk.
Sunday 26 November, 2045

For the first time in the six days since they'd taken Mary from her home, Holly had enjoyed a relatively undisturbed night's sleep. As she emerged from her slumbers, she remembered where she was, in a new 'safe house' to which Tom had brought them, along with Wilfred and Eversley, the previous afternoon. Slowly, she was conscious of an unfamiliar but pleasant sound. It was coming from downstairs and it was the unmistakable tones of a saxophone. For a few moments she lay in bed enjoying the music as Jake lay at her side apparently oblivious and undisturbed by Wilfred's playing.

Holly's waking thoughts were a mixture of comfort and worry. The thought that today was the day when Wilfred's saxophone composition was to be premièred was genuinely a source of joy for her even though she had never been that interested in music. But the lack of definite news about her father was disturbing. Apparently he was alive if the call he'd attempted to make to her a few days ago was genuine. But, even though she'd tried him several times since, there'd been no response. What was he up to? Maybe, even now, he was in Hunstanton? She was mystified as to why they had not heard from him again.

Holly went downstairs, exchanged pleasantries with Wilfred and made herself some breakfast. It was still before nine and through the window it looked to be a crisp, bright autumn day. She would love to go for a walk along the beach with Jake and forget about all the anxieties they had heaped upon themselves by undertaking the mission to save her grandmother. But she knew that was impossible for now.

As she daydreamed, a key turned in the lock of the front door. A momentary surge of anxiety quickly dissipated when the familiar figure of Tom Blatchford walked in offering his usual cheery greetings. Behind him followed two men breathing heavily, one of them clearly overweight and sweating profusely. They struggled through the doorway with what Holly soon realised was a small electric piano. Tom instructed them on where to put it and then they went out, returned a few moments later with a series of heavy cases which, Tom confirmed, contained a drum kit.

"Right, we're all set up then. One composer. One saxophone. One piano and pianist, yours truly, plus a drum kit complete with drummer when he deigns to get out of bed. Plus, a violinist on her way as we speak."

The two men who had done the heavy lifting declined the offer of a cup of tea and bade their farewells as Tom and Wilfred thanked them extravagantly for their efforts. Holly could sense that Wilfred was barely able to contain his excitement as he tinkled on the piano, repeated notes on the sax and tried to help Tom unpack the drum kit. Moments later Jake, woken by the activity below, had joined them downstairs. Then, as the drum kit was being assembled, another knock on the door announced the arrival of the violinist, a woman whose age, Holly thought, was difficult to assess. She looked too young to be a remainder but she found it increasingly difficult to guess ages.

For the next half an hour or so, the front room of the house was a hive of activity, a mixture of setting up equipment, tuning up instruments and consuming breakfast. This house, the second refuge in Hunstanton for Holly, Jake and Mary and for Wilfred and Eversley, was considerably more spacious than their previous abodes. Like much of the property in the colony, it was rather unloved and clearly little had been spent on decoration for many years. Holly, normally bothered by appearances and how things looked, surprised herself by being able to ignore the surroundings.

Jake made some breakfast and came and sat next to Holly.

"I've just been reading about Hunstanton. Fascinating stuff. Do you know that many of the houses here have disputed ownership? There are lots of long-running legal disputes. Owners who had fled the town when it was abandoned after repeated flooding have made legal claims but some remainders had simply occupied abandoned houses and now claim squatters' rights."

"Do you know, Jake, I'm not sure I care about that very much. I doubt there's much chance of us being evicted."

As the preparations continued for the first performance of Wilfred's piece, Holly observed how the composer gradually took charge of the proceedings. He spent a few minutes with each of the other musicians, giving them the chance to run through their parts. The violinist wanted to keep practising. Jake and Tom, on the other hand, seemed happy to wing it. This didn't surprise Holly. Then, Wilfred declared that they were ready, asked everyone to take their places and prepared to start.

But, at this point, Tom, never one to miss the opportunity to make a speech, interjected.

"Wilfred, may I just say a few words, please before we begin?"

Wilfred nodded his agreement. Tom continued.

"All I wanted to say was just how pleased I am that we've been able to make this happen this morning. I'm happy for you, Wilfred, because I know how much it means to you to be able to get this piece performed. But I'm happy for another reason. The reason some of us try to help people escape the

90 Law is not simply to enable people to prolong their lives. It's to enable them to continue their lives with meaning. It's to recognise the fact that everyone, whatever their age, has something to contribute. So, this is an important statement of principle. That's enough from me, though, so let's make music! Take it away Wilfred!"

Tom's words elicited a response from Wilfred.

"Thank you, Tom for making this happen and thank you to all of you for helping with this. I know that the law of England says that my life will have run its course in a matter of days. When Eversley and I set out on our journey a couple of weeks ago, never did I imagine I would be sat in a house in Hunstanton performing a piece which, when we started our travels, was far from finished. So, I am enormously grateful to my dear son for persuading me to leave home because, in a way, it has been the experience of this journey which has inspired me to finish it and which now means that I can say that my journey is over.

"Whatever happens to me after today, I believe I will feel that my life's work is finished. And that work, I now realise, has been about bringing people together. It has been about the slow process of integrating the traditions of my heritage with the traditions that were already on these islands before that ship docked at Tilbury almost a century ago. And, even though we may all have many misgivings about how our country is being run now, I am still glad - very, very glad that my parents made that journey to England all those years ago.

"So, if you are all ready, here's the world première, I suppose we can describe it, of what I am going to call 'Homage to Hunstanton - a Concerto for Saxophone.'"

There were several moments of silence in the room as Wilfred steadied himself. The only sound was a gentle breeze blowing outside and Holly thought she could make out the distant sound of the sea. Then Wilfred took a deep breath and the first haunting notes of the piece rang out from his saxophone. Holly noticed that Eversley was smiling for the first time since they had met.

Gradually, over the next few minutes, the piano, then the violin and finally the drums, joined in at the appropriate times. The audience of three, Mary, Holly and Eversley, sat fully engaged with the music. The concentration on the performers' faces was intense. Wilfred played his part on the sax, smiled broadly in the interludes between his contributions and, from time to time, conducted the others. Even Holly, with her limited musical appreciation, knew it wasn't perfect and they all lost their way at various points but that hardly mattered. All that mattered was that an original piece of music, written by a man days from his legally mandated death, was finally getting its première, albeit in a run-down semi in a sad English seaside town.

The overture lasted around seven minutes and when it finished, in line with normal orchestral tradition, no one clapped, although nearly everyone allowed the odd cough to escape their lips. After thirty seconds pause, Wilfred brought the scratch orchestra to attention and they began the second movement. As this progressed, Holly thought that the ensemble seemed to gain in confidence. Wilfred and Jake, in particular, became more expressive in their playing. Tom added the occasional improvisation on the piano and even the nervous violinist let slip the occasional smile. All three in the audience were obviously enthralled as the soaring melodies of the piece, led by the saxophone, reached deep inside them. It wasn't long before Holly noticed tears on Eversley's face and a broad smile on Mary's. It was, she thought, as if the world did not exist beyond the four walls of this borrowed house.

In a matter of moments, though, the mood was shattered,

slowly at first but then rudely. Holly had deactivated her I-COM and switched to her hand-held but left it on vibrate. Even on the first vibration, the hand-held rattled against the glass surface of the scratched table where she had placed it. She ignored the first few disturbances but when Eversley's attention moved from the musicians in front of him to the phone, Holly leant over, grabbed the hand-held and stood up apologetically. She hurried up the stairs and was pleasantly unsurprised to see 'Dad' on the caller ident. She slipped into the room she and Jake were using as a bedroom and answered.

"Holly, it's time to come home now. You've had your little adventure but it's over. I need to look after your grandmother in her final few days. Now I'm recovering from my injuries, I must be in charge again."

Her father sounded far from recovered to Holly. His voice was much weaker than normal and lacked its normal bravado.

"Dad, you can't do this," said Holly calmly. "Gran wants to live. You have no right to deny her that."

"I have every right, Holly. I'm afraid you have no rights in this matter," replied her father, his voice now sounding stronger and louder down the hand-held.

"I don't want to fall out with you and I know you love your grandmother. Let's work together to make her last few days special. I can't do it on my own, Holly. Please come and help me."

"What happened to you Dad?"

"I crashed the drone when you rang."

Holly noted to herself that her father was already perhaps laying the blame at her door.

"I suppose I must have been distracted and ran into the exclusion zone round Heathrow and had to make a big override to change course but I over-reached and tipped it over. I tried to right it but I couldn't and I was dropping fast. Thank God

I managed to pull it round before I hit the ground so I didn't land at full speed. I can't remember anything after that until I woke up in hospital."

Holly could feel herself welling up inside. She had delivered a guilty verdict already. It was her fault. If she hadn't made that call, her father wouldn't have crashed.

"I'm sorry. I'm sorry," was all she could manage.

"Holly, don't blame yourself. I should never have accepted the call."

Even though her father's absolution sounded genuine, it didn't diminish the guilt she had already apportioned to herself. Then she remembered she hadn't yet asked about his condition.

"What are your injuries? How badly hurt are you? Is it serious?"

"Lots of broken bones. Lots of bruises. Bad concussion. I've still got terrible headache despite the painkillers. But no brain injury. The worst thing is my right leg which must have got crushed when I was trapped. They say it'll take a while before I can walk again."

"Oh, Dad. I'm coming to see you straight away. Where are you?"

"Still in hospital but I've been transferred to the Princess Royal. I should be able to go home in a couple of days."

"Why didn't someone contact me?"

"I didn't want anyone to know where you were or what you were up to. Anyway, how is Hunstanton?"

Holly was so overwhelmed by the extent of her father's injuries that she hardly registered her father's question.

"Stay on the line. I need to tell the others."

She went out of the bedroom, shot down the stairs, and, holding the hand-held up, interrupted the music.

"Sorry. I'm really sorry but it's Dad. He's badly hurt. We need to go, Jake."

For a few seconds, the music continued as each of the performers realised at their own speeds what was happening. Gradually, they all stopped apart from Wilfred who was so engrossed that he seemed oblivious to what was happening around him. Holly went across and spoke directly to him. He stopped. The room fell silent. All that could be heard was a voice from the hand-held.

"Holly, Holly, what's going on? What's that music? Where are you?"

"Dad, it's too complicated to explain but we are safe but we'll be back soon. Don't worry about us. Take it easy."

"Let me speak to Gran. I need to hear her voice."

Holly flicked the hand-held onto speaker as David announced to the room,

"Mum, it's time to come home with me now. I need you to come back so I can look after you properly."

His voice was barely raised but its tone distinctly determined. For a second or two, everyone else in the room froze. Then Jake, still brandishing the drum sticks he had been using to make music moments before, lurched towards the hand-held shouting.

"David, you can't do this. Mary wants to live. You have no right to deny her that."

"Jake, this is not your business. It's for Holly and I to sort out and we've agreed that Mary is coming back now."

At this, Jake's temper rose instantly and he stabbed at the hand-held with a drumstick. A tirade exploded peppered with expletives. Tom intervened, restraining Jake who then turned his fire on Holly.

"What do you think you are doing? We are not going back. I won't let you."

Before Holly could reply, everyone in the room heard David again through the hand-held in what Holly thought was a remarkably calm tone.

"I am her son, her nearest relative. I will decide what's best for her."

"You have no idea what's best for her," snorted Jake in response but Holly felt that he was already accepting defeat.

The awkwardness in the room was unexpectedly punctured by Mary.

"How nice to hear you, David? Are you alright?"

"I'm fine, Mum. Don't worry about me and we'll be getting you back home very soon."

Holly stood silent and motionless, looking straight at the hand-held with a blank look. Everyone waited for her response but none came. Jake broke the silence.

"Holly, don't let him ride roughshod over you. Stop him. This mustn't happen."

Tom, still holding Jake away from Holly, and who had said nothing until now, spoke quietly.

"Holly, I will do whatever you want me to do. It is not my role to get involved in family matters. I said I would help you bring your grandmother to safety and that's a promise I will still do my best to fulfil even now if you want me to. For what it's worth, I believe it is not for us to decide when death should come. I'm not a religious man but I think fate determines when we must go. And it's natural that each of us clings on as long as we can, often in the face of great challenges, to eke out the last drops of life. But, Holly, you must decide."

There was another short period of silence. Holly could sense all the eyes in the room trained on her.

"Come on Gran, we're going home."

Holly walked across to Mary, helped her from her chair and guided her upstairs. As she did so, she ended the call with her father.

"We need to pack your things. I'll help you."

For the next ten minutes or so, Holly busied herself packing Mary's things and her own. She sent Jake away when he came upstairs with a last ditch attempt at protest.

Half an hour later Holly, Jake and Mary were ready to go. They had decided they would leave the refuge that, only a few days earlier, had seemed the best option for Mary's safety. It took only ten minutes for Tom to organise to have their driverless brought to the house. Hasty farewells were said. Holly couldn't hold back her tears as Wilfred and Mary embraced warmly. Just as they were about to head out of the door, Wilfred insisted they stay just a few minutes longer and they were treated to a final reprise of the main melody from the abandoned concert.

Holly's mind was in a fog. She was worried about her father, worried about her grandmother but somehow she also felt strangely liberated. Her father had taken away the responsibility for Mary's future from her. Now she just wanted to get out of Hunstanton as fast as possible. She felt like a fugitive from a war as their driverless negotiated the back streets out of the town. Even though it was still quite early on a Sunday morning, they could hear sirens. Holly recognised the road out of the town, the one they'd entered nervously only days before. Their mission was over.

CHAPTER TWENTY-TWO

City of Westminster, Greater London.
Tuesday 28 November 2045

The serenity of the Rose Garden on a bright November morning contrasted sharply with the political storm brewing around the Prime Minister. As Edward Watson glanced out of the window, he saw the Downing Street gardener going about his work tidying away the vestiges of summer, cutting back and clearing the autumn fall of leaves. At this moment he envied someone whose job involved simple, clearly defined tasks and where, apart from the vagaries of the weather, success or failure was in his own hands. Today, however, was going to be the most difficult of his own political career. But, as he put the finishing touches to the speech he would make in a couple of hours in Parliament to try to convince MPs to retain the current euthanasia laws, his mind was wandering.

The days that had passed since his explosive TV debate with Evie Smith had been especially challenging for him. He had been lobbied by people from every section of his Party, those wanting to keep the status quo, those wanting the termination age raised to this age or that, and those who wanted the whole thing swept away. It reminded him of the Parliamentary debates forty years previously about changing the age limit for abortion. Then the argument had been all about the beginning of life, a subject on which there was now little disagreement. The argument now about the ending of life was much more heated and vitriolic. Today was the day when it would all come to a head in the big set-piece debate.

The meetings and phone conversations of the past few days that troubled him most were the lobbyists with vested interests.

Hearing people argue passionately about the rights and wrongs of terminating life at ninety were fine when he believed them to be motivated by genuinely held views. However, the lobbying of politicians by people representing all sorts of commercial and other pressure groups seemed to have reached a new level of intensity. So, he'd agreed to a call from a woman who quite unabashed told him why increasing the termination age to ninety-five, or preferably 100, would be excellent news for the care home sector which she represented. On the same day, he'd met another lobbyist who spoke for the organisation representing termination clinics who naturally wanted the status quo to stay. The lobbyist had made no effort to dress up his arguments as public benefits but quite unashamedly said any change would damage his members' profits. However, the Prime Minister knew that his view on the subject would not be influenced by the strength of arguments but by the size of the donation.

If all of this wasn't enough for Edward to process, there remained the dilemma of his father. He'd not visited him since their tearful encounter just over two weeks ago but he'd spoken to him several times. He was deeply troubled by the conflicting emotions he was balancing within himself. He wanted his father to stay alive but he had suffered considerable political damage since the revelation during the TV debate about his opposition to his dad's wish for voluntary euthanasia. But it was deeper than that. Never mind the political fallout, he was becoming increasingly unsure about his own refusal to accede to his father's wishes. All that had to be for another day, though, as he tried to focus on the important task rushing out of the future towards him right now.

He read through his speech again. He had rehearsed likely questions and answers with his advisors the evening before. He remembered what his dad had said to him when he had fretted over exams as a teenager about the dangers of over-preparation. He had ten minutes before the car would arrive to take him to the Commons. He flipped through some of the front pages of the papers. He had already read the digest prepared by his team earlier but he still liked to read some of them for himself. The Daily Mail, once a great supporter of Conservative governments but now the self-styled 'voice of the people' had somehow survived. Many other papers had fallen by the wayside, victims of commercial pressures or, more worryingly, political pressure. The British Press was still in theory free but there wasn't much of it and its influence was much reduced. Today the Mail's headline, quoting a survey carried out in the previous few days, thundered 'Stop it now – bring termination to an end'.

Fortunately, a knock on the door announcing the arrival of his car meant that Edward was spared the details of the Mail story and he consciously expunged it from his mind as he gathered his papers, put on his coat and headed for the door. Emerging into the Downing Street sunshine, he was greeted by a scene that had not changed in a hundred years. The media pack gathered behind crowd barriers on the far side of the street shouted their predictable questions at the Prime Minister. He ignored them and disappeared into the car which left quickly.

Richmond House was literally just across Whitehall from Downing Street and Edward often walked there but, as the euthanasia debate had intensified in recent weeks, his security advisors had forbidden it. The journey by car actually took longer because it was necessary to turn left up Whitehall and then double back. But just as the car went through the security gates at the entrance to Downing Street, Edward's secure hand-held rang.

"Prime Minister, a call for you that I think you will want

to take."

"Who is it?" asked the Prime Minister, struggling to contain his irritation.

"The League, Sir."

Edward accepted the call. It didn't matter that the time in the car was short because the caller had a short, sharp message which only required a few seconds to deliver. Nor did it invite a reply.

"Good morning Edward. It's an important day for you. For all of us. Smith appears to have stirred things up rather a lot. And the King is supporting her. So I thought I would remind you why you need to remain firm. The reasons we need termination at 90 haven't changed. If you give any concessions, it'll be the beginning of a slippery slope. We'll have another care crisis. We'll have younger generations up in arms again. But most of all, you'll see the League really flexing its muscles. The police are useless. The NARA have lost the plot. It's the League who will help you keep order. What you've seen in Hunstanton is just for starters. And never forget how we helped you into power. We made sure that those nice reasonable people in your Party were silenced. We made sure that Labour became a spent force. We made sure that older people were 'persuaded' to give up their generous pensions. You need us, Edward. Don't forget that. Have a nice day."

The call ended as the car drew up to its destination. Edward didn't have time to dwell on the call other than its simple message. But he did just have time to realise that it was a familiar voice, although one that he hadn't heard for a long time. As the door was opened for him, his brain delivered a name – David, yes it was David, the drone guy, from a long time ago. But, for Edward that was now an irrelevant detail.

Parliament had moved to Richmond House twenty years before as a temporary measure to allow the refurbishment of the Palace of Westminster. But the economic crash of the mid-2020's had caused the project to be delayed and then postponed indefinitely and MPs were still in their 'temporary' home and unlikely to leave anytime soon. But the Prime Minister was still focussed on the chilling phone call he'd just received and not on the recent troubled history of the Parliamentary estate. Once again, he found himself having to try to banish negative thoughts from his mind to stay focussed as he got out of the car and walked the short distance into the building.

CHAPTER TWENTY-THREE

Bromley, Greater London
Tuesday 28 November 2045

About twenty kilometres to the south, Holly was only paying partial attention to the live images of the Prime Minister arriving at Parliament showing on the news channels being flicked through by David now in the lounge of his mother's home in Bromley. Holly, Jake and Mary had come straight back from Hunstanton two days before and David, now discharged from hospital, had come to stay there. Mary was sat on her sofa with the 1960s retro clothes she'd bought for today still lying there as they had been on the day she was taken by Holly and Jake. She was looking at the screen, but Holly could not be sure that her grandmother was unaware of the potential significance of the news for her.

"Dad, can we switch it off?"

David complied. Then, after a nervous cough, turned to his mother.

"Mum, you have remembered that it's your birthday today, haven't you? Your ninetieth birthday and your Happy Deathday. Some of the family and a few friends will be arriving soon for lunch. And then a bit later on, the nurses will be here to help you go to sleep."

Holly winced at her father's description but before she could add something to soften the message, Mary responded.

"Yes dear. You've told me about this before," was her reply, as though the information he was imparting was about just another day when nothing out of the ordinary was going to happen.

Holly had persuaded her father not to complicate matters

further for Mary and so didn't mention the Parliamentary debate coinciding with her birthday which could change history and determine her grandmother's fate. Over the past twenty four hours, Holly had flicked back and forth in her emotions. When she saw her father being brought in a wheelchair up the driveway of Mary's home the previous evening, she had been flooded with a mixture of guilt and sympathy. She had caused the crash. He had been badly injured. He was going to need further operations to try to repair his leg. He would possibly not be able to walk properly ever again. It was yet more evidence that she had failed to be a good daughter, failed to perform the role of nearest relative, even though her father never allowed her that close. She spent the evening sorting out a room for her father, making him a meal and, with Jake's help, lifting him from the chair into bed. For the first time in her life, she had helped him in the bathroom.

All of this meant she was almost able to push her grandmother's fate somewhere near the back of her mind but when she had fallen into bed exhausted the previous night, her conflicting views resurfaced. By this morning she felt as though her doubts about what was going to happen to Mary were outweighing concern for her father and her natural desire to please him.

Holly was relieved when Mary's best friend and neighbour, Jean, arrived earlier than expected. She came into the room, hugged Mary warmly and asked her,

"So when are you going to put on your special outfit, Mary?"

Mary smiled, apparently understanding, and Jean used this as a cue to take her away to her bedroom and help her change.

Holly was left alone in the lounge with her father. She knew this would be the last chance. She took it.

"Do you really want this to happen, Dad?" she asked

quietly.

"It's for the best, Holly. Look at her. She doesn't know what's going on."

"But what about the vote? We can't go ahead if the law is going to be changed."

Holly had checked the news feeds herself and, remarkably, it was unclear when a new higher termination age, or even a complete abolition of the law, would come into effect if passed by MPs. So, as her grandmother's death day dawned, it was far from certain that she would no longer be alive by tomorrow.

"I've tried to check that. The answer was not entirely satisfactory. We will apply the law as it stands at the time, was the best I could get out of the agency," replied her father.

He paused, cleared his throat and then continued.

"But I expect the law to stay as it is. I've spoken to the PM. He will stand firm."

"You've spoken to the PM? What do you mean? When?" Holly couldn't believe what she was hearing.

"Earlier today. We keep in touch. You know we were close when I was active in the League. It's important we keep everything as it is. And it's best for Gran."

"I don't understand, Dad. On this day of all days, I just don't understand."

Holly suspected that her father wasn't going to concede anything or show any weakness. Even though he had been through a major trauma, even though he himself could have died just days before, he seemed unwavering in his belief. She wanted to know why. What was the real reason? Would she ever know?

To fill time, she picked up the documents about the termination. Her father had printed them all off and had them neatly organised in a special plastic folder. The arrangements for termination were disturbingly clinical and bureaucratic. A month or so before someone's ninetieth birthday, an old style letter arrived through the post reminding people that it was their legal duty to respond indicating whether they wanted to die at home or at a termination clinic. The letter asked them to pay the termination fee in advance and reminded them of the severe penalties if they attempted to evade death on their due date. Holly thought the tone of the letter was a bit like a reminder to pay car tax or to fulfil some other mandatory civic duty.

Her father had told her that he had completed the documentation and paid the fee a couple of weeks before. He had discussed it with his mother, as he had on previous occasions and, as ever, she had said little and certainly asked no questions.

By chance, David had booked the evening slot for his mother's departure from this life. The nursing company offered three slots, morning, afternoon and evening. David had told Holly he thought it would be nice for his Mum to have a modest lunch with a few family and friends, then maybe a walk with close family in the afternoon before the nurses arrived.

Holly placed the documents back in the folder and returned them to the table. She looked at her father trapped in his wheelchair. He appeared lost in his own thoughts. Holly realised how unusual this must be for him. He rarely had quiet moments of doing nothing. He was always doing something, usually working, planning, organising something or other, or sorting out his mother, something that he often undertook, it seemed, as another item on his to do list. Then, out of the quietness, he spoke.

"It'll be funny without her," he said, "In about ten hours' time, she will probably be dead. Her death will be painless and it will release her from the torment of dementia. It is definitely the right thing for her. But there'll be a gap. Like there was a gap, a very big gap when Emily went and when Hazel went."

This was the first time Holly had heard her father talk like this. When her sister had died, Holly was too young to understand her parents' reaction. When her mother died, her father had briefly allowed his feelings to show but not for long. But now, this small opening of an emotional window and the pitiful sight of her father stuck in a wheelchair moved Holly in a way that would normally seem uncomfortable.

"Oh Dad, it doesn't have to be this way."

But, as she moved towards her father and before he could reply, their attention was dramatically diverted by the reappearance of her grandmother in the room. Holly had never seen her dressed like this before. However odd it looked, Holly could see that it was making her happy. She had a beaming smile and she was talking animatedly about going to dances as a teenager wearing mini dresses and patent high-heels. Here she was at the age of ninety recreating her youth in retro clothes. Holly didn't know whether to be happy or sad about this.

"Oh Gran, you look very glamorous."

David didn't seem to know where to look. He confined himself to complimenting her weakly on her appearance. But it didn't sound that convincing.

Over the next hour or so, a small group of family members arrived for lunch. It was a modest affair, just a buffet of salads, quiches and the like. On the day which was certainly her birthday but which also might be her deathday, Mary was surrounded by her son, her granddaughter and his partner, a few more distant relatives as well as a few close neighbours and friends. Holly was pleased that her father had realised that speeches were not the order of the day. Instead he confined himself to inviting the guests to raise a glass to Mary to congratulate her on reaching her ninetieth birthday. Maybe he just didn't feel up to making a speech, although she doubted that would have stopped him. Then the second tier of the deathday cake was produced and cut into small pieces and offered to the guests. There was no mention of death.

Mary alternated between lapsing into lucid nostalgia, mostly of early memories with her late husband, and quietness as others talked around her. Holly noticed that guests seemed unsure how to behave, something which would probably have been true even if Mary's deathday hadn't coincided with the parliamentary debate. But this was undoubtedly accentuated by the political drama about to unfold. Concern for David provided a welcome distraction for them all.

Holly was glad when David called the proceedings to a close announcing that Mary needed some fresh air before it got dark. It had been decided that only David and Holly would be with Mary to the end, her only child and only grandchild, a decision that no one else in the family contested, even Jake.

Then, as the departing family members and friends made their farewells, there was a mix of sadness and relief in the room. No one lost their composure. There were many firm hugs, affectionate kisses and kind words. Holly was conscious how, in years gone by, before the 90 Law, some of those in this small group had been through the experience of saying goodbye to the dying, expecting it to be the last time they would see someone but not always knowing for certain.

Today in theory was different. They all knew for certain that Mary would die that night, peacefully and painlessly, mandated by the law of the land in her best interests and those of her fellow citizens. Except that they didn't, because everything might be about to change. But even that knowledge didn't change their behaviour. Holly was glad because it would have been unbelievably cruel to have raised any false hopes of survival, particularly to a woman with dementia whose grasp of reality was intermittent at best. More than that, though, Holly suspected that most, including still part of herself, thought it for the best.

The last guest to leave was Jake.

"Are you certain you don't want me to stay?"

"No, Jake, I'll be fine."

Holly knew that having Jake there would add extra tension and she would have another set of emotions to manage. She was pleased Jake put up no further fight, hugged her and left. For a few minutes after his departure, Holly, David and Mary sat silently in the lounge. Holly naturally waited for her father to announce the next stage in proceedings. That was what he did. And that was what she did. Waited for her father. But this didn't happen. He just sat, looking ahead with a look of vacancy on his face, a look Holly thought she had never seen before. It was a look that frightened her. She wanted to ask him what he was thinking. She wanted to ask him what he wanted to happen. She even wanted to ask him about the court case she had read about concerning his company. But she did none of this. Instead she moved the proceedings onwards.

"OK Dad, let's go for a look round the garden. It's not raining and I don't think it's too cold. Gran, would you like to have a look round the garden?"

"That would be nice, dear."

Holly busied herself for a few minutes finding coats for her father and grandmother, threw on a woolly jumper of her own, and wheeled her father onto the patio. Holly pushed the wheelchair containing her father while her grandmother steadied herself by holding onto Holly's arm. It wasn't a large garden but it had been well looked after, first by Mary and Colin but, more recently, by a gardener. For the next ten minutes or so, this sad procession of three generations made its way around the lawn, stopping at various features to admire the autumn colours and the few remaining flowers. Holly had hoped her grandmother would add a running commentary but this time she just looked intently at everything without comment. It was as though she was committing it all to memory.

Holly steered them towards the small pond and bench at the point furthest from the house. She parked her father next to the bench where she and her grandmother sat. Holly noticed a neighbour looking discretely from an upstairs window, no doubt wondering why these three should choose to sit outside in the fading light of a November afternoon. Unexpectedly, her father spoke.

"I remember you building this pond. Dad sweated over it for months. I should have helped him."

"You were too busy, David. You didn't have time. Anyway, Colin enjoyed having a project."

Holly kept out of this conversation as the older generations reminisced. But she detected a different mood in her father. He seemed more reflective. But what really struck her was how her grandmother seemed to be at peace. This was, she thought, how she had imagined it. How it should be when people died. No uncertainty. No fighting to the last. Just acceptance. Dignity. Quiet. At this moment, she too felt some sort of peace.

They were probably on the bench for ten or fifteen minutes before Holly, starting to feel the cold despite her jumper, suggested they go inside. She helped Mary up, took the brake off the wheelchair and the three made their way back towards the house. As Holly opened the patio doors, Mary tapped her on the arm.

"Just a minute, please, dear."

Her grandmother stood, turned towards the garden, looked ahead intently, turned back and stepped towards the door.

"Thank you."

By the time Mary, David and Holly were back inside, the light was fading fast and lights were coming on in houses in the street and away across the South-East London landscape. Holly imagined the cosy suburban scene playing out all around them, with children arriving back from school, adults from work, and all settling down for an evening in the warmth of their homes. But on this day across England, around 1,000 lives would be coming to an end as Mary's was about to. 'Happy Leavers', they were known as. Many weren't happy. Some tried to flee. Some took voluntary euthanasia at younger ages. But it seemed that most accepted it. Even she had. It had become the new normal.

It was now coming up to 5 p.m. Mary was sat on her sofa motionless. Holly wanted to know how the debate was going in Parliament but she was reluctant to risk upsetting the equilibrium. But, not for the first time, Mary surprised her.

"When are they coming, then?" she asked addressing her question to her son.

"When is who coming, mother?"

"The nurses, of course, David."

"In about an hour," he replied, trying to conceal his surprise.

David seemed to think this exchange gave him permission to switch on the BBC News Channel. The coverage of the debate in Parliament was in full swing. The number of MPs had been cut to 495 at the same time as the Lords had been abolished. However, just about every one of those 495 wanted to be seen to have their say on this matter. It seemed like every possible view on euthanasia was aired from both extremes of the argument. There were those wanting repeal of all the euthanasia laws, including voluntary euthanasia, even to those wanting the compulsory termination age reduced to eighty-five. As they watched, it was the middle of the time allowed for debate and Holly saw a series of backbenchers, some in the chamber itself but many joining virtually, have their moment in the Parliamentary limelight. Mary was looking at the screen but registered no comprehension.

After a few minutes listening to backbenchers, Holly felt none the wiser about which way the vote was likely to go. She picked up the remote, flicked through the channels and found the Political Editor of Times TV speculating. It was going to be very close but the informed view, he said, was that Evie Smith would not get a majority for an outright repeal. Behind the scenes, according to his sources, discussions were going on about a compromise between repeal and the status quo. The outcome was on a knife-edge.

CHAPTER TWENTY-FOUR

City of Westminster, Greater London
Tuesday 28 November 2045

Indeed it was. Just as the political pundits were sharing their speculation with the nation, the real stuff was happening away from the cameras. The Prime Minister's Commons office, on the top floor of Richmond House, was a surprisingly modest place although it did command an impressive view across the London skyline. Edward Watson had been out of the Chamber for an hour or so. He'd made his opening speech and felt pleased with how it had gone. Then he'd stayed long enough listening to the first few backbenchers so as not to appear rude but then had slipped out to the sanctuary of his office. His advisors had tried to get him to spend a bit of time on other pressing matters, like the latest twists and turn in the deteriorating relationship with Russia. He knew he wouldn't be able to focus on anything else until the vote had happened. And he knew that the next few hours would not be a matter of just waiting. At some point deals would be offered and would need to be assessed.

Sure enough, that moment arrived sooner than he had expected. As Edward made a poor attempt to read and digest a Foreign Office briefing paper on Russia, there was a knock on his door.

"Prime Minister, Ms Smith would like a quick word if you're free?"

"Yes of course. Show her in," he responded, glad of the interruption to his Russian reading.

Smith walked in confidently, with the unmistakable glow of confidence she always seemed to radiate. Edward noted that she had returned to her trademark flat shoes.

"Well, Evie, nice of you to call in. I thought we each put our case well earlier?" offered the PM in an attempt to create a mood of friendliness.

"I agree," replied Evie rather curtly. "May I come straight to the point, Prime Minister. We've done our soundings, as I'm sure you have. And this is how we see it. We are probably about ten votes short of getting a clear majority for repeal. However, we believe your chances of getting a vote for the status quo are rather worse. So, if our assessment is correct, we might lose the vote at 10pm but, if we still believe this to be the case closer to the vote, we'll put down an amendment for a compromise of raising the termination age to ninety-five which I'm sure we'd win. I would have thought that you would not want to be in the position of having to argue for the status quo against ninety-five which sounds like a much less attractive place for you to be than defending the status quo against complete repeal. So, to save yourself a lot of aggravation, why don't you just agree to this now and we can make a joint statement to the effect that we are withdrawing the repeal proposal and both supporting an increase to ninety-five?"

Edward had been weighing up his options as Evie spoke. His team had done the soundings and broadly they had delivered the same expected result. His instinct was to tough it out. If the repeal vote was lost, that would be the end of it for now. The current law would stay in place. He would have won. But he also knew that the issue wouldn't go away and, as night follows day, his opponents would be back with a new proposal to raise the age, probably in a matter of weeks. As he made to respond, Evie added a final thought.

"Just one more thing, Edward, to help you make up your mind. I know I've been making your life very difficult in recent weeks. It's nothing personal but, if you agree to the compromise I'm suggesting, I can promise you that I'll be fully cooperative in the coming months on all the other issues that you're trying to resolve – Russia, the transport crisis etc. If on the other hand, you dig in your heels, then I wouldn't be surprised if there are calls within the Party for a leadership challenge, not that I will be initiating them."

It took every ounce of willpower for Edward to restrain himself in response to this. He knew full well that if he agreed to the compromise, Smith would claim it as a victory despite what she had just said about being supportive. On the other hand, if he stuck out for the status quo and lost, there would likely be a leadership challenge straight away. He was between a political rock and a hard place.

He knew he should mull it over, speak to his advisors and then get back to her. But he was tired. He was worn down by it all. He was, if honest with himself, intimidated by Evie, intimidated by her confidence, by her youthfulness. She was the future. He was the past. He doubted there was enough fire left in his belly, even though the League of Youth's warning from this morning was still ringing in his ears. But he would keep her waiting.

"I hear what you say, Evie. I'll let you know when I have had a chance to think about it. I won't take long."

"Thank you Edward. I'll wait to hear from you."

She stood up, smiled directly at him, turned and walked out. Edward would make her wait but he had already made up his mind.

CHAPTER TWENTY-FIVE

Bromley, Greater London
Tuesday 28 November 2045

As this decisive conversation had been going on in the corridors of power, Holly was looking out of the window of her grandmother's home. She was expecting what she saw next. A small, white van drew up outside. 'Croydon Care Solutions' was imprinted in reasonably discreet lettering on both sides. People made fun of the names chosen by these termination agencies, so some had started using unmarked vehicles. But it was a highly competitive market and they needed to advertise. Two people, one man and one woman, got out, went round to the back and removed a number of boxes and cases, locked the van and walked towards the house and pushed the entry bell. Holly switched off the news channel and went to the door.

"Hello, it's Croydon Care Solutions. I think you are expecting us."

"Yes, of course, do come in," replied Holly pressing the switch to let them through.

Once inside, the two termination nurses introduced themselves as Oliver, a slightly gaunt-looking man, probably in his forties and Gemma, a bit younger and slightly over-weight. Holly examined them intently as they started going through the documents with her father. She was trying to imagine who would want this job. Killing people for a living. They were business-like and gave the impression of wanting to get on with the job in hand. They had a plan, a running order and they were not to be diverted from it. When her father asked a question, they were polite in their response but sounded just a little exasperated.

The first half an hour was taken up with checking and double-checking the documents and getting David to sign what seemed like endless consent forms. Mary was in the room but Gemma and Oliver only involved her in the conversation in what Holly considered a perfunctory and slightly patronising way. Eventually, they seemed satisfied that everything was in order and were about to embark on explaining what was going to happen next. David, however, had a further question.

"Holly, please can you wheel me through to the dining room?"

Holly realised he wanted a private conversation with the nurses. She went across, manoeuvred her father and signalled to the two nurses to follow. Holly went back to the lounge and sat with Mary but she could hear what was being said despite the lowering of voices.

"Look, I know you are just here to do your job," started David, "but I want to know how what's going on in Parliament as we speak will affect all this. It looks likely the law could have changed by ten o'clock tonight so what happens then?"

It was Oliver who assumed the leading role to respond.

"We are of course aware of that, David, but we haven't yet been given any instructions from our office. As the law stands, your mother's termination must happen before midnight tonight and that is the position we are assuming unless we hear to the contrary."

"That doesn't sound very satisfactory, if I may say so. Even though my mother is, it would appear, blissfully unaware of what is going on, it seems very unfair that we should all be on tenterhooks waiting for news. Do we know if the law will be changed straight away?"

"I am not a legal expert but I assume any change in the law will need Royal Assent which I imagine will not happen straight away so my guess, and it's only a guess, is that the law is likely to be the same as it is now by midnight tonight, whatever has happened in Parliament."

The conversation from the dining room went quiet. Holly expected her father, who liked certainty, who liked a clear plan, to object further. But he didn't and he reappeared in the lounge, his wheelchair pushed by Oliver. At this moment, Holly felt a sudden pang of nervousness grip her. She felt a growing sense that the loss of her grandmother, now potentially only a few hours away, was something for which she hadn't properly prepared. The process was underway. The train was leaving the station.

"I think we should make a start," suggested Gemma, with a more sympathetic tone than Oliver had managed.

Gemma then took charge of the proceedings and, unlike Oliver earlier, she addressed her explanation of what was going to happen mainly at Mary but in a way that included David and Holly.

"In a few moments, we will go through to the bedroom, Mary. I understand from your son that this is where you would like to spend your final evening. What we will do is get you comfortable in there. I think you'll maybe want to get changed into something more suitable? It's a nice dress, you're wearing, Mary but probably not right for this evening."

This was a sentiment with which Holly wholly but silently agreed.

"When we've explained everything, perhaps you and Holly would like to go through there and I'm sure she can help you get changed. When everything is ready, we will give you a little drink which will help relax you and then you'll probably feel you want to lie down in bed. Then Oliver and I will just stay in the background and you can chat to your son and your granddaughter. I see that Holly has got a digital album here for you all to look at. That'll be nice. Then a bit later, when you're feeling nicely relaxed and the three of you have said all you want to say, I'll be giving you a small injection in your arm. You'll feel very drowsy and sleepy and you'll find yourself drifting off very soon after that. It'll all be very painless. We just want to make it as pleasant as we can for you and your family. Do you have any questions, Mary?"

There were several seconds of silence. Mary stared straight ahead. She appeared to be unaware that she'd been asked a question. Holly felt she should repeat Gemma's question.

"Gran, did you hear what the nurse said?"

"Yes dear, it all sounds fine to me," she replied straight away.

Holly thought it sounded as though she was assenting to a trip out, the choice of recipe for dinner, or the selection of a film to watch for the evening.

Holly and Mary went through to the bedroom leaving Oliver and Gemma busying themselves preparing their drugs. Holly sat Mary on the side of her bed. She knelt on the floor, removed the patent shoes and took them round to a wardrobe where she hid them away. She returned to Mary, asked her to stand up and was thankful that the dress had a zip which she undid, allowing the dress to come off easily. Mary complied uncomplainingly and unaware that Holly was having a flashback, a flashback to the many times she had done this for her mother when she was ill. She had helped her dress and undress and helped her in the bathroom. So she was already over the awkwardness of attending to the personal needs of a close family member but it reminded her of her Mum and the way she had gone and the way she had helped her.

Banishing these unhelpful thoughts from her mind, she found her grandmother's nightdress, helped her put it on and suggested she sat in a bedside chair.

"We're ready," she called through.

After a few moments, the two nurses came through to the bedroom. Holly collected her father. Just as he was about to enter the bedroom in his wheelchair, David got a news alert on his hand-held. The Times TV Political Editor was reporting that Westminster was awash with rumours of a compromise proposal before the vote.

"Turn it off, Dad," hissed Holly, a message reinforced by Oliver.

Once they were all in the room, Oliver and Gemma proceeded quickly and efficiently. With Mary sat in a chair next to her bed, they offered her a small plastic beaker.

"Just drink it down at your own speed, Mary," said Gemma.

CHAPTER TWENTY-SIX

Bromley, Greater London
Tuesday 28 November 2045

There were two subdued bedside lights and a standard lamp in the room giving out an orange glow. The curtains were drawn but a fanlight window had been left open allowing a faint rumble of the evening traffic to permeate the room. Life was going on as normal outside this space which death was about to invade. For several minutes there was silence in the room, interrupted only by the occasional sounds of Mary swallowing the liquid which was preparing her for her death. Eventually, Holly broke the silence.

"Gran, shall we have some music? I've put together some of your favourites."

The opening bars of Fleetwood Mac's 'Albatross' started to fill the room. Holly moved to sit on the bed next to her grandmother who was still in the chair.

"Do you remember this, Gran?" she asked as she flicked on the digital album which was displaying holiday photos from a family trip to southern Spain.

David, who might normally hold back from these types of nostalgic conversations, seemed to want to be part of it. He leant across in his wheelchair, alongside his daughter, and looked at the images which Holly was showing.

"Yes, that was a great holiday. It was the year before the Pandemic. Look at Holly, there, Mum. She must only have been about five or six."

"I was older than that, Dad - the Pandemic started in 2020," Holly corrected her father.

Holly knew that her father's attention would not be

focussed on the date of his daughter's birth but on the pictures of his late wife, Hazel, Holly's mother. Since her death, they had rarely looked at pictures of her together. How attractive she was, Holly thought, and how much her father had loved her mother. She was convinced of that. She was sure also that their marriage had been an overwhelmingly happy one. Then the conversation had moved on to other more recent family events sparked by the pictures Holly had selected. Mary joined in intermittently, sometimes apparently achieving perfect recall of events many years before, but other times offering only a vacant stare.

Twenty or more minutes passed like this with the two nurses remaining unobtrusively in the background. But then, exactly as they had predicted, Mary started to feel sleepy.

"I think I need to lie down, dear," she said, directing her remark to Holly.

As the three family members started to rearrange themselves, Gemma intervened.

"Perhaps you should just make a quick trip to the bathroom, Mary, before you get into bed?"

Without waiting for a response, she guided Mary towards the bathroom, leaving Holly, David and Oliver in the bedroom. Somehow this seemed perfectly normal as this was now becoming a medical procedure, albeit one conducted in the comfort and familiarity of home. Several minutes later, Gemma and Mary emerged from the bathroom.

"Everything done in there. That's good," announced Gemma, clearly pleased that this no doubt final round of ablutions was out of the way.

Holly helped pull back the duvet and Gemma guided Mary, now visibly drowsy, into the bed where she let out a deep sigh as her head hit the pillow. Her eyes closed and she lay motionless on the bed. Holly couldn't help but move forward towards her, suddenly fearing that the process was going faster than she had anticipated. Irrationally, she suddenly thought that Gemma might have administered the lethal injection in the bathroom even though she had been clear earlier that the family would be there at every stage.

"Have you given it to her already?" she said accusingly in Gemma's direction.

"No, of course not, Holly. It'll be another half an hour or so before we are ready for that. Just keep talking to your grandmother. She'll be able to hear what you're saying."

Holly pulled the chair up close to the bed. Holly had thought about this moment. She had rehearsed it. She felt able to start the conversation with her dying grandmother without showing any self-consciousness. She felt empowered to block out the other three people in the room. For a few minutes, she spoke of her early memories of her grandmother and told her how much she had enjoyed being with her when she was a child. Then she talked about more recent times. How her grandmother had been such a support when Holly went through difficult times as a teenager and, even more so, in the last few years.

"Gran, you've been like a mother to me since Mum died. Even since you've been ill."

"I love you Gran. I love you. I'll see you again one day."

She lay with her head resting on Mary's chest and the room was filled with Holly's gentle sobbing. Mary put her arm across Holly's back. As she lay there, Holly hoped her father would now say his last words but she knew he would find it difficult, very difficult. He was a man who had the gift of the gab but for business, for politics, for organisational matters but not for expressing his emotions. She was alarmed when he spoke.

"I just need a few minutes, Holly, to go to the bathroom.

Will you please take me?"

Holly released herself from the loose embrace of her grandmother, and wheeled her father out of the room and into the bathroom. She helped him stand up, checked that he felt steady and left him. Holly imagined that, knowing that it must be his turn next to say his farewells, he was composing himself. As she waited, she glanced out of the window. The vehicle hadn't been there earlier when the nurses had arrived. But, parked right by the entrance to the driveway, blocking it in fact, was the unmistakeable shape of a narabanc. Even in the darkness, there was no mistaking it.

Her father called out that he was ready and Holly re-entered the bathroom.

"Dad, why is there a narabanc outside?"

"It's standard practice, Holly, just a precaution to make sure people comply with the law."

"It's sinister, Dad. It makes me feel sick."

David ignored her comments.

"I'm just going to check the news."

He switched his hand-held off silent. Laura Kuenssberg's voice filled the bathroom.

"The BBC is predicting the closest of results which could hang on what was said by the two leading protagonists in their closing speeches before the vote. We are expecting those speeches any moment now. I reckon it's unlikely to be much more than fifteen minutes before the result is known."

Holly wheeled her father back into the bedroom, positioned the wheelchair right next to the bed and stepped back into the shadows, allowing her father to take centre stage.

"They're about to vote and it's going to be very close, by all accounts," he announced to the room.

Gemma and Oliver offered no reaction as though this information was completely unconnected to the task at hand.

David leant over his mother who seemed to be fully asleep. Her breathing was loud but not laboured. She hadn't said anything when Holly had spoken to her. He started to speak.

"You've been a very good mother to me. Thank you for everything, Mum. I know I've not always paid you as much attention as I should have done. I was difficult as a teenager. Then when I left home, I was so focussed on my work. I didn't spend as much time with you and Dad as I should have."

Holly was surprised at her father's eloquence.

"Then when I got married and had the girls, there was another excuse for not paying you enough attention. But you never complained and you were always there and interested when I did make an effort. And you've always been brilliant with Holly. But I hope I've been better in recent years. I've tried my best to do what I thought was right for you since you became ill. Sorry if it's not been good enough."

With this, he let out an anguished sob and tears streamed down his face. Mary stirred from her slumber.

"David, are you alright?"

"Yes, I'm OK, Mum," he replied unconvincingly, as Holly crossed the room to comfort her father, something she could only remember doing once before, on the day of her mother's death.

Gemma and Oliver, well-versed in witnessing scenes like this, remained visibly unmoved in the background. Mary lay motionless in the bed with Holly now cradling her grandmother's head, and David slumped awkwardly half out of his wheelchair with his head on Mary's stomach.

After three minutes at most, and just as Gemma was preparing herself to propose they move to the next stage of the process, the pathos of the moment was shattered by the buzz of a news alert on David's hand-held. He must have left it on after consulting it in the bathroom.

He pulled himself up from the bed, pressed the hand-held and read the headline to the room.

'Closing statements by PM and Evie Smith in 90Law debate starting now'. Without hesitation he pressed 'Watch Live Now' and the sound of the House of Commons filled the room where death was imminent. All five occupants listened as first Evie Smith spoke. It was a short speech.

"The choice before the House tonight is simple. Continue with the unjust and immoral law that our country misguidedly adopted ten years ago. Remain a pariah among nations for such a draconian and divisive measure which abrogates the natural laws of the universe. Continue breaching the universal moral code, common standards of decency and a sense of what we all know in our heart of hearts to be right and instead usurp the right to take life away when we know that is a choice God never intended us to have. That is one option. The other, better, option would be to rid ourselves of this law once and for all. However, we recognise that may be a step too far tonight. So, we propose that this great nation should begin a process and come to its senses and take a step on the road to a more just, a more normal, a more rational system. We should do this by increasing the termination age to ninety-five thus sparing hundreds of thousands of mainly fit and healthy people an untimely death and offering them five more years with their loved ones and friends."

Smith sat down to cheers and applause which continued as Edward Watson rose and started his statement. Almost as soon as he opened his mouth, Smith realised that what was about to happen was not in the script.

"Tonight, my friends, you may have two choices on paper but, in reality, only one. You might think the difference between ninety or ninety-five as the age of termination is unimportant. If we increase the age to ninety-five, that will make a lot of

people happy but still preserve the principle that life should
be brought to a definite end at a mandatory age. But I tell you
that this will be a grave error, a slippery slope leading to the
eventual return to unlimited lifespans and all the grief that
will bring in its wake."

There were howls of protest from the Commons' benches
as MPs realised that the Prime Minister had ripped up the
agreement, apparently reached only an hour or so earlier. He
ploughed on.

"I won't rehearse all the arguments again but briefly
remember why we introduced the 90 Law ten years ago. It was
because of the terrible injustices wrought upon our younger
generations, not to mention the terrible conditions our older
people lived in. What we gave people instead was fairness
but above all certainty and dignity. Don't throw it all away."

The Speaker of the Commons struggled to make herself
heard above the hubbub as the Prime Minister sat down with
opponents booing him loudly and his supporters cheering. She
eventually brought the House to order and instructed MPs to
use their electronic voting pads, those in the Chamber and
those involved remotely.

Back in Mary's bedroom, Holly hadn't noticed Oliver
taking a syringe from its packet, slowly filling it from a vial
he had taken from his case and then moving close to the
bed. Gemma walked with him and said more loudly than she
would normally in order to be heard above the feed from the
Commons.

"It's now time, Mary, to go to sleep. Do you want any
final words, David? Perhaps you could turn off the news
feed now?"

David said nothing. It took Holly a few seconds to register
what was happening. She experienced the next few moments
as though she were an observer hovering above the scene. She

saw herself swing round and lurch towards Oliver.

"They're about to vote. We need to wait."

Oliver ignored her and continued to come close to the bed. Holly saw herself react instinctively. She lunged at Oliver, knocking the syringe from his hands. Oliver said nothing, stooped down and started gathering the splintered remnants from the floor. Maybe this had happened to him before with grief-stricken relatives trying to frustrate the enforcement of the law? But not surely, thought Holly, in circumstances like these?

Then, just a few seconds later, the news feed burst back into life, 'Result imminent... Result imminent...' it declared.

Everyone in the room froze as the camera on the news feed focussed on the result board. One second, two seconds, three seconds and then it was there, and a reporter recited the result as it appeared, "In favour of increasing the age to 95, 338; 157 against. 338 in favour, 157 against."

The cheers and claps echoing round the Commons disappeared slowly as David decreased the volume on his hand-held and then muted it completely. There was a moment's silence in the room. Holly looked at her father. Gemma for the first time looked uncertain. Oliver was kneeling on the floor, pausing in his task of clearing the mess Holly had created. It was she who broke the silence.

"She must live. You must leave now please."

Gemma and Oliver didn't protest. They gathered their stuff quickly. Holly held her grandmother's hands. David sat back in his wheelchair, motionless. After two or three minutes, Gemma and Oliver said they were ready to leave. Holly took them to the door, opened it and ushered them out. Gemma hesitated, turned back towards Holly, looked in Mary's direction and said,

"God bless you, Mary."

She turned and followed Oliver towards the gate. Holly saw the narabanc still parked in the street at the end of the driveway. Holly whispered a goodbye in the direction of the nurses and shut the door behind them. A few moments later, as people in Mary's street were glued to the screens assimilating the dramatic news from the Commons, the small white van drove slowly away into the evening darkness.

PART THREE

PART THREE

CHAPTER TWENTY-SEVEN

Downing Street, Westminster, Greater London
Thursday 30 November 2045

On the morning of Thursday 30 November, just two days after
Parliament had voted to raise the compulsory termination age
to ninety-five, Edward Watson was pacing up and down the
Cabinet Room in Downing Street unable to confirm what
he instinctively knew to be inevitable. Since the vote, the
clamour for his resignation had become a crescendo. The party
grandees had been to see him. He had discussed his position
with advisors, with friends and with family. A few had said
that he shouldn't allow his premiership to be defined and ended
by this single issue. But the majority had politely refused to
contradict him when he had suggested that his authority in
the party, and probably the country, was now shot through.
Most notably, there had been silence from the League and
silence from those who had supported him. Edward thought
the silence spoke a thousand words.

Shortly before midday, he dismissed his closest advisors
from the room and rang his wife to confirm that he was going
to resign. Sophie had made no further attempt to dissuade
him. Even then, he couldn't quite bring himself to make the
call. For a few moments, he gazed out into the garden. Once
again, the same Downing Street gardener was at work as two
days before and still seemingly oblivious to the national crisis
unfolding around him. This cameo of simple job satisfaction
gave the Prime Minister the courage to confirm his decision to
give up the highest office in the land. He reached for the phone.

"Organise a podium outside for half an hour please," was
his simple message.

For the next twenty-five minutes, he sat alone composing the few words he planned to deliver to the nation to announce his departure. He spurned offers of help from his speech-writers and forcefully refused to allow the Downing Street Communications Chief from seeing the text in advance. At 12.27 he was told that all was ready outside. He composed himself, looked in the mirror and walked towards the door. Just as he was about to leave the room, his private hand-held, which had been left on his desk, rang. Normally, he would have ignored it. But on this occasion, something made him turn around and answer it. Maybe, sub-consciously, it gave him the excuse of delaying the unpleasant task ahead, if only briefly.

"Thank you for letting me know. I will see you shortly," was all anyone heard him say in responding to the call.

He left the room, went out into the hall of Number 10, and, before the door was opened, he whispered to his chief advisor that he needed a car ready immediately after his statement. He went out into the November sunlight, walked confidently to the podium, and briefly scanned the waiting media pack. Then he launched into one of the shortest resignation speeches ever delivered by a resigning Prime Minister. It took less than a minute.

An hour and ten minutes later, a car drew up outside the Robinson Care Home in Cambridge. The car had come directly, ignoring the tradition of a courtesy visit to Buckingham Palace to inform the Monarch. Out stepped a man who once would have attracted a crowd, sometimes of supporters but often of opponents. On his last visit here, he had been Prime Minister but now he was, or would very soon be, just plain Edward Watson MP and his arrival was unaccompanied by fuss or demonstration. He walked into the home and was greeted by the Chief Executive, less obsequiously than previously. He was guided towards the familiar room where he had been a visitor on many occasions before. A policewoman stood guard at the door. She moved to one side. He entered.

Edward was alone in the room. The curtains were drawn and the only light was a small lamp on a table near the window. His father's body lay covered with a sheet except for the head left exposed as though to create a last lingering connection between this life and whatever might follow. Edward moved next to the bed, stood above his father and stared straight at his eyes.

"I'm sorry I didn't get here in time, Dad."

He bent over, bringing his face close to his father's. He imagined he could hear his father's breathing. He half expected to hear his father's voice. Last time he had been in this room, he had broken down sobbing. Today, although too late for his father to appreciate it, he was going to keep his composure. He lowered his face and placed a single kiss on his father's cold cheek.

"Thank you. Thank you for everything."

As he stood up again, he could feel a solitary tear rolling down his face. He stood for several minutes more, lost in a mixture of confusing thoughts. The only sounds were the sound of clicking heels in the corridor outside and the intermittent hum of driverless. Then he took the last look he ever would of his father, turned away and walked to the door. He went outside, smiled at the policewoman and walked to the office of the Chief Executive.

"Would you be so kind, Rachel, as to organise for my car to be brought round to the back?"

"Of course, Edward. I will do that straight away."

For the few minutes that it took for his wishes to be executed, he sat alone opposite the pictures which recorded the academic history of this building before it had become a home. But he studiously ignored the pictures which marked his role in that history. The Chief Executive came out of her room, confirmed that the car was ready and guided him through the corridors to the back entrance.

"Goodbye Edward. And good luck."

"Thank you for calling me. I'm glad I was able to come but I wish I could have got here sooner. My good old Dad saved me another difficult decision, didn't he, by dying naturally. But what timing, eh? I'll be in touch about the arrangements."

Without waiting for a reply, Edward got into the car and was driven away. For the journey back to London, he sat looking out of the window, numb rather than grief-stricken. For now he was nowhere near being able to think about his personal or professional future, or able to care about what would happen to the money.

CHAPTER TWENTY-EIGHT

Bromley, Greater London.
Thursday 30 November, 2045

Later that day, Holly was at her grandmother's house in the London suburbs, looking out of the window, thinking about nothing in particular. This morning she had needed to spend several hours fending off colleagues and clients who were starting to be curious about her extended absence from work. She had agreed it with her boss, but the work that only she could do was backing up with deadlines approaching. None of this mattered much to Holly who was still in shock after the events of two nights previously. Jake had gone to work but was due to join them by lunchtime. Holly had somehow persuaded her father to go back to bed and rest after he had complained of nausea when he had woken up that morning. Mary was sat on the sofa with her deathday clothes neatly folded and inside a box waiting to be wrapped and returned to the shop.

As she waited, Holly's attention was suddenly drawn to a vehicle heading down the street. It was similar to the white van that had been at the house two days earlier. It was making its way slowly past. Exactly at the moment it passed Mary's house, one of the people in the driverless turned towards the house. Holly recognised the face as that of Oliver, one of the nurses from two nights ago, and for a second their eyes met. A momentary shiver swept through Holly as she contemplated the fact that people were still being euthanized either voluntarily or simply because they had reached their ninety-fifth rather than their ninetieth birthday. The van, of course, gave nothing away. Voluntary or compulsory made no difference to the process.

Holly turned on a news channel and live pictures were being relayed from Hunstanton. A funeral cortège was passing along the seafront. The voice-over explained how hundreds had turned out to pay their respects to a man in his nineties who had died after being stabbed by a League of Youth rioter in the remainder colony. At first Holly didn't register the name but then it hit her. Tom Blatchford, the man who'd taken risks to help them only a week ago, had been killed. The news report explained his criminal past and his role in the colony leading opposition to the euthanasia laws. There were many close-up shots of people visibly upset as they lined the route, but also of those who were angry, holding banners demanding further reform of the laws. Just as the report came to an end, there was a buzz on the entry phone. It was Jake. Holly went to the hallway and let him in.

"Tom Blatchford is dead. Stabbed by a Leaguer."

"That's terrible. He was a brave man."

Somehow, though, Holly felt disconnected from the news, from Tom, from Hunstanton, even though she was saddened. Their brief stay in the colony now felt unreal. She was back on familiar safe ground and her grandmother had been saved both by her and by the vote. Jake came over and hugged Holly. They held each other in a longer than normal embrace. Holly knew she was still processing everything – their escape attempt, her father's crash, the events of two days before.

"You were right to grab that syringe. That's all that matters now. You saved her, Holly. Even if they'd known about the vote, they would have carried on. So would your father."

"I'm not sure about that, Jake. Dad was having his doubts. At the eleventh hour, it hit him."

"We'll see. We'll see how he is now about it. Mary still has dementia. And he still wants her money."

"Jake, don't say that."

They went through to the lounge.

"Hello Jake, you disappeared without saying goodbye after lunch," announced Mary to Holly's astonishment.

"It's not lunchtime yet, Mary, and I've only just arrived."

"No, no, I mean the other day."

Holly then realised that her grandmother was remembering what had happened on the day of her planned termination. What else did she remember? She had fallen asleep after the nurses had left on Tuesday, slept soundly until well into Wednesday morning without apparently then having any recall of the previous evening's events. Holly had decided that it was right to try to explain to her what had happened about the vote in Parliament. Mary's response was not the one Holly had been expecting.

"Oh well, never mind. These things happen."

Importantly, though, for Holly was the fact that her grandmother appeared not to have remembered that drugs had been administered to her as a precursor to being put to death. Nor did she seem to have been aware of the commotion which led to the termination being aborted. It would best if it stayed that way. The years that potentially now lay ahead for Mary seemed to Holly like an unexpected holiday or, maybe more accurately, an extended sentence.

"Gran, what would you like to do this afternoon?"

"Could we go for a trip in David's drone?" was the unwanted reply.

"No, Gran. We can't do that. You know that Dad had an accident in his drone. It's badly damaged and he's badly injured and will not be getting in a drone for a very long time, if ever."

Mary seemed to accept this response. Holly tried another tack.

"Let's go and have a walk round the garden."

"That would be nice."

Just as Holly was about to put this plan into action, she heard her father calling from the makeshift ground floor bedroom they had created for him. She went to him, helped him out of bed and into the wheelchair and wheeled him through.

"Hello Mum, how are you today? Hello Jake," he said but with a flat voice completely devoid of the cheerfulness, however contrived, that he usually managed.

Holly looked at her father and thought he looked like an old man, stripped of his power, his raison d'etre and his identity. This was the time to tell him straight out. This was the time, perhaps for the first time, to say what she really thought.

"Dad, I think we should have a celebration. A celebration of the fact that Gran is still with us. A celebration of the fact that Parliament did the right thing, well at least moved in the right direction the other night. I know now that I was wrong and that you were wrong. Killing people just because they get to ninety can't be right. The League of Youth had a point. It still has a point. But the way to make life fairer for the young is not to end it prematurely for the old."

David did not reply straight away but then, turning to look straight at his mother, said, "Of course, I'm glad you're still here. The rest is for another day. Am I allowed to have a glass of wine, Holly?"

Jake fetched a bottle and some glasses, poured four generous measures and handed them round. They toasted.

"To Mum."

"To Gran."

"To Mary."

"To me."

They drank. Holly looked round the room. Jake smiled at

her. The vacancy which so often occupied Mary's expression had gone. But, when she cast a glance at her father, he still looked worried and full of doubt.

CHAPTER TWENTY-NINE

Wilfred David Hall, Manchester,
Greater Manchester
Friday 30 November 2046

Holly could not remember going to a concert like this since she had been a child. Classical music had never really been her thing. But today here she was, sat right in the front row of the dress circle looking towards the stage where the Halle Orchestra were warming up. Violinists were tuning. Woodwind and brass instruments were letting slip tantalising fragments of what she recognised as the main melody. The audience were taking their seats. Old, young, black, white. Formally dressed, casually dressed. There was a buzz of conversation and she could feel the anticipation in the Hall.

Suddenly, a hush descended followed quickly by enthusiastic applause which grew to a crescendo in a matter of seconds. Then cheering as a spotlight homed in on a box of seats on the left hand side near to the stage. Holly realised why. King George had just taken his seat. He stood up, acknowledged the applause, waved and then sat down. Holly thought he then looked in her direction and smiled. The Hall fell silent. Then three further rounds of raucous applause and cheering greeted first the conductor, then the pianist and then the saxophonist as they came onto the stage, bowed to the audience and took their places. The lights were dimmed. A few coughs broke the otherwise perfect silence. The conductor raised her baton. Holly felt Jake squeeze her arm. Then it began.

Holly found herself almost immediately transported back to a front room in Hunstanton. In the year since then, the piece had been adapted for orchestra but somehow what she was hearing now was the original composition performed shakily in a run-down house in a shabby street by the sea. Holly looked to her right. Her grandmother was looking straight ahead, concentrating intently, it seemed. Beyond her, Eversley smiled in a way that she didn't remember seeing before. His daughters likewise. Holly was sad that her father was not also there. Even a year after his accident he was still having trouble walking more than a short distance and he had used this as his reason for not travelling to Manchester, a reason doubted by Holly.

After three or four minutes of teasing by piano, by violins and nearly every other instrument, the saxophone started, quietly at first but before long much louder and, it felt to Holly, overriding all other sounds. Within a few seconds, applause began breaking out, first from the depths of the stalls at the back of the Hall, then, taken up like a Mexican wave, through the rest of the stalls and up into the dress circle and then above. The boxes joined in, even the Royal box. Cheers erupted at this. The King smiled. The band played on, despite the breach of orchestral convention.

After a while, the audience returned to quiet appreciation and 'Homage to Hunstanton' progressed through its first, then its second and finally its third movement. Holly found her mind drifting as she remembered how much had happened in the last year. First, the call from Eversley who'd had contact from the King. The King had heard about Wilfred's last composition and now he wanted to put on a royal performance for him. It was amazing how the idea had gained momentum. The Halle had got involved with an offer to add a full orchestration of the piece. Plans to hold the concert in London had been shelved. Instead it would be in Manchester, nearer to Wilfred's home.

As these thoughts subsided, Holly refocussed on what

was happening inside the Hall. She knew the final movement must be nearing its conclusion. She glanced again at her grandmother who by now had tears streaming down her cheeks. Holly put her hand on Mary's and squeezed it gently. Her grandmother squeezed back. Holly looked towards the stage. The saxophonist seemed to be reaching every note possible as he swayed to and fro, long since having abandoned his chair. The first and second violins were bowing and plucking their instruments with frenetic intensity. Every part of the orchestra seemed to have nothing left in reserve. Finally, the conductor jumped up on her podium to bring down her baton with so dramatic a flourish to signal the final note for every instrument bar one. Then, for a full twenty seconds, guided lightly by the conductor, the saxophone played the last few bars alone.

It took two or three seconds for even the most knowledgeable to realise it had ended. Once they did, the Hall erupted, clapping, cheering, stamping, whistling and with the least inhibited in the audience hugging their neighbours. Hardly a soul was left sitting. Holly looked straight ahead clapping enthusiastically. She wanted to take in the moment and cast her glance around the Hall scanning the front of the stalls below, then taking in the circle behind her. As she was about to return her gaze to the stage, her attention was caught by a lone figure. High above the circle, away to Holly's left, there was a box, otherwise unoccupied, with a man seated alone, clapping but otherwise showing no emotion. Holly instantly knew who it was. It was a man who had hardly been seen in public for a year. A man about whose future, and past, there was endless speculation in the media. It was Edward Watson.

A cheer going up above the clapping dragged Holly's attention away from the former Prime Minister back to the stage. The conductor was using her baton to signal to the King to join her on stage. After a few more swings of encouragement from her baton, the King turned around in his box and left it by the door. The cheering intensified. Holly then noticed a steward coming to the end of the row where she was sitting and guiding Eversley from his seat. To the cheering was added rhythmic clapping. Holly stole a glance behind. Edward Watson was now standing alone in his box, clapping more enthusiastically than he had been moments before. She turned back. It seemed to take an age but then, as though choreographed carefully beforehand, the King walked onto the stage from the left just as Eversley did so from the right. But it was not just Eversley. Holly could hardly recognise the person in the wheelchair which Eversley was pushing. She hadn't expected this. The audience hadn't expected this. But it didn't take long for the recognition of the composer to sweep round the audience. Holly had been told by Eversley that Wilfred wasn't able to come to the concert. He was in too much pain and he had become increasingly confused and forgetful in recent months. The conductor ushered the King onto her podium, stepped to one side, and signalled to the audience to be quiet. They obeyed instantly, cutting off in an instant the sound of whispering around the hall as Wilfred's presence was acknowledged.

"Good evening."

The King was only able to utter these two words before another round of applause broke out, this time not for Royalty but for Wilfred. The King let the applause continue but then waved his arms to request silence.

"Thank you to all of you for coming here this evening. It's nearly a year since I first heard about Wilfred David's latest composition. I decided that we should make sure that this piece could be performed in one of our great concert halls. As you all will know, Wilfred was one of the greatest musical talents in Britain in the earlier part of this century. He did much to ensure that the musical traditions of his community became mainstream and loved by people of all backgrounds. Perhaps, in recent years, he hasn't received the recognition he deserved. I am determined to put that right. But perhaps more importantly than that, I just wanted to give you all the chance to hear a superb piece of music. Until a few hours ago, I understood that the composer would not be able to join us tonight but, as you can see, he has taken me, and all of us, by surprise and given us all a wonderful bonus by honouring us with his presence."

More clapping and cheering interrupted the King. Holly instinctively rose to her feet on the balcony, cheering and clapping without reserve. Through the tears now streaming down her face, she could see Wilfred, now turned by Eversley in his wheelchair to face the audience, lift his left arm to offer a weak wave. Holly could see how much he had changed since she had last seen him a year ago. She wanted to rush down onto the stage and embrace him. Then, as the King tried to bring the audience under control, Holly could see Wilfred trying to signal that he wanted to say something. It was this that silenced the Hall. The King stood still. For several seconds, Holly and everyone in the Hall held their breath. Wilfred managed just two words and only very faintly.

"Thank you."

But that was all that was necessary as another eruption of clapping and cheering filled the hall, eventually subsiding as the King started to speak once more.

"Thank you, Wilfred. And everyone here will, I know, join me in wishing you all the very best. But tonight I want to say a little more about Wilfred. He is a great musician, of that there is no doubt. He also represents something else very important in the story of our country. What some of you may not know is that, his son, Eversley, who is on the stage with us, had taken his father, first to the Scottish border and then to Hunstanton, to try to avoid Wilfred being compulsorily terminated. It is of course for our elected politicians to decide the laws of our country but, for what it's worth, I believe that a man who tries to save his father from death in these circumstances is to be commended."

A polite applause started around the Hall, quite tentatively at first. Holly joined in. She looked around. Most people were clapping but with varying degrees of enthusiasm. She was keen to see the reaction of the former Prime Minister. He too was clapping. The King resumed his speech.

"I have one final thing to do. I am delighted to be able to reveal this evening that the Trustees of the Bridgewater Hall have agreed to my proposal that this great auditorium, recently refurbished and restored to its former glory, is to be renamed in honour of the man whose music has filled these walls with such a rapturous reception. I would like to ask his son Eversley to unveil the plaque to mark the renaming of this building as the 'Wilfred David Hall'".

To Holly, and it seemed nearly everyone inside the Hall, this came as a further surprise. The whooping, stamping and clapping broke out again and continued for several minutes as the King and Eversley, pushing his father, were eventually led from the stage. As the excitement slowly died down and the audience drifted out, Holly gathered up her party, Mary, Jake, Eversley's partner and children, and they made their way slowly to a small room behind the stage where they had been invited to a VIP reception.

As she entered the room, Holly could see the King some ten metres ahead talking to guests. She had never met the King before. He turned and walked towards her and Mary and Jake. They were introduced. An informal conversation started. But, after only a few moments, the King's attention was distracted. He made his apologies, walked towards the door. Holly turned to look in the direction the King had walked. There, standing in the doorway, was Eversley with his father in the wheelchair in front of him. Instinctively, and throwing protocol to one side, Holly ran towards Wilfred, knelt down in front of him and threw her arms around him. A stream of words left her lips – later she wouldn't be able to recall what she had said to Wilfred nor how she had apologised to the King for interrupting him. All she knew was that this was, at one and the same time, one of the happiest and saddest moments of her life. Wilfred said little in response but smiled broadly.

Mary was ushered over to see Wilfred whose smile increased. The two ninety-year-olds seemed immediately to connect emotionally but with few words. Holly knew from their body language that both knew the other and it was as if they were taking up where they had left off a year ago in Hunstanton. A disjointed conversation involving Mary, Holly, the King, Eversley and, in a limited way, Wilfred continued for a few minutes. Holly could see Eversley looking anxious and took this as a signal to help him extract his father from the scene.

"Wilfred, it has been so good to see you again. And we all absolutely loved the music. Look after yourself."

With this, she knelt down, embraced Wilfred again before standing up, hugging Eversley and then stepping back and guiding her grandmother away. Eversley bade his farewells, said a final thank you to the King, pushed his father through the doorway and disappeared.

After Wilfred's departure, the room fell into a series of small group conversations but only a few moments had passed before the door offered another surprise. The King seemed to be among the first to notice him standing in the doorway.

Holly's gaze followed him as he walked purposefully across and offered his hand to the new visitor who bowed slightly awkwardly before accepting the proffered hand. Seen at close quarters, he was much shorter than he appeared on television but Holly was sure he had lost weight and looked gaunt in the face. His suit looked a size too large for him.

As Holly and the others looked on, it was clear to her that the former Prime Minister was anxious. He looked like a man with all the cares of the world still on his shoulders even though he had left office a year ago and resigned as an MP a few months later. The King and Edward came over to where Holly was standing. Everyone was introduced. There was some chat about the music and then Edward asked if he could say a few words.

"You may be surprised to see me here tonight but I felt that I should come. I wanted to do so unobtrusively. I didn't want to be the story. I am not the story. This is Wilfred's story. But I do just want to say sorry to you all. I shouldn't have hung on to the idea for so long. I shouldn't have convinced myself for so long that it was for the best. People shouldn't be condemned to misery and indignity in old age but it should be their choice, not the state's. Oh, by the way, Holly, give my best wishes to your father but tell him from me that it's over. That was all. I will leave you to enjoy the rest of the evening."

With that, he turned around, declined the King's invitation to stay with them for a drink, and left the room. The King left Holly's group to do his duty and talk to others. Holly wandered over to the window, looked out, reflecting on the emotions of the evening. She was thinking about her father's absence, thinking about what the King had said, thinking about what Edward Watson had just said but, above all, thinking about Wilfred.

She turned, looked back into the room and saw her

grandmother in what looked like animated conversation with the King. She wondered how much of what Mary was saying would make any sense. In the past, she would have worried about that and intervened. Today, though, she left them to it and looked out of the window again. As she was doing so she noticed the distinctive, dark shape of a narabanc gliding past beneath a headline scrolling on a news ticker on a building opposite, which read 'Govt blocks early vote on 95 Law'. The image of her father flashed through her mind but, for tonight at least, she felt at peace even if the fight she now knew to be hers, still had to be won.

CHAPTER THIRTY

Fairfield Hospital, Bury, Greater Manchester
Monday 3rd December 2046

Eversley walked slowly but purposefully along Rochdale Old Road in Bury and turned towards the entrance of Fairfield Hospital. Wilfred, wearing his favourite overcoat and a woolly scarf and hat, was in his wheelchair with a small case balanced on his lap. Progress was slow and Wilfred could see that Eversley, even though physically strong, was struggling to negotiate the uneven pavements and difficult kerbs. He knew he had been a bit selfish earlier, insisting that they struggle on to the bus rather than getting a special taxi. But he wanted this journey to be by bus. He liked buses. He always had.

They paused by the hospital entrance, studied the large sign announcing the various departments, and walked through a maze of corridors to find their destination. They opened the door, and Wilfred announced himself at reception.

"Good morning Wilfred, come with me," responded a nurse.

Eversley hesitated momentarily but Wilfred took control, signalling to his son to start pushing the wheelchair to follow the nurse. Since Friday's concert, Wilfred had felt stronger, physically and emotionally, and he had been more talkative. He knew exactly what he was doing and why. Father and son followed the nurse along several more corridors before being shown into a small but well-furnished room. It contained a single bed, two well-upholstered chairs, and a small table with a vase of what looked like freshly-picked flowers. The room looked and smelt fairly recently painted and the curtains were in good condition. The nurse signalled for them to enter and he closed the door behind them. They were instructed to wait. Someone would be with them very shortly.

The two men sat in silence. Wilfred had chosen hospital rather than home. Less fuss was his justification. But he had wanted to see his granddaughters and his daughter in law. So, the previous evening, Annie and Helena, and Eversley and Emma had assembled at Wilfred's house. They cooked him a meal before sitting around a table in his cramped and cluttered dining room. The conversation had flowed with Wilfred joining in more than of late. Music, including some of Wilfred's, had blared out from the speaker, and there had been a few tears, mainly from his granddaughters. But Wilfred knew he was doing the right thing.

Now, the moment was upon him. The door opened and two nurses, one man and one woman, came in. Wilfred found himself focussing on the details. The small stain on the front of the man's white coat. The missing button on the blue jacket worn by the woman. He also noticed how Eversley was uncharacteristically quiet but he was fairly sure his silence now signified assent rather than just acquiescence.

"Good morning, Wilfred," said the man introducing himself as Will. Wilfred thought he must only be in his twenties.

Alice, who stood behind her colleague and made it obvious by her body language she was less senior, was nevertheless probably well into her forties. She took a set of documents from a brown shoulder bag and laid them carefully on the table in front of Wilfred. Life had become largely paperless but not, Wilfred thought, death. For almost half an hour, the two nurses went through the documents, explaining everything in some detail before obtaining Wilfred's and Eversley's signatures many times.

"OK. That's all the paperwork done. Thank you for that," announced Will. "Now we can move to the next stage if you're feeling comfortable."

Wilfred noticed Alice picking up a small black case, which she placed on top of another table near the door of the room. She opened it and started unpacking some of its contents. The blinds covering the two windows in the room were only partially preventing the strong winter sunshine from penetrating inside. Wilfred put his hand up to protect himself from the sun.

"Oh, shall I just close the blinds a bit tighter, Wilfred?" suggested Will.

"No, no, I don't want to shut out the world just yet. Thank you."

"In a moment," continued Will, "we will give you the drink as we just explained and then we'll leave the two of you for a while. We'll just be along the corridor. Just press the buzzer if you need us."

Will pointed to a red button on a white socket in the middle of a wall.

Alice came across towards Wilfred.

"Just something to make you relax, Wilfred."

"I'm perfectly relaxed already," replied Wilfred, smiling broadly at Alice and even eliciting a weak smile from his son.

Wilfred allowed himself to be helped from the wheelchair by his son and he sat down on a chair by the bed.

Wilfred drank the liquid quickly, placed the now empty plastic beaker on the table, reached into the inside pocket of his coat and took out an envelope.

Alice and Will left the room as Wilfred handed the envelope to his son. Once the door was shut, the room was quiet. Wilfred could hear the siren, presumably of an ambulance, coming very close to the room where he and Eversley were sitting. He thought to himself that, even as death approached, the business of saving lives carried on. Once the noise disappeared, Wilfred turned and addressed Eversley. It was the most lucid he had been for a while.

"Thank you, my dear son, for what you've done. My time is up. I am tired. Read this afterwards."

He paused. Eversley put an arm around his father. Then a second arm and they embraced. A tight embrace but one without tears.

Over the next thirty minutes they sat together quietly as Wilfred produced lists of tasks for his son. He wanted to make sure that Eversley would sort out his house, his papers, his music and his money. There was actually quite a lot of that, Wilfred remembered, not because he'd ever made that much from his music but because he had never been extravagant with it. Wilfred had never been a great organiser but now, in his final moments, he had the urge to get things straight. Once this was done, he let out a sigh, stood up and took off the overcoat, which he had probably worn every day for at least the last twenty years, and placed it neatly on the arm of a chair.

"I'd like to lie down now."

Wilfred saw Eversley press the red buzzer. He heard the door open. He saw Will and Alice come round to the side of the bed. He thought he probably smiled at them. He remembered having operations years ago and the moment just before the anaesthetist leant across. He convinced himself it was just like that. Then he heard the music. Eversley showed him the hand-held on which he'd recorded it in Hunstanton. Wilfred definitely smiled at that point. For a few seconds he tried to look around the room and take in this final stopping point but he couldn't. Then it was just the music.

At some indeterminate point later, Wilfred felt as though he was in a drone. He had never been in a drone but he felt at that moment to be flying. He couldn't really make out where he was but he assumed it must still be the hospital. 'Homage to

Hunstanton' was playing, loudly and getting louder still. And then he saw him. Maybe he looked a little pale but otherwise he seemed untroubled as he walked along a pavement in the winter sunshine. He saw him hurrying, quickening his pace almost to a run as though he wanted to distance himself from the scene as fast as possible.

Then, once he was out of the hospital grounds, he saw him stop and sit on a seat next to a bus stop, the one they had arrived at earlier. He could see him reach into his coat pocket and take out a tissue and blow his nose. There he sat apparently oblivious to the world around him, and the bus which stopped a few moments later assuming him to be a waiting passenger. Wilfred observed that it took him several minutes to compose himself and then to take the envelope from his coat. He sat there, his head down, reading as several more buses stopped, opened their doors and then closed them without taking him on board. Now Wilfred knew that Eversley would understand. The music played on.

Colin Philpott

'Deathday' is Colin Philpott's first work of fiction. Previously, he has written three books about twentieth century history. 'A Place in History'– the stories of places in Britain touched by news events; 'Relics of the Reich' – examining how Germany has dealt with the buildings left by the Nazis; and 'Secret Wartime Britain' – about hidden places in Britain that helped the war effort in the Second World War. Colin worked for the BBC for twenty-five years as a journalist, programme-maker and senior executive. Later he was Director of the National Media Museum in Bradford. He lives in Yorkshire.